# GRAVEYARD SHIFT

## CHRIS WESTWOOD

SCHOLASTIC PRESS
New York

# For Gill

Library of Congress Cataloging-in-Publication Data Available

ISBN 978-0-545-39919-7
10 9 8 7 6 5 4 3 2    12 13 14 15 16
Printed in the U.S.A.          23
First American edition, July 2012

The text type was set in Minion Pro.
Book design by Phil Falco & Becky Terhune

# 1

# MR. OCTOBER

The first time I set eyes on Mr. October, he didn't look like anything special. He didn't look like a man who'd stand out in a crowd, let alone a man who could change anyone's life, turning everything inside out. But that's what he did to me, and that's why I have to explain what I did and how it all came about.

It wasn't my fault, that's all. It wasn't his fault, either, but sometimes I think it would have been better if we'd never met, if my life had turned out to be normal like everyone else's.

I was wandering through Highgate Cemetery at the time. It was a late Saturday morning with low clouds and a thick, muggy atmosphere. By the time I arrived, visitors were flocking through the north gate and following tour guides down the paths, but I'd found another, cheaper, way in, over the fence down the hill.

Inside, the place was a maze, and without a map I hadn't a clue where anyone was. Karl Marx was here somewhere, and George Eliot and Henry Moore, but I was more interested in the stones themselves, the way they leaned at strange angles as if they'd fallen from the sky and landed just so. I liked the way bright, shiny new monuments rubbed shoulders with chipped and broken tombs overgrown with ivy and moss.

I found a stone with no name on it and sat to eat a chicken salad sandwich and sip bottled water from my packed lunch. The clouds parted and patterns of light and shade played on the paths between the headstones. I wished I had a camera to capture the scene, but I did have my sketch pad and pencil. On a clean page of the book, I outlined the path where it forked in two directions with the stones on either side of it and the trees running alongside.

A group of four girls with Liverpool accents strolled past, heading down the path to the right. I paused until they moved out of the frame before going on. It was hotter now, and a bead of sweat fell from the tip of my nose and hit the page, creating a smeared shape in front of one tomb. It looked like a blurred, ghostly figure.

When I looked up again, a shape like the one the sweat had made on the page was standing in the near distance, sixty feet or so up the slope. The tomb behind him was a creamy off-white, nearly the same color as his suit, so I didn't see him clearly until he began to move.

He seemed to be waving or gesturing to someone and

mopping his face with a handkerchief. It took a moment before I realized he was in trouble. Wobbling on his feet, he stopped near the edge of the path, falling side-on against a marble cross. He looked about ready to keel all the way over.

"Mister?" I said, but he didn't seem to hear. "Mister, are you all right?"

Dropping my sketch pad, I started up the path.

He didn't look up as I approached. He simply gripped the cross with one hand, holding out the other for balance.

"My," he gasped. "Oh my, sometimes it's all too much."

As I came up beside him, catching him by the elbow, his legs buckled and he fell against me with his full weight, which didn't feel like much at all. When I was sure he wouldn't fall, I walked him to the path and sat him down on a flat square stone. He looked around as if he didn't know where he was.

"Should I get help?" I asked.

He looked up at me with misty gray eyes and a weary smile, the look of a man with the weight of the world on his shoulders.

"No, I'll be fine in a minute. It's only a spell."

"Are you sure?"

"Yes, young man, I'm sure."

I ran for the water bottle, uncapping it on my way back and handing it to him. He took it and sipped slowly, staring into space. Looking at the brown liver spots on the backs of his hands and his white-whiskered jaw, I wondered how old he might be. Seventy, maybe. Probably older. Sunlight flared off his bald head like a halo.

He swallowed more water and settled a little, breathing more easily.

"Thank you," he said at last.

"That's OK. I didn't do anything."

"Oh, you did more than you know." He offered his hand, which felt clammy when we shook. "I'm Dudley October. And you are?"

"Ben. Ben Harvester."

"Ah, one of the Harvesters. An interesting name."

"Not as interesting as October, I'd say."

His gray eyes held mine until I had to glance away.

"I think I met your father once," he said. "Long time ago, but I remember him mentioning you, saying how proud he was. Jim Harvester, isn't it?"

It was a shock to hear Dad's name on this stranger's lips. "I'm not sure I did anything to make him proud," I said.

"Whoever said you had to *do* anything to make your dad proud?"

Mr. October drained the rest of the water. I waited until he looked ready to move, then helped him to his feet and walked him along the path to where I'd left my belongings.

"Did you meet my mum too?" I asked.

"Not that I recall, but I've known many Harvesters in my time. In my line of business, you get to meet all kinds."

"What line of business is that?"

"Oh, mostly clerical work, filing and so forth, which I'm sure sounds to you like the dullest job in the world."

We stopped while I put away the sketch pad and shouldered

my backpack, then I steadied him past the queues at the exit gate. As we reached the road outside, he turned to me with a sadness in his eyes and said, "It's been good to meet you, Ben Harvester."

"You too. Can you manage from here by yourself?"

"Yes. I may be fragile, but I'm very resilient. I'll cope." He cleared his throat, watching the traffic. Then he said, "Hope it's not inappropriate of me to say, but I'd like to pass on my best wishes and deepest condolences to your family. Regarding your Aunt Carrie, I mean."

We hadn't seen or heard from Aunt Carrie for years, and I had to think twice who he meant. For one reason or another, she and Mum had been off each other's Christmas card list for as long as I could remember.

"Thanks," I said. I didn't know what else to say.

The last I saw of him as I set off down the hill, he was waiting at the roadside to cross. I walked to Gospel Oak from there and caught a train to Hackney Central.

We'd moved last month into a maisonette on Middleton Road where we had the top two floors. We'd been told we would have a view of the park from there, which was true if you stood out on the balcony and leaned over as far as you could, craning your neck.

It wasn't the quietest place. The neighbors downstairs liked their drum and bass music loud, sometimes cranking it up late at night and all weekend. But it was cheaper here and we had to cut costs now, Mum kept reminding me. We'd had to struggle ever since Dad left home.

To get to our place you had to enter via a security door and take two flights of stone steps up a stairwell. Then you had to sidestep the mess of plant pots and hanging flower baskets Mum had placed everywhere on the balcony. Our old house in Swanley had a garden and greenhouse, and less than half of our things would fit into the new place. The rest was in storage now.

The front door was propped open, the way Mum had kept it since the hot spell began, but indoors still felt warmer than out. In the kitchen I pulled a Coke from the fridge and stared out the window, wondering if Mr. October had gotten home safely. What he'd said about Dad had started to bother me for some reason. Had he seen Dad since I last saw him? I should've asked about that.

"That you, darlin'?" Mum called from the living room. Her voice sounded sleepy and slow, and she was rubbing her eyes and stretching on the sofa when I came through. "Ah, there you are. Finished your graveyard shift, have you?"

Mum thought there were better places for a guy to spend his time. Idling around cemeteries seemed somehow morbid and unhealthy to her. I didn't want to get into it now, so I just nodded, sipping the Coke.

"I thought we might go to the park this afternoon," she said. "Get acquainted with our new surroundings. Unless there's something else you'd rather do."

"Can you give me an hour? There's some work I'd like to finish first."

"Whatever you like, hon." She yawned and settled again. "Give me a shout when you're ready."

It wasn't exactly work and it wasn't that important, but I was thinking of the sketch I'd started at the cemetery but left unfinished. Upstairs in my room, a much smaller space than I'd had at the other house, I sat on the bed and opened the pad, touching a finger to the smeared shape in front of the tomb.

The bead of sweat had dried in the shape of a man, but a man without any clear features. I could still picture Mr. October's face, so I added a line here and a squiggle there to make the figure complete. After roughing in a few wisps of cloud, I was adding a Celtic cross to the background when I heard the telephone ringing downstairs.

At first I didn't pay it much attention. Mum answered, her voice the softest murmur. Then a long silence, broken by the sound of sobbing, a sound I'd only heard from her once before.

When I ran down to the living room, she was still clutching the phone, staring at it, aghast, and her eyes and cheeks were dark with tears.

"Mum!" I said. "What's up, Mum?"

She shook her head, straining to catch her breath, and it took a long time before she could force out the words.

"It's OK, darlin'. Everything's OK. It's just a shock after all this time. I don't suppose you even remember Aunt Carrie, do you? She passed away an hour ago."

# 2

# AUNT CARRIE

A little over a week later, I saw him again. Again it was at a cemetery, this one built around a hulking Norman church outside Seaborough, on the northeast coast of England, where Mum's family originally came from. We were there for Aunt Carrie's funeral.

The church service was well attended, but most of the congregation were strangers to me. The pastor spoke about Carrie's life and how we were here to celebrate it. He spoke about everything having an appointed time and place and being part of a larger plan, and a few mourners started sobbing when he read from Ecclesiastes and when Carrie's favorite Beatles song, "In My Life," began playing.

As we filed outside afterward, some of the strangers greeted Mum with hugs and kisses, and some shook my hand when we were introduced. It felt awkward meeting anyone for the first time when they had tears in their eyes.

But I couldn't cry for someone I'd hardly known and barely remembered. If something had happened to cut Mum and Aunt Carrie off from each other for so long, no one was making anything of it. Mum's family had never been good at keeping in touch, but it had always been good at keeping secrets.

At the end of the burial ceremony, we moved in a slow procession past the grave, collecting handfuls of earth from the funeral director's assistant to sprinkle over the casket. I let mine fall and stood a moment, watching it settle, then followed the others to the gravel path between the church entrance and the gates, rubbing my hands together.

That was when I saw him. Mr. October stood some distance away beside a white granite plinth, head bowed and hands clasped together as if praying. A warm breeze cut across the churchyard, turning the air dusty with dandelion spores. The old man didn't move a muscle and didn't look up. If he sensed me watching, he didn't show it.

I had an urge to go to him, to leave the group and just walk over. For one thing, I wondered what he was doing here. For another, there was something important I needed to ask. But this wasn't the time or place. It would be too hard to explain to Mum.

Along the path, the others talked in small groups, saying how lovely Aunt Carrie was and how she'd gone before her time, and how sudden it must've been because a few short months ago she'd seemed such a picture of health. You never knew what was in the cards, they said, sniffing and wiping their noses.

In twos and threes they began peeling themselves away and heading for their cars at the gates. There were farewells and promises to keep in touch from now on, and I wondered how many of them I'd ever see again.

Mum took my arm, steering me toward the gates.

"Our train leaves in twenty minutes," she said.

When I looked back at the church, Mr. October was moving away, his back toward me and his right hand reaching as if he were holding someone else's. As far as I could tell there was no one with him, but for a second the cloud of white spores seemed to arrange itself into a human shape and follow him step for step.


On the train to London, I skimmed an Iron Man comic while Mum opened a paperback book on the fold-down table in front of her and turned the pages, not really reading. She didn't look up at me as she said, "Well, there she goes. She's on her way."

"She's at peace now," I said. It was the kind of thing you were supposed to say.

"You must wonder why I brought you," she said. "Why I even came myself. We hadn't spoken for so long."

"She was your sister. It would've been odd if you hadn't gone."

She nodded, watching the last of the blue-gray coastline through the window before the train altered course, heading inland. "Yes, it would. And it wasn't so bad after all. They could've made me feel unwelcome, but they weren't there for that; they were there for her."

"Yeah."

"Do you remember when Dad left?" she asked.

"Not really. Not well."

"You were young. Just nine."

"Yeah. And we've hardly talked about it since."

"Only because I didn't want you to be hurt."

"Did he leave because of me?"

She looked at me as if I'd just sworn. "God, no. Is that what you think? Don't ever think that, Ben. It wasn't anyone's fault — at least not yours."

"Then why did he go?"

A white butterfly had somehow found its way inside the car. It fluttered above our heads, tapped the window a couple of times, then dipped out of sight behind us.

"Everyone goes eventually," Mum said. "When they do, the timing never seems right. It always seems too soon."

But the pastor had said everything happens as part of some plan, always in the right way at the right time. Confusing. I didn't know who to believe. I thought about what Mr. October had told me, what Dad had never told me himself.

"Was Dad proud of me?" I said.

"Of course. What kind of question is that?"

I shrugged and turned in my seat. I couldn't see the butterfly now. It must have followed us through the open door at Seaborough and stayed with us ever since. Mum read for a while, or pretended to, but she hadn't finished saying her piece yet.

"Anyway, I'm sorry," she said. "We were stupid, Carrie and I. We shouldn't have let it drag on so long. We should've worked things out like grown-ups. And now I wish I could've seen her one last time to let her know everything's really all right."

"I'll bet she knows," I said. "Wherever she is, I'll bet she knows."

The train rolled on between small brown towns and across expanses of flat green country, and I imagined Aunt Carrie out there in the land, sitting by a shallow stream, dipping her feet in the water to cool them, happy and at peace and everything forgiven.

I still didn't know what the secret was or what should be forgiven. Maybe I wasn't meant to know. Closing my eyes, listening to the rhythm of the train, I thought, *Suppose what I saw today, the figure made out of white pollen dust, was her? Where could Mr. October have been taking her? Why on earth was he there? And how come he knew what had happened to her so soon, before everyone else?*

By the time we were back in London, I'd decided I had to find him again. As our train settled at its platform and the doors swung wide, the trapped butterfly shot out just ahead of us into the noise and steam two hundred miles from home.

# 3

# MASQUERADE

Nothing moving. Everything still. The next few days were even hotter and the air felt like a clammy skin. On the bed in my room with the windows open, I waited for a breeze that never came. It was like waiting for a miracle, a sign to point me toward Mr. October.

"Get out!" Mum said one morning as she rushed around getting ready for work. She had a waitressing job at a greasy spoon on Mare Street where breakfasts cost four pounds any time of day or night. "You can't lie around here all day. You have a talent, so why not exercise it? Go out and fill your sketchbook with everything you see!"

She meant parks with wide-open spaces, well-tended green grass, and lakes replete with birdlife. But I preferred places where everything grew wild and tangled with thorns and mosses and things half buried. I liked to see what nature did when people didn't interfere.

"Just don't go to the cemetery," she said. "If you do, I'll know."

She didn't say how she'd know. And she didn't say what was so wrong about it, either.

Morbid curiosity, she called it. But there were entire histories there. You could read the inscriptions and piece together the stories of folks who'd lived and grown old or who'd gone too soon and while they'd lived they may have changed the world in some way. They may have invented something, or written a great book, or painted a famous portrait or posed for one. Or maybe all they'd done was be a good mother or father to the people buried alongside them.

She knew I liked the kind of stories where flesh-eating creatures came alive underground, pushed up soil and stones and lumbered into the dark. She knew the comics and books and action figures that filled the shelves in my room meant more to me than almost anything. But she didn't seem to know I knew these things were make-believe.

"Promise you won't go," she said, halfway out the door.

"I promise."

"Do something positive with your day. Don't waste it. Life's too short."

"How short?"

"Don't be smart. You know what I mean."

She pulled me toward her, quickly pecked the top of my head, and set off for work.

I didn't need to lie because I didn't think I'd have to go looking in cemeteries for Mr. October. He couldn't spend all his time in them. After Mum left I went through the phone book, but I couldn't find anyone with his name. Maybe he was listed in the business section, I reasoned — he'd said he worked as a clerk — but the book only included local businesses and I'd seen him two hundred miles away in Seaborough. He could be anywhere.

I decided the reference section at the library might help me cast a wider net. I went out and crossed London Fields, which was crammed with early sunbathers setting up barbecues, and turned along Lamb Lane.

Even in the daylight, the closed workshops and warehouses under the bridge looked like they were hiding something. The sudden crash of corrugated iron shutters made me start and hurry the rest of the way to the thoroughfare. A thick, yeasty smell from a nearby bakery followed me on the air.

At the end of Lamb Lane, there's a short alleyway with a bicycle lane just before the pedestrian lights on Mare Street. A man was lying there, flat on his back, belly up. His chest rose and fell with each breath he took, and his stringy hair was peppery gray like his beard. The scruffy clothing he wore looked like it might have something living in it besides him.

He looked harmless enough, I thought, but passersby took one glance and walked quickly away. Some didn't glance toward him at all.

I stood over him, not sure what to do. I was worried he might be sick. I didn't get too close, though, because of the scent coming off him, sweet and sour like the yeasty smell from the bakery.

Despite myself, I yelped and stepped back sharply when he opened one eye — a filmy green eye with the tiniest pupil — and looked straight at me.

"Who are you?" he growled. "What d'you want?"

It took me a second to find my voice. "Thought you were in trouble, mister. Thought you needed help."

"Go away," he said. "Go on, kid, get lost. Don't need any help."

He closed his eye and drifted away again.

Something told me I should stay. I'd seen others like him before, broken men with sunken eyes and rank hair sleeping in doorways or hunched up in cardboard beds. I'd seen Mum hurry past them like everyone else, and once she physically dragged me away by my arm. You see this kind of thing every day and it terrifies people, but I don't know why.

The man was snoring now, his face beaded with sweat, and the yeasty factory smell seemed worse than ever.

"Mister," I said. "Don't you have somewhere to go? It's way too hot outside to sleep on concrete. There's a place across the street for guys like you. They might have a room."

The man groaned, covering his face with his hands.

"You still here?"

"What are you doing down there?" I said. "What happened to you? Why won't you let me help?"

His lungs whistled as he inhaled and exhaled.

"Are you married?" I said. "Or were you married before?

Don't you have friends and family who might be missing you, wondering where you are?"

He shifted onto his side, propped himself up on an elbow, and glared at me with his one sleepy green eye. The other eye still rested shut.

"Now I've got a question for you," he said. "Why don't you please bugger off?"

He sat up sharply, faster than I'd imagined he'd be able to move. For the first time I began to feel scared.

"Sorry," I said. "I didn't mean anything. I was just trying to —"

"Don't worry. I won't eat you alive. But didn't your mother ever tell you to let sleeping dogs lie, Ben Harvester?"

"Pardon?"

I backed up, not sure I'd heard him correctly.

"That's right," he said. "Ben Harvester, turned twelve years old in May. Son of Jim Harvester and Donna Harvester, formerly Williams of the Williamses of Seaborough. How do I know this? I know your entire ancestry, boy. And here's another lesson your mother and father never taught you: Never poke a dead thing with a stick unless you're sure it's dead. Otherwise it might jump up and bite."

His second, lazy eye opened and his gaze was suddenly twice as intense. The green irises seemed grayer and shone so brightly, I had to look away for a second. Then his frown faded and he began to grin, the wrinkles and cracks of his face twitching, rearranging themselves into a different shape.

When he got to his feet, even his clothing seemed to fit

differently. These weren't the same stinky rags he'd had on before. They weren't fashionable or expensive, either, but more like the kind of grungy, dark clothes you might find at a secondhand stall in Camden.

I looked around, up and down Mare Street, not sure what was happening to him but hoping someone else might see. The traffic was light, except for the odd vehicle buzzing past like an angry insect. For the moment there were no other pedestrians anywhere in sight.

It was just him and me.

"Who are you, mister?" I said.

"Guess what," he said. "You're about to find out."

And then the transformation began.

"Now," he said, "look, see, and wonder."

I'd seen magic shows before — disappearing acts, quick-change artists, death-defying stunts involving fire and water and chain saws — but I'd never seen anything like this. And it was happening right in front of me.

The man spread out his hands as if to say, *See here? Nothing up my sleeves.* With bony white fingers he began very slowly to massage his scalp, moving his fingertips in small, regular circles. Then all at once he pressed and pulled sharply downward to his jaw, and the face I'd seen a second ago folded over itself and came away with a dull, wet snap, like surgical gloves being peeled off.

Underneath was another face, thirty or forty years older, with soft gray eyes, a shiny bald pate, and white-whiskered chops — a face I recognized at once.

"Gotcha!" he said, nearly choking with laughter.

"Mr. October!"

"I knew you were looking for me, young man. Thought I'd save you the trouble."

"How did you know?"

Mr. October just smiled.

In his left hand he held the remains of the face he'd removed. It hung there limply, wrinkled and expressionless except for the faintest of smiles on its lips. He let it fall to the ground, where it lay for a moment like a snake's cast-off skin. Then the breeze from a passing 55 bus swept it up, whipping it through the air until it broke apart into dust and scattered across the street.

I stared at him, terrified. His features were restless, as if ready to change again. Nervous ticks dragged at the corners of his mouth, pulling his smile out of shape.

"How . . . how did you do it?" I asked. "What kind of trick was that?"

"Trick? That was no trick," he said, again reaching for his face and pulling. "That was who I really am. But so is this, and this!"

With the swiftest, smallest of movements, Mr. October tore off the old man's face, and the face beneath that, and the one beneath that. One moment he was a boy not much older than me with mischievous eyes and a lopsided grin, the next a tanned, clean-cut, middle-aged man who might've been a lawyer or banker. Then another familiar face, the surly derelict with stringy hair.

"Oh, I've done that one already," he said and quickly moved on, becoming an actor I recognized from old black-and-white films, then a politician who'd passed away last year. Very briefly I found myself staring into the eyes of a huge-headed snake, scaly and shining dully, with a darting forked tongue.

Mask after mask came away in his hands, torn free and discarded, blown to dust on the breeze. It was like a living slideshow made of flesh and bone. No two faces were ever the same. None kept their shape for long.

"This," he said, ripping and tearing, "is who I was yesterday, and this is who I'll be tomorrow. Every man has more than one face, Ben, one for every occasion. I just happen to have more than most."

"Who are they?" I asked. "Where did you get them?"

"You're all questions, Ben Harvester, but I'll give you a hint. It's all you'll be able to understand until I've shown you everything else."

The slideshow seemed to have stopped. He'd settled on a face that made me think of a pirate's — long dark hair swept back from a high swarthy forehead, a stud earring in one earlobe, narrow black eyes with bushy eyebrows that nearly met in the middle. A rash of dark stubble covered his neck and jaws, and when he looked at me squarely the lines of his brow formed a capital Y.

This was still Mr. October, just not the Mr. October I'd expected to find. This one made me more than a little anxious.

The next time he spoke, it was in a rasping sandpaper voice I didn't recognize.

"You can't expect to understand yet," he said, "but I'll tell you this for free: Everyone you meet, everyone you help or who helps you, and everyone you love or hate or who loves or hates you back — they all become part of you, for better or worse. These faces are all the people I've ever crossed paths with. Some I've crossed swords with too."

"And the snake . . . ?"

Mr. October shrugged. "Sometimes you try to help and get bitten for your trouble. Hence, I'm one percent reptile."

He flicked out a forked tongue to prove it.

"Anyway, Ben, put it there," he said, offering his hand. "I'm glad to have found you."

We shook, and his grip had the same clammy coolness I remembered from the first time.

"I thought *I* found *you*," I said.

"Yes, but you wouldn't have tracked me down in a lifetime if I hadn't allowed you to."

"Suppose not, you being the master of disguise and all."

"Exactly."

"Then why?"

The Y of his forehead shrank as his features steadied. He smiled, all dull gray teeth except for a single silver front tooth so polished, I could see a tiny version of myself reflected in it.

"You're a good kid," he said. "A born helper. You saw an old man in distress at the cemetery and you made him comfortable and gave him your last drop of water. You saw a homeless guy on the street and didn't look the other way like everyone else. It's as simple as that."

"Never really looked at it that way," I said.

"No, because you didn't do what you did to score points. You saw someone less fortunate than yourself and tried to lend a hand."

I had to stop him there. "Fortunate? I wouldn't say I was that. Dad's gone and who knows if he'll ever come back, Mum's stressed and too tired to speak to me half the time, we're broke and in a new place where I don't know anyone and don't know what to do with myself."

He wasn't impressed. "That's not so bad. It's an ideal situation, if you ask me. No ties, nothing to hold you back, no one to stop you."

"Stop me from what?"

"From finding your destiny," Mr. October said, black eyes shining. "Your true calling."

Across the street, a handful of pedestrians were waiting to cross at the light. In the hazy heat, their features were blurry and melting, as if they were about to change too. A few others walked past us: an arguing couple with a three-wheel stroller, a gang of teenage girls eating pink ice cream. None of them paid us any attention, but they didn't hurry away like the others had. For a moment I wondered if we were invisible, if everything Mr. October had shown me had taken place in another dimension.

"Funny old day," he said, watching the sky. "Look there."

Above the baking hot city, above the world, a full moon floated in a cloudless sky, so bright I had to shield my eyes to see it.

"So what's my true calling?" I asked. "Are you going to tell me or what?"

He grinned and stretched out his arms, locking his fingers together until the joints crackled and clicked.

"My, but you're hard work," he said. "Always the questions. But I'm hungry! Let's take a walk."

# 4

# THE SUNGLASSES THIEF
# AND THE CLOVER CHAIN

We set off along Lamb Lane and crossed London Fields through a fog of barbecue smoke. Everywhere in the park, sun lovers were roasting themselves alive in shorts and swimsuits. On Broadway Market, cyclists swarmed in all directions between the chic coffee shops and stalls of brightly colored fruits and vegetables, not slowing or giving way, so we had to duck aside to avoid being clobbered.

We turned off at the bridge, heading down to the canal. It felt cooler alongside the water, and the pale moon's reflection on its surface kept pace with us as we went.

"Tell me the truth," I said. "You're no ordinary office clerk, are you?"

"That's right," Mr. October said. "But, then, my office is no ordinary office. Here, have an apple."

Wiggling his fingers, he reached up to his right and picked one from the air and handed it to me, rosy and red.

"Good trick," I said, "but I bet you stole it from one of the stalls."

"If that's what you'd like to think," he said, plucking another for himself as if from an invisible tree.

I was cautious at first about biting into the fruit. If it hadn't come from a stall, then where? But it tasted delicious, bitter and sweet and crisp. We walked on, munching, not speaking for a while.

"So what else can you do?" I said. "Read minds? See the future?"

"Not exactly, not the way you mean, but something tells me if you don't step this way right now, you'll regret it."

Before I could fathom what he meant, he'd taken my arm, yanking me to his side of the footpath just as a girl cyclist went flying past at top speed exactly where I'd been walking. I caught a glimpse of her scraggy fair hair and wraparound sunglasses as she whisked by.

"God, how about that?" I stared after the girl as she shrank into the middle distance. "She would've flattened me if you hadn't done that."

"Some people have no morals," he said, a note of anger in his sandpaper voice. "She stole that bike, you know. And the sunglasses too."

"How could you know a thing like that?"

"I saw her leaving a shop back there on the street. Saw the

look on her face and knew at once. I pick these things up from people."

He was glaring after the bike in the distance when the girl seemed to lose control, as if she'd hit a stone or a crack in the path, and went skewing to her left toward the bank. The cycle struck the edge and upended, carrying the girl into the water with an almighty splash.

"Nothing to do with me," Mr. October said innocently. "If she hadn't been thieving, she wouldn't have been in such a rush, and that would never have happened."

We headed to where she and the bike had hit the water. The bike had already sunk without a trace and the girl was splashing frantically a good distance from the bank.

"Can't swim," Mr. October confided. "That's how it looks to me."

"She's gonna drown," I said.

"Not only that, but she's lost her sunglasses." He didn't seem at all concerned. "All that fuss and trouble for nothing."

"But aren't you going to help? Maybe I should go in after her. . . ." I was starting to panic.

"There you go again: born helper." He patted my shoulder. "Don't worry. Someone else will be along in a minute. And besides, she's not what she seems. She's not on the list."

No sooner had he spoken than a small group of people — two more cyclists, a trio of joggers — appeared in the distance, heading our way. Mr. October set off along the bank, ignoring the girl's screams and splashes. It took me much longer to drag myself away.

She vanished below the surface, then shot up again spitting water and thrashing her arms. It wasn't right to leave her like this, but the others were closer now and had seen what was happening. They would help.

"It's OK. You'll be out of there in no time," I called to the girl, but I couldn't be sure she heard. Then what Mr. October had said began to dawn on me, and I set off after him, running.

"What list?" I said. "I don't understand."

"Everything in its own time and place, Ben. Just like the preacher said." He stretched through a yawn, wiggling his fingers. "All this excitement is making me hungry again. Fancy a hot dog?"


The hot dog he plucked from the air for me came with both ketchup and mustard and an extra helping of caramelized onions. We ate in silence for a time, and then Mr. October let out an appreciative burp, which I matched with one of my own. We both laughed.

"My, I feel as stuffed as a taxidermist's cat," he said.

Farther along, the canal path was busier, with a constant stream of cyclists and joggers. None of them got too close, as if they sensed what had happened to the last cyclist who'd done so. Instead they slowed down, easing around us at a respectful distance. Even so, they were a source of irritation to Mr. October.

"We came here for a quiet chat, but look at them — they're thick as flies. I can't hear myself think." He clicked his fingers a couple of times, and the pathway ahead suddenly appeared silent and clear. "That's better," he said.

"Did you do that?"

"Do what?"

"Clear the path. There's no one else here now, just us."

"It's only a lull. There'll be more along soon."

All the same, as we strolled on I noticed how still the water had become, with the moon's reflection frozen on its surface like a snapshot. Overhead, a few small white clouds stood fixed against the sky, not moving. In the last few seconds, the roar of traffic on a road bridge nearby had faded to nothing. This was becoming stranger, more unsettling, by the minute.

"It's like being inside a bubble," I said.

He gave me a quizzical look. "How so?"

"Like before, on Mare Street, when no one noticed us. And the street went quiet for a time and it was just you and me. Like being inside a bubble where we could see everything but we were unseen."

Mr. October considered this, then a broad grin broke across his face, his silver tooth sparkling. "I knew I was right about you. I knew you had the gift the first time I saw you. Congratulations, young man."

Now he'd confused me again. "Congratulations for what?"

"You've passed all the tests so far. You've shown just the right qualities for the job. And as soon as I've run my report past my superiors, I think we can move you along to the next level."

So far he'd answered none of my questions; all he'd done was invite many more. What list? What job? What true calling? I was still pondering all this when he clicked his fingers down by his hip and the traffic noise returned to the bridge and the roads around Victoria Park. Light and movement quivered across the water again, and seconds later I noticed the first cyclist pedaling toward us around the bend.

That was when I knew for sure: He had powers I couldn't even begin to imagine, the kind I'd only ever seen from heroes and villains in comics. If only for a minute, Mr. October had stopped the world.


Leaving the canal towpath, we cut across Victoria Park to the lake. It was quieter and less crowded there than London Fields nearer home. Families of swans and geese idled on the sparkling water.

Mr. October sat with me on the grass in the shade of a gnarly old oak, his nimble fingers knotting together a chain of four-leaf clovers.

"Count yourself lucky," he said, passing me the chain. "Some people wait their whole lives and never find what they're looking for. Some go looking in all the wrong places. Others are too lazy to look in the first place. They think, *This is my lot, these are the cards I've been dealt, this is as good as life's ever gonna be."*

"That's sad. I'd hate that."

"Good for you, then, because destiny tapped you on the shoulder today. Tapped you right on the shoulder and took you on a ride to see the sights."

"Is that what this is?"

"It's only a start. There's so much more."

"Why me, though?"

"Because I've been in this line of work longer than I care to say, I've lost count of the people I've seen come and go, and I've never seen anyone so right for the task as you. That's the crux of the report I'm filing with my superiors, anyway."

"Who are your superiors?" I had to ask.

"The Overseers," he said quite seriously. "All you need to know for now is that our work is vitally important. Top secret. Highly classified. Not to toot my own trumpet, but without us the world would be in an even worse state than it is now. The whole thing would come crashing down. The natural order of things would change."

"Wow. Sounds like a big responsibility."

"Yes, it's huge."

"I'd be scared to take on something like that."

"Nothing wrong with being scared," he said. "Nothing worthwhile's ever achieved without fear. If I'm wrong about you, I'll throw up my hands and say, 'Sorry, my mistake.' But come with me and you'll have the answers to all your questions, even the ones you haven't thought of yet. Questions about your father and what I was doing last week at Seaborough churchyard."

He closed his eyes for a moment. Dappled patterns of brightness and shade played through the oak's branches above us, falling on the intricate chain of four-leaf clovers and making them appear to squirm between my fingers.

"Well, duty calls," Mr. October said. "We've come a long way together today, young man. We've got a lot further to go. I'll check back with you next week about the trainee position. But now I've got work to do."

I stood to watch him walk away toward the lake, a tall raggedy man dressed head to toe in darkness. As he neared the water, a frantic scratching behind me drew my attention away. A red squirrel scrambled up the tree trunk, freezing in its tracks when it felt me watching, its bright button eyes staring straight into mine for perhaps a full minute. Then it skirted around the far side of the tree, out of sight.

There were countless gray squirrels in the park, but I'd never seen a red before. I'd never seen a four-leaf clover for that matter, and here I was holding a string of them in my hand, standing on a green carpet of thousands.

*Magic,* I thought. *Something like magic. Everything's alive!*

Folding the chain into my shirt pocket, I scanned the lakeside for Mr. October. There was no sign of him now, and the only movement near the water was that of an urban raven taking flight.

The bird soared into the air and soon became a dark dot above the trees. The moon had sunk from the sky, and I stared into the hazy blue until I grew dizzy. Then I set off toward home.

The first true breeze of the day wafted down the roadway as I came up from the towpath. I hadn't seen anything of the sunglasses thief on the way back. Whatever she'd done wrong, I hoped she was safely back on dry land by now. But what had Mr. October meant, she wasn't what she seemed?

On London Fields the barbecues were still going strong. The smoke made everything soft and distant. Near the fence along Lansdowne Drive, a black mass of ravens were fighting among themselves over a pile of bread someone had dumped in the park. As I got to the path that crossed the park from Lamb Lane, I saw Mum coming back from work, carrying a shopping bag and jumping aside to avoid a cyclist.

"Summer in the city! Don't you just hate it?" she said when she saw me. "Ever noticed how *cycle path* sounds like *psycho-path* if you say it three times quickly?"

"Cycle path. Cycle path. Cycle path."

"So how was your day, love?"

"Oh, you know, not bad."

"You're a mine of information. But I can't help noticing you don't have your sketch pad with you. Remember what I said about not wasting your God-given gift."

I felt a flush of guilt about that, but I couldn't tell her what I'd really been up to. She'd think it was a lot stranger than frequenting cemeteries.

"Anyway, you can tell me what you *did* do," she said, and twitched her bag, showing me the parcel of takeout food inside it. "You can tell me over a supper of wonton soup and shredded chili beef — your favorite."

"But we can't afford . . . ," I started to say. "Can we?"

Mum shook her head, then ran a hand back through her dark blond hair. "No, we can't. And you know what? I don't care. You have to live a little now and then, otherwise you'd go mad. Do us a favor, hon, and carry this for me. My arm aches."

"You're in a good mood," I said, taking the bag. I hadn't seen her so buoyant for ages.

"Well, I should be, considering I got the biggest tip I've ever seen in my life today."

"Really? Who from?"

"Some man in a suit, very posh and smart and well spoken. A fish out of water where I work. Hands me a twenty-quid note for a six-quid roast dinner and tells me to keep the change."

"Blimey."

"I know! So I ask if he's made a mistake, does he know he's tipping me fourteen quid, and he waves me away like it's nothing. 'See you again,' he says as he goes out the door. Oh, I hope so."

"Me too. Maybe he'll come back again and sweep you off your feet and . . ."

Mum clammed up then, lowering her gaze as we left the park. I knew right away I shouldn't have said it. Perhaps because of the way Dad had left us — it had never been that clear to me — she never spoke to me about men.

We crossed Lansdowne onto Middleton Road. Mum didn't speak again until we'd climbed the cool stairwell, the coolest place in town today, and negotiated the planters and pigeon droppings on our balcony to unlock the door.

"Anyway," she said, unpacking the food in the kitchen, "that's dinner from Hai Ha's with change left over. Only thing that bothers me is, he said I looked like I could use the money. Now I feel insulted."

"He probably didn't mean it like that."

"What else would he mean?"

"Where you work. It's a bit of a dive. He probably thought you must be hard up to work there."

"Hmm."

"That's probably all he meant."

"Probably. But still. All the same."

We felt stuffed after the meal, and I told her my day had been a good one without explaining the reasons why. I did mention the squirrel but not the four-leaf clovers, and I mentioned the girl in the canal but not Mr. October's part in what happened. I even told her I'd had a hot dog for lunch but not where I'd gotten it.

She seemed satisfied by my story, anyway, and by the time I'd cleared the plates from the breakfast bar she was nodding over the table, close to sleep.

Another day's waitressing had worn her out, and I felt sad that she'd been so happy over a lousy fourteen pounds. By the time I'd washed up, she'd crawled from the kitchen to the living room sofa and was drifting away in front of the TV.

Upstairs, I opened my sketch pad for the first time that day and began to draw, just doodling at first. I was trying to picture the faces Mr. October had shown me on Lamb Lane, but now they all merged into one. The only one I could see clearly was the dark-eyed pirate type with the slicked-back hair and silver tooth.

The sketch didn't turn out well — it didn't look anything like him — so I put the pad and pencil aside and rolled back on the bed with my hands pillowed under my head. I wouldn't tear up the sketch, I decided, even if it wasn't much good. It was the only memento I had from the day to prove that any of it had really happened.

That and the four-leaf clover chain inside my shirt pocket.

# 5

# THE FIRE CHILDREN

The hottest days passed and the air became breathable again. One night, the equivalent of a whole month's rain fell in a hundred minutes. Torrents and droughts. Life was like that. One day with Mr. October had opened my eyes, and then came day after day of nothing at all.

Every morning at seven o'clock sharp, a wiry gray-haired man in army fatigues and scruffy sneakers came rummaging through the trash bins outside our building. If he found anything of interest among the cat litter and rotting fish heads in the bins — old clothing, an unfinished bottle of wine — he would stuff it into the pack he carried on his back. Then he would continue along Lansdowne Drive and turn into the Blackstone Estate.

Watching from my window, I wondered if he might be one of Mr. October's many personalities. In the end I decided he wasn't, but Mr. October might turn up again anywhere, anytime, with a different face. I might have seen him ten times on the streets without knowing it. That day by the canal seemed so distant, I might've dreamt it up, and as the days spun out I began to think I'd seen the last of him.

And then there was school.

Monday morning — my first day at Mercy Road School near De Beauvoir Town. Mum bustled around the maisonette, twice as flustered as usual. The only thing worse than her being late for work was my being late for school on day one.

"Tickets. Money. Passport. Apple for the teacher. Are you sure you haven't missed anything?"

"Yeah, I'm sure."

"Then off you pop." She smoothed out her clothes, checked her face in the living room mirror. "Do I look OK? Will I pass?"

"Does it matter when you work in a greasy spoon?" Seeing her hurt look, I quickly added, "Fine. You look fine, really great."

"No need to be facetious," she said.

She'd been preoccupied since the previous Friday when the businessman had again entered the café, ordering a sandwich and latte and leaving another large tip. She'd gotten it into her head that he fancied her, and she didn't know how she felt about that or how Dad would've felt if he'd known.

"But Dad's been gone four years," I reminded her, following her down the stairwell. "Don't you think he'd want you to be happy?"

"You're just a kid. You wouldn't understand."

"Then explain and I'll try to."

"One day I will. This isn't the right time."

It was never the right time.

We exited the building and stood on the path outside. By the cold light of day, the worry lines and dark circles around her eyes were more obvious, but she didn't need to hear that from me.

"Right, then," she said. "Do your best, try to make friends, and if the teacher asks what you do in your spare time, don't mention graveyards."

"OK."

She straightened my tie and picked a few invisible specks of dust and fluff off my blazer.

"What's up?" she said.

"Nothing." I shrugged. "I just wish you'd talk about . . . you know what. I don't like seeing you sad. I might be able to help. I'm a born helper, you know."

"You're funny. Now get along before I clip your ear."


The school was an old Victorian building whose red bricks had darkened almost to black over time. From the outside it looked cobbled together, with turrets and cupolas and windows too dim to see through. It was easy to imagine ghosts hiding inside. The playground was narrow and long with jungle gyms at one end but no athletic field like I'd had at my last school.

Inside, the classrooms faced one another along two dark corridors which crisscrossed at the center of the building. The rooms were small, divided by newly painted partition walls, with desks crammed closely together. The ceilings were low, the fluorescent lights hurt my eyes, and by the end of first period, I was suffocating.

We began with attendance in our homeroom, classroom 8C, then had algebra with Miss Neal, a large and matronly woman with impatient, small eyes and a slow, booming voice. Through most of the lesson, I stared out the window at the small gray chapel across the street. A sign outside advertised cheap lunch specials downstairs in the crypt.

By midafternoon I'd decided I didn't care much for the other kids in 8C. There were two in particular, twin brothers Dan and Liam Ferguson, whose cold stares and sly smiles made me think they were sharing telepathic jokes about me. There was Tommy Farley, a red-haired kid with permanently encrusted snot on his upper lip like a silver-green alien mustache; Raymond Blight, who whispered "Fish" behind my back and spent most of English flicking tiny paper balls at other students whenever Mr. Glover looked away; and Mel Kimble, a girl who finished every other sentence with the word *innit*.

"Mel, you can kick us off by reading the first page," Mr. Glover said at the start of the period.

" 'It was the best of times, it was the worst of times,' innit?" Mel read.

Mr. Glover blinked at her over his half-moon spectacle

lenses. "Sorry to interrupt, but I think you'll find that's a spurious word not found in the original text."

"Just reading what's on the page, sir, innit?"

Mel wasn't so bad. That was just her way. Some of the others were probably OK too, but on day one none of them said hello or otherwise did anything to make me feel welcome.

There was a gang of six who sat together in every class, stayed together during break, and ate together at lunchtime — Matthew, Ryan, Curly, Devan, Kelly, and Becky. They were the smartest and best-looking in 8C, and they seemed to know it. They never fussed for attention or argued or bickered or made much of a noise.

They didn't speak to me, either, but sometimes I caught them looking my way as if trying to decide whether I was animal, vegetable, or mineral. Matthew was long and lanky and constantly grooming his fingernails. Kelly was dark and icy, looking straight through me but never at me.

Becky Sanborne was the most interesting one, I thought. She had a round cherub face with cool green eyes and a lightly freckled nose. She never stopped chatting and smiling except when she looked at me, and then she became serious and silent. Once I thought she was mouthing something across the class to me, but that turned out to be a yawn.

At lunchtime I went to the crypt. The cool, dark space was full of warm-coated senior citizens who'd claimed all the tables. Their chatter and the clink of their spoons amplified off the stone walls under a low, curved ceiling. I bought a hot dog at the counter and ate it outside on the chapel wall across from the school. The hot dog was tasty, but not nearly as tasty as the one Mr. October had given me.

In the afternoon, French with Mrs. Radcliff was followed by social studies with Miss Whatever. At least, that's what the other kids called her. Her real name was Whittaker. Jolly and energetic, she had a habit of going, "Now, children," in a way that made everyone squirm, which was the worst you could say about her. But during her class, our last of the day, something happened — something that turned my first day at Mercy Road from a bad day into a disaster.

We were doing an assignment she called From the Headlines. Miss Whittaker explained as she handed out newspapers that we should each choose one story to present to the class. Later we would have to research these in greater detail and write essays on our subjects for next week.

Raymond Blight chose a football story from the *Daily Mirror*. Mel Kimble spoke about a pop star's arrest for drunk driving. Matthew from the gang of six preferred a more sober story about the current economic climate — the latest unemployment figures had just been published — while Becky found a bizarre one in the overseas section of *The Independent*. "42 DIE IN FIGHT OVER WRISTWATCH," the headline read.

No one believed it, not even Miss Whittaker, until Becky showed the paper to the class. What began as a dispute over the ownership of a watch between neighbors in a small Afghani village had soon escalated into a full-scale riot between rival gangs.

"Remarkable," Miss Whittaker said.

"Worst fing I ever heard," Mel said.

"Incredible but true," Becky said, "and it's worse that the story's only a small piece on page nineteen. It should've been on the front page, but it isn't, because it didn't happen here."

As Becky returned to her seat, Miss Whittaker signaled me to the front. The story I'd found was closer to home, from page three of the *Metro*. I opened the paper on Miss Whittaker's desk, stooping over it to avoid eye contact with the class.

"By the way, I believe you're new here," Miss Whittaker said. "Have you met Ben, everyone?"

"Nnn."

"IImm."

"Uh."

I'd never liked speaking in public, let alone in front of strangers. Standing there, I felt like an exhibit, a curiosity at a circus sideshow. Taking a breath, I began to read.

Three mornings earlier, after Mum had left for work, I'd done what she'd been encouraging me to do and taken my sketch pad to London Fields. The first of the barbecues was already smoking and more were being set up. My idea was to capture the park, the trees, and houses beyond before it became too busy.

It was a fine morning, still warming up, and the air had a golden glow. Even the wisps of barbecue smoke would add something to the picture. I took an empty bench and set to work, roughing out the scene on an empty page. Sometimes it felt good to draw just for the sake of it; the subject didn't have to be anything special. After half an hour I stopped and looked up, wondering if Mr. October would appear if I waited long enough.

The barbecues were multiplying. Already there were twice as many as when I had begun. Sun worshippers spread towels on the ground, threw Frisbees and played cricket with tennis balls and plastic bats. I watched with the smell of smoke clinging to my nose and listened to the sudden rise and fall of a siren a few streets away.

The newspaper story brought it all back. It seemed so vivid, I could smell the smoke right there in the classroom.

About the same time I was opening my sketch pad in the park, Kevin Willow, 36, and his wife, Hannah, 33, were locking up and leaving their second-floor apartment on Henryd Street five minutes away. They'd planned to leave the building just long enough to buy bread from Gossip café on Broadway Market and stamps from the post office. They didn't know as they set off that a small fire was kindling in the apartment below theirs. They didn't know it would spread so quickly, tearing up through the complex like a ravenous beast. They didn't know that safety regulations had been overlooked in their building and the fire escape outside was hazardous.

Why they decided to stay at Gossip for coffee instead of going straight home was anyone's guess. Instead of taking five minutes, their outing ended up taking thirty. By the time they turned the corner onto Henryd Street, the place was ablaze, thick black smoke billowing around and above it.

The fire department was already on the scene.

Two engines had arrived together, a minute or so before the ambulance, and almost ten minutes before the Willows.

Ten minutes too late to save the two children trapped inside.

Molly, 6, and Mitch, 4, perished from inhalation of smoke while they slept. The emergency services did all they could, but were hampered by the loose and rusting fire escape and a stairwell between floors where the worst of the blaze had taken hold. They managed to lift the children out through an upstairs window, but neither brother nor sister survived as far as Homerton Hospital.

" 'An investigation is under way,' " I finished. " 'An electrical problem on the ground floor is suspected.' "

I closed the paper and looked at the class. No one spoke or moved. A chair scraped somewhere near the back. Raymond Blight stared, bored, out the window.

And still I could smell the smoke.

" 'Orrible," said Mel. "Them poor kids."

"So sad," Kelly whispered to the gang of six.

Becky stared misty-eyed at the floor.

Miss Whittaker cleared her throat. "Indeed. And what will you do, Ben, with a story like that? There doesn't seem to be much to add."

"Dunno, miss." I shrugged. "It just makes me think."

"About what?"

"I suppose about me being in the park around the corner

at the time." I paused. It was hard to explain. "All those bar-becues, all that smoke. If they hadn't been there, someone might've seen the smoke from the house and done something about it in time."

"See what you mean, Ben," Miss Whittaker said. "It'll be interesting to see what you come up with next week."

"You can still help," a small voice said at the back of the class. It sounded more like rustling leaves than a voice.

"Help how?" I said.

"Help us. Help *them*."

I hadn't noticed them there before. They must've just entered the class. The way the light angled across the room from the window, the three figures were in semidarkness, seated together at a desk-table near the door.

"I don't understand," I said, leaning forward for a better view. "Is there something I should do? Something I should've done?"

"Not before, but now," the voice answered. "Help now. We're still in the fire."

"Ben?" Miss Whittaker's voice was barely audible. "Ben, is everything all right? Look at me."

I was inside a tunnel, all soft and dark at the edges. All I could see was hazy light at the end and the three figures waiting there for me.

Three chairs scraped back at once. Three figures stood up.

"Who are you?" I said. "Tell me and I might be able to help."

"You know who these two are. Help them first."

It was the tallest of the three who'd spoken, the one with the rustling voice. Standing behind the desk was a man about six feet tall, blackened and scarred from head to foot, his charred clothing hanging off him like rags.

From what I could see of his face, there wasn't too much of it left. Most of the flesh on its left side was gone. Half of his hair had been singed away, leaving a scorched black scalp.

Standing on either side of him, holding his hands, were the two children from the blazing building I'd read about, Mitch and Molly. It had to be them. They looked the right ages. They weren't in the same terrible shape as the adult, but their little round faces and clothing were sooty and smudged.

The girl wore a pale yellow nightdress and clutched a rag doll to her chest. The boy had on blue pajamas and held a teddy bear. They had the same shiny fair hair and sleepy blue eyes. They could've been twins.

"I need to sleep and I don't know how," the boy murmured, rubbing his eyes.

"We're lost," said his sister. "We're locked in and can't get out."

"And you," I said to the burned man. "Were you in the building too? How come there's no mention of you in the newspaper?"

"Ben?"

Miss Whittaker again, still a murmur, even farther away.

A distant sound of stifled laughter. The gasp of twenty-four students catching their breath.

Across the room, the threesome began slowly backing up to the door. "Help us," they said, all three together. "Help us sleep."

"But how? Tell me how. I don't know how!"

Uncontrollable tears filled my eyes, throwing everything in front of me out of focus. I took a step around the desk, meaning to follow them. The sudden pressure of a hand on my shoulder brought me back.

"It's all right," Miss Whittaker was saying. "Whatever you saw isn't there now. Come with me."

She took my arm, guiding me past the desk to the door. I couldn't look at the others as we passed.

I didn't need to, either. I knew they were staring at me in openmouthed wonder.

Sniffing back tears, I wiped my eyes with a forearm and followed Miss Whittaker out.

"This way, Ben, this way."

She ushered me out to the dim corridor, her hand still holding my arm.

"We'll get you to the nurse," she said.

"I don't need a nurse."

"Let her have a look at you all the same, just to be sure." Poking her head back inside the classroom, she said, "Now, children, no noise. Matthew, you're in charge while I'm gone."

As she closed the door, I glanced inside the room. The man and the children were gone. She'd been right about that, even if she hadn't seen them herself.

There was a dark patch on the varnished floor more or less where they'd been sitting. Ashes, maybe, or a fragment of burned clothing. Or maybe only a scuff mark caused by the friction of chair legs scraping back and forth over it all down the years.

# 6

# THE PORTRAIT

Through the closed door of the nurse's bright but small office, I could hear them whispering out in the corridor.

Miss Whittaker said it must be first-day nerves, a little migraine perhaps. She said I seemed to be highly strung.

The nurse, dark-haired with a thin, unsmiling face, shone lights in my eyes and checked my throat and took my temperature. Temperature was a tad high, she said, but otherwise I was well enough to go home.

She scribbled something in a notebook, gave me an aspirin with water, and sent me on my way. It was a waste of time, and I didn't dare imagine what the others thought of me after what had happened back in the classroom.

But I knew what I'd seen.

\*     \*     \*

Before going home I cut around from Middleton Road onto Henryd Street. If anyone had asked why I'd gone there, I wouldn't have known how to answer, except to say I needed to.

Above the fence that had been erected to protect the remains of the building, I could only make out the very top of the roof. Blackened and slimy, with smoke still rising faintly above it, it looked ready to crumble apart. The air still hung heavy with the stench of soot.

A TV antenna was still in place up there, warped out of shape by the heat. A raven perched on one of its conductors, staring straight down at me.

It sat there a minute or so, not moving. Then something disturbed it — the slam of a car door up the street. The bird took off above the rooftops, heading for London Fields.

Around the side of the block, the top of the fire escape was just visible. It had blistered and broken loose and now hung slack against the wall like a busted limb.

I turned toward home. I didn't feel like looking anymore, and I didn't know what I'd expected to find. It must've been the thought that Mitch and Molly might come back here. Then again, if they were lost, how would they know where to go?

Mum was still at work when I got home. In the kitchen was a note she'd left in a shaky hand reminding me not to eat too much; she'd treat us to more takeout tonight. I poured a glass of milk and drank it on the balcony, watching workmen at a house they were refurbishing across the street. From there I could see barbecue smoke drifting above the park, and a handful of urban ravens above that.

Up in my room, I tried to sketch the two children from memory. They were still fixed clearly in my head, and I caught their likenesses much better than I had Mr. October's. At first their eyes came out too dark, so I softened them by dabbing away with a small round of Blu-Tack. Soon I was staring into the same sleepy gazes I'd seen in the classroom.

But I found I couldn't do the man at all. His injuries were so severe, there weren't many features to draw. What I didn't understand was what he'd been doing there, what connection he had to the children.

Maybe he'd been in one of the other apartments and they hadn't found out about him yet. Or maybe he'd been in another fire at another time.

*Born helper.* That's what Mr. October had called me. And now I was being asked for help and I didn't know where to begin.

*Help how?* I thought. *Help* who?


Days two, three, and four at Mercy Road weren't much of an improvement. The word about me had spread, and it wasn't only 8C who kept their distance now, watching me for signs of another meltdown. Kids from other years gave me a wide berth in the yard and corridors. Teachers spoke to me in hushed tones, the way you might speak to an elderly relative at the funny farm.

They all treated me with respect — the kind of respect that comes out of fear.

All of them except Raymond Blight, who didn't care either way.

"Weirdo," he whispered behind me during algebra on Tuesday morning. "Crybaby. Space cadet."

At lunchtimes I went to the crypt across the street. No one else from school went there, so it seemed the best place to avoid them. Midmorning and afternoon breaks I spent in the library. I went back there each day after school, killing time until I could be sure the other students had left.

Sometimes when other kids see you as different, especially when that difference makes them afraid, they tend to pull together against you. They keep you outside. Sometimes they even attack.

No one had attacked me yet, except Raymond, and he'd only done it with words. It was only a matter of time, though, I thought, before things got worse.

I couldn't talk to Mum about it, couldn't tell her truthfully how things were at school or about the fire children or anything else, just as she couldn't talk to me about Dad.

On Thursday night we ate supper in silence and watched an hour of TV. Afterward I lay awake in bed till the early hours, unable to settle, dreading the first light of Friday.

\*       \*       \*

Three things happened that Friday. Three things that turned the week around, that in the end turned my whole life around.

The first involved Becky Sanborne from the gang of six; the second, Mr. October, just when I'd given up any hope of seeing him again; the third, a red-haired woman in a green dress throwing a tantrum on a street corner in Soho.

I would never be any kind of hero, not in 8C or anywhere else, but by the end of day five at least I wasn't a zero anymore. And I'd begun to understand what my true calling was.

The art room at Mercy Road was upstairs and faced due south, so the lighting there was the best in school. At the start of last period, Mr. Redfern explained the day's assignment. He would divide the class into pairs, with each pair sketching a portrait of their partner using pencil, Conté crayon, or any other drawing medium of their choice.

Then he moved around the class, naming names. "Raymond and Mel. Curly and Tommy . . ."

Chairs scraped and crashed as students flitted between tables.

"Dan, you go with Liam. Matthew with Ryan. Becky with Ben."

Everyone stopped at that. You could tell from their faces that Becky had just drawn the short straw. She'd landed the weirdo.

I picked up my things and started toward her desk, but she was already on her way to mine and motioned me to sit. Her face was pink with embarrassment. Slapping her bag on the desk with a sigh, she looked back at her friends as if pleading for help. She took pencils and an eraser out of her bag and set right to work.

Becky had a hard-set expression, which I preferred not to draw. It wasn't a natural look, but I couldn't think of how to make her relax. A joke might've helped, but I'd forgotten the punch line of the only joke I could think of. It wasn't that good a joke anyway.

On a clean page of my sketch pad, I roughed out the general shape of her head and shoulders, then softened the lines with my thumb. After ten minutes her outline seemed about right and her features were coming together. It felt strange, though, having to draw someone while she was drawing me. All I got were concentrated frowns, plus Becky had a habit of poking her tongue from the corner of her mouth, which I decided not to include. It didn't flatter her.

As the period went on, she spent more time checking what I was doing than focusing on her own work. Her lines were too clean and precise, and although I was seeing it upside down on the desk, I could tell the portrait looked nothing like me.

"Very good, Dan," Mr. Redfern said, moving between desks. "Too harsh, Kelly. You're not supposed to carve it into the page."

Apart from Mr. Redfern, you could've heard a pin drop. Everyone was engrossed in their work. For once there were no blank stares, no whispered insults from Raymond.

"Raymond," Mr. Redfern went on. "You're a budding Picasso. Nose on one side of the face, eyes on the other. Intriguing. And Mel? Some advice if I may. Look closely and you'll see Raymond has two eyes, not just one slap-bang in the middle of his forehead. Observe!"

Then he stopped behind me. My pencil faltered over the page. I heard the whistle of his breath above my shoulder, but he didn't comment before moving on.

I was close to finishing. All I had to do now was correct the light in Becky's eyes, soft white orbs, which I managed with a tiny ball of Blu-Tack, dabbing it around them. I did the same to lighten the freckles on her nose. Becky watched in wonder as if she'd never seen a blob of Blu-Tack before in her life.

The portrait looked as close as I could make it. I put down my pencil and turned the sketch pad around to show her.

She flushed, not looking at me as she spoke — which was the first time she'd spoken to me at all.

"That's really good. Wow!"

Then she looked at her own unfinished effort and planted her forearms across it to cover it.

At the end of the class, we were invited to circulate the room to see what everyone else had done. Constructive criticism was encouraged. Smart remarks and insults were not. The wide variety of styles included stick figures, abstracts that looked nothing like human beings, and one portrait in two separate pieces which Kelly had torn apart in frustration. Oddly, Mr. Redfern had chosen to seat the twins together. Their work wasn't bad, but it was hard to tell whose portrait was whose.

Most of the class crowded around the desk I'd shared with Becky, pushing and prodding one another and straining their necks for a view. There were gasps and approving looks I hadn't seen before, even an admiring nod from Devan, one of the gang of six.

"Looks just like her," he said to Ryan, loudly enough to make sure I heard.

At the back of the commotion, out of earshot of everyone else, Mr. Redfern waved me toward him and took me aside.

"Exceptional, Ben. Looks like we've found ourselves a talent."

"Thanks, sir."

The last bell sounded, and while the rest of 8C were packing up and leaving, I noticed Becky still at the desk, going through the other work in my book. She paused at each page, taking it in, then moved on to the next without comment.

"You coming, Becky?" Matthew called from the door.

"Yeah, just a sec."

With a fleeting glance at me, she followed him out, leaving me alone in the room. As she went, I heard Raymond Blight's voice booming in the corridor.

"What a creep. Thinks he's something special."

Then a heartbeat later another voice — Matthew's.

"Give it a rest, Blight. You're so boring."

I knew then that if I ran into the others on the way home,

it wouldn't be too bad. I'd shown them something I could do well, something that might make me less of a freak and a joke around class.

So I decided I wouldn't kill time in the library that night. No need to hide. At the same time, I wasn't in a hurry to catch up with anyone, either. They'd liked my work, but that didn't mean anything else had changed.

Hanging back in the classroom, I listened to the voices and footfalls fading away downstairs and outdoors. From the window I watched them pouring out of school: a sea of gray-and-maroon uniforms spreading along Mercy Road like a soccer crowd after a match.

Some headed for the bus stop. Others piled into parents' cars, which clogged the street from end to end. One by one the jammed-up vehicles drove away at walking pace, and a silence fell over the school.

Leaving the art room behind, I set off into the gloom. Stale smells of varnish and cafeteria food followed me along the corridor and into the stairwell. Halfway down, I heard sounds from a downstairs classroom — a faint scratching and squeaking like a rat clawing its way through a baseboard.

It sounded louder from the heart of the building where the two corridors met. As far as I could tell, it seemed to be coming from one of the rooms at the north end.

Miss Whittaker's room.

I started toward it, pausing along the way to listen. Perhaps the children were there again, waiting for me. Perhaps they — or the burned man — would be able to explain what was happening and what I was supposed to do.

As I peeked inside through the glass panel, another door slammed elsewhere in the building. I froze on the spot. Some of the staff were bound to still be in the building, and if they found me they'd question what I was up to down here by myself.

I waited a moment, but no one appeared. A telephone rang and rang, but no one answered. Inside the room the clawing noise stopped abruptly. I grabbed the door handle and pushed.

Goose bumps crawled over me the second I stepped inside. A window was open and a cold breeze whistled across the desktops. On the teacher's desk was a pile of newspapers, their pages fluttering open and shut in the breeze.

"Anyone here?" I whispered.

The sun moved behind a cloud and the classroom suddenly dimmed, its corners filling with shadows. I looked at the long desk-table where the three figures had sat. Moving closer, I could see the mark on the floor was only an ink or paint stain. It had probably been there for years. Taking hold of the nearest chair, I swept a hand across the seat to be sure no one was sitting there invisibly, then flopped down into it myself.

Staring around the room, into the dark corners, I wondered where the children were now. Not here, not at the place on Henryd Street. Why had they shown themselves in the first place if they weren't coming back?

"*Are* you coming back?" I asked the empty room.

And then I saw it. I saw what was written on the board, and my blood turned to ice. Suddenly I knew what the sound had been, the scratch and squeak that had brought me here.

Across the board, in bright blue letters large enough to fill it from top to bottom and end to end, the message read:

*Welcome to Pandemonium, Ben.*

# 7

# BECKY

I didn't waste another second in there.

First I read the message through in one fell swoop. Then again slowly to be sure I wasn't seeing things. After that, I grabbed my things and ran.

I legged it along the corridor to the heart of the building, then right to the main doors. I stumbled outside, heart pounding, not slowing down until I reached the gates.

The open window. Anyone could've come and gone from the classroom that way and written the message as a practical joke. Raymond Blight seemed the most likely. But how would he or anyone else know I'd hear anything and go to investigate? How would they know I'd be the last in school?

They wouldn't. They couldn't. It had to be someone or something else — someone or something that knew my name.

*Welcome to Pandemonium, Ben.*

I didn't even know what *pandemonium* meant, but it couldn't be good.

The school looked darker and more imposing than ever as I left it behind, hurrying out onto Mercy Road. Just as I came through the gate, a bus roared past. Its noise and heat rocked me back on my feet. For one mad second I almost thought some great fire-breathing beast had followed me outdoors.

Two-thirds the way up Mercy Road, the gang of six were waiting at the bus stop. The bus pulled over, doors wheezing, and five of them clambered aboard, leaving Becky alone at the stop.

She waved good-bye, watching until the bus turned left past a phone booth two intersections away. As she checked the street, ready to cross, she saw me heading toward her and seemed to stiffen and straighten up. The last of the parents' cars had gone and the street was clear, but she stood nervously tapping her foot against the curb as if waiting for me to catch up.

"Hello," she said as I came nearer. "I'm Becky."

"I know. I'm Ben."

"I know."

"Well, hello."

"Everything all right?" she said. "You look a bit rough."

"Just running," I said.

"For the bus?"

"Nah. Forgot something and had to go back for it."

She nodded, watching the empty street.

A small, dark bird, probably a raven, fluttered from the school roof to the chapel spire and settled there, *caw-cawing* across the rooftops.

"Which way are you going?" Becky asked matter-of-factly.

"I'm near London Fields, just off Lansdowne Drive."

"Me too. How come I've never seen you around?"

"We only moved there last month, Mum and me. We're still settling in."

Without agreeing to, we set off in the same direction at the same time, past the chapel, toward De Beauvoir Square. Above us, gray clouds blotted out the sun. It felt like rain. The raven left its perch on the spire to hover above a chimney off to our right.

"So, it's just you and your mum," Becky said.

"That's right."

"Your parents split up or what?"

"I guess so," I said. She gave me a look. "I mean, at least I think they did."

"How can you not be sure if your parents split up or not?"

"Dunno."

"Are they divorced?"

"Separated. Separating." I was digging myself into a hole, so I added quickly, "Mum never likes to talk about it. It's complicated."

"Sounds like it. Never mind. Do you want anything from the shop?"

At a grocer's on the corner of Northchurch Road we

bought Hula-hoops and Monster Munch, which we ate on the way, not speaking for a time. I was glad of the silence while it lasted. Talking about my folks made me uneasy.

Becky must've realized that, because when she spoke again she changed the subject.

"So how do you like your new school, Ben?"

"It's dark," I said.

"Dark. That's an odd way to describe it."

"Well, I don't just mean dark. It's old and creepy. Do you think it might be haunted?"

Becky laughed. "You don't believe in ghosts, do you?"

"Ghosts in the school?"

"Ghosts anywhere."

"Course not," I said, kicking a stone across the street. "I was just thinking about it, that's all."

The stone ricocheted off an aluminum can in the gutter with a tinny gunshot noise that startled the raven from its rooftop vantage point.

"Anyway," I said, "I didn't have a good first week."

"It'll get better when you get to know everyone."

"Hope so. But I think Raymond Blight hates me."

"He hates everyone, or pretends to. Forget about him. He's just a negative person."

"And what about you?"

She slowed, watching me with her head cocked slightly to one side. "What *about* me?"

"You and your friends didn't exactly make me feel welcome."

"Oh, they're all right. They just think you're weird."

"Ah."

"They wanted me to talk to you, though. We're not what you think. We're just a tight-knit group. We've known one another since we were babies."

"So they sent you to investigate."

"Something like that. They're curious about you. They'd be curious about any newcomer."

"And what will you tell them?"

Becky's face lit up as it only ever seemed to when she was with the gang. A mischievous glint had entered her eye. "I'll tell them you're even weirder than they thought."

"Thanks a lot."

On Kingsland Road we had to wait ages for the traffic to clear before we crossed to the top of Middleton. As we reached the other side, Becky said, "Actually, the truth is they think you're interesting. And that portrait you did is incredible. My friends were buzzing about it after class. How do you do it?"

"What do you mean?"

"I mean I wish I could do what you do, picture something in my head and put it down on the page as I see it. Sometimes I get really clear ideas about what I want, but it never turns out right. It must be a gift."

"Maybe it is. That's what Mum says."

"So who are the kids?"

I looked around, thinking she meant someone she'd spotted on the street. "Which kids?"

"The ones in your book. The young children."

I checked myself before answering. "They came into my head once and, you know, I just drew what I imagined."

"They look so sweet and sad," she said. "Like they've got a story to tell. That picture makes me want to know more about them — who they are and what made them so sad."

I nodded.

"Ben?" she said, watching me closely. "That day in Miss Whatever's class . . . you saw something in the room, didn't you? Something the rest of us didn't."

"Maybe." I couldn't think fast enough. "No, probably not. It was a migraine. I had a migraine. That's all it was."

"But you were talking to someone. I could've sworn you were."

"Dunno. Don't remember."

"It's OK." She watched the traffic, lost in thought, then turned back to me. "I only thought, if you *had* seen something — which of course you didn't — it might've had something to do with those kids."

I looked away, shaking my head. "What makes you think that?"

She waited for the war whoop of an ambulance to pass by, fading on its way to Dalston. Then she said, "Because of the news story you read. Because of the picture you drew. And because I passed that same room the next day and thought I heard children crying inside."

"Oh?"

"I could've sworn I did. I still heard it when I went inside, but I didn't see anyone there. So maybe it was nothing, just someone with a baby on the street."

"Yeah, probably outside," I said.

"Anyway, your picture reminded me of that," she said, "and I wondered if you were thinking of the kids in the fire when you drew it. But you know something, Ben?"

"What?"

"*I* believe in ghosts, even if you don't. I've seen more than one."

I thought she was putting me on, but she looked deadly serious.

"Tell me about it," I said.

She shook her head. "I'll tell you when I see you again, but only if you'll tell me what you saw in that classroom." She lingered a few paces behind me at the start of Middleton Road, so I guessed she wasn't going my way from here. "Do we have a deal?" she asked.

"I'll think about it."

"You do that." She half turned away. "OK, then. See you Monday."

"Monday. Yeah."

She was heading for Richmond Road when the thought struck me, and I called her back.

"Becky? You can have it if you want. Your portrait."

"No!" Her mouth formed a wide O of surprise. "Are you serious?"

"If you like it that much, it's yours."

Taking out the sketch pad, I carefully teased the page loose and peeled it out.

"Only if you're sure," she said. "But could you roll it up? I don't want to get it creased." She put out a hand to stop me before I could start. "Funny, didn't notice that before. The lights in the eyes are shaped like four-leaf clovers."

"Are they?" I looked again. "You're right."

I'd put a lot of work into getting the eyes right, but hadn't noticed that, either. I rolled up the page and handed it over.

"Hope, faith, love, and luck," she said, balancing it between her hands.

"What?"

"It's what the four leaves represent." She flashed a smile before setting off again. "Dead grateful, Ben. Wait till my folks see this."

Watching her go, I thought over what I'd learned during our walk from Mercy Road. She liked my work, no question, and I didn't mind giving it away. But her wanting to get to know me probably had more to do with my outburst in class than my skill with a pencil.

The rain I'd sensed in the air was beginning to fall, misty and fine. It began as a drizzle, but the sky looked set to burst wide open. I took off down Middleton Road.

A breeze was picking up, driving the rain. Trees and hedgerows nodded at me over garden walls. A plastic supermarket bag whistled past my ear. Torn scraps of newspaper, potato chip bags, and candy wrappers fluttered at my feet across Queensbridge Road.

A raven kept pace with me as I went, gliding above the rooftops along the nearest row of houses. Every so often it slowed and hovered, as if waiting for me to catch up. I lost sight of it when it dipped down into a yard farther up the street.

It couldn't be the same bird I'd seen above the chapel on Mercy Road — that would be highly unlikely — and yet something told me it was. Slowing to check the yards to see where it had landed, I nearly collided with a figure stepping out from between two parked cars right in front of me.

"Hey you, watch out!"

His sturdy hands caught me by both shoulders before I could smash straight into him. He let me go and took a step back, looking me up and down. His face was inscrutable, his eyes concealed by a pair of mirrored sunglasses. He towered above me, tall and well dressed in a dark suit. In the lenses of his shades I saw myself reflected twice over, looking shaken and small.

"Sorry, mister," I said. "Wasn't looking. Didn't see you there."

"Nothing damaged. No harm done."

He flipped the sunglasses up to his forehead, studying me with deep brown eyes. As he did, a peal of thunder sounded far away across the city. Something cool and moist brushed the back of my neck, the tip of a branch poking over the wall beside us.

As soon as I saw his face, I realized I knew him from somewhere. But I couldn't place where. The dark eyes glinted with good humor and the thin lips smiled. He seemed amused by a private joke.

"Well, I'd better go," I said. "Looks like we're about to get soaked."

"Is that what you think?"

"Yeah, just look at it."

"Don't think so," he said. "Brighter spells later, the forecast says."

As he spoke, a mass of dark cloud peeled back from the sun and warm sunlight drenched the pavement where we stood. The rain was now only a faint prickle on my skin.

"Told you," he said. "Sometimes the forecasters get it right, sometimes they don't. And sometimes big changes come right out of the blue."

A tree's skeletal shadow played over his face, making his features appear to quiver and twist. When his thin smile broadened into a Cheshire-cat grin, I suddenly knew where I'd seen him before.

Doctor or lawyer or banker or whatever he might be, there was no mistaking him. This was one of the faces he'd shown me on Lamb Lane.

"Mr. October?"

"Got it in one," he said through a laugh that sounded like wind groaning through eaves in the night. "Sorry if I startled you, son. I'm just back from an important meeting and I haven't had time to . . . change. It's been a heck of a day."

"I thought I'd seen the last of you," I said.

"Ah. Sounds like you've had a rough week too. Well, the good news I'm bringing will give you a boost. Apologies for taking so long, but I've been meeting myself coming and going all week. One of my assistants had to be suspended after misfiling a vital document. Big disappointment. It's hard to find good help these days, and now my workload has doubled. But that won't be for long — assuming you're interested in the job I'm offering you."

"You want me to take his place?"

"Eventually, but not until you're ready, and not until you've seen the nature of our work and decided it's what you want."

I thought it over a moment. Whatever it was, it sounded important. "What would I have to do?"

"We begin tonight," he said. "So your first task will be to leave your home without being noticed. Do you think you can do that?"

"Yeah, I think so."

"Good. I'll be waiting. There's some traveling to do. I'll take care of the details."

"What makes you think I'm right for the job?" I said. "I mean, you hardly know me."

"I could give you a million reasons," he said. "But here are just three: because it's in your nature to help. And because you can see what others can't, like the three souls you saw in your classroom."

"You know about that?"

"Of course."

I guess I shouldn't have been so surprised.

"And the third reason?"

"I can't afford to be mistaken. There's no room for error — none at all. I've made a case for you to the Overseers, and I don't expect you to let me down." He paused there, watching me with a critical eye. "So, young man, what do you say? Are we set?"

"Yeah, I think . . . I mean, yeah, we are."

"Very good. Then welcome to the Ministry of Pandemonium, subdepartments of registration and salvage. You'll soon see for yourself what an honor that is."

"Pandemonium." The word stuck in my throat. "Like the message on the blackboard."

"Yes, the message I wrote for your eyes only," he said. "No one else could have entered that room and seen what you saw. That's proof enough of your talent for me."

"And what does the Ministry do exactly?"

"Everything that matters," he said. "But essentially we're in the business of cleaning. Life is short and messy, and we're there to tidy up when it's over. We seek out the lost and the soon-departed and show them where to go. We comfort the living. We work with the dead."

# 8

# NIGHT SHIFT

Mr. October's words clung to me all the way home. He never failed to make an impression on me, but this time he'd put my head in a spin.

The dead were everywhere among the living. I'd seen them for myself: the nameless burned man; the fire children, Mitch and Molly. I'd known they were lost and needed help, and now Mr. October was giving me a chance to help them.

I couldn't have slept after what he'd told me, so it was just as well that we were to begin on the late shift.

We'd meet at nine, he told me as we parted. I left him standing in the sunshine and ran ahead to the corner. Waiting there for a car to pass, I looked back and saw him step behind a hedge into a house's front yard. An instant later, with a flurry of feathers and scattered leaves, a raven shot above the hedge and flew up the street in a steeply rising curve.

It could have been the same bird I'd seen a few minutes ago, or another of Mr. October's disguises. Then again, I thought as I ran toward home, couldn't it have been both?

Mum came home at six, more sprightly than usual. She had the weekend off. The businessman customer had visited again, leaving another sizeable tip.

"Does he wear mirrored shades?" I asked.

"No idea. Not in the diner," Mum said.

I wondered if Mr. October had the idea that by helping her he could help me. But Mum was unclear when it came to describing her customer: kind of stylish, kind of OK-looking, neither short nor tall, not the kind of man who'd stand out in a crowd.

It might have been him. It could've been anyone.

Apart from when we spoke about the businessman, Mum seemed distracted, nodding as if she were listening to me talk when I knew she wasn't digesting a word.

"So everyone loved my picture," I said. "Things were a lot, lot better today."

"That's good."

"And I think the school could be haunted."

"If you say so, darlin'."

By eight o'clock she was spread out on the sofa, sleeping with her fists bunched under her chin. Fighting, I thought. Fighting to survive, for us, for me. But with no fight left by the time she finished work each day.

I waited for nine o'clock to come. It took, or seemed to take, forever. I sat in my room, watching the hands on the bedside clock for signs of movement. For half an hour, our downstairs neighbor played drum and bass loud enough to crack the plaster. When it finally stopped, sounds of angry voices and breaking glass drifted up from a nearby street. The start of the weekend. Oh joy. If Mum slept through it, she'd sleep through anything.

I fixed my bed, placing pillows end to end under the blankets to resemble a sleeping figure. It had worked for Frank Morris and the others who'd escaped from Alcatraz in the 1960s, and if Mum came to check on me later on, then she might be fooled as the prison guards were.

The clock's hands were at two minutes past when I heard it: a soft but rapid beating of wings followed by a solid thud as something touched down on the balcony.

I went to the window, leaned out, and looked down. In the pool of darkness on the floor below there was movement, a small huddled shape slowly inflating itself into something larger. I heard a rattling noise like the scraping together of old dry bones. Then I caught my first sight of Mr. October, raising himself up to full height.

I didn't wait for him to finish. Dry mouthed, I crept downstairs and past the living room where Mum was still sleeping. Then I let myself out.

There was no moon out, and with the streetlights at his back, Mr. October was nothing more than a silhouette. The raspy sound of his breathing reached me on the air, and I heard the *crack* of his knuckles at his side. His ragged weather-beaten outline suggested he'd returned to the swarthy pirate guise.

A sudden blast of headlights on Lansdowne Drive caught his shiny stud earring, and one silver tooth gleamed out of the black.

"Good work," he said. "You're right on time. You've kept your part of the bargain, now I'll keep mine. Are you ready?"

I nodded, too nervous to speak.

"Then it's time," he said. "But before we begin there's something you simply must see."


Watching the lights from a roof garden forty-six stories above the city, I felt I was standing on top of the world.

"I've only ever seen things like this in photos and films," I said. "It's so far away. The lights are like stars."

"A city of tiny stars, yes."

"Millions of them."

If I'd known he was bringing me to this high spot, I might have expected him to do it by magic — to bundle me up and sprout wings and fly. But Mr. October never did the expected thing. Instead we'd traveled by Tube and taken two elevators to the top.

Now he paced slowly around the edge, his ragged clothing flapping in the wind, sweeping his arm in a wide arc that took in the city.

"All this can be yours, son," Mr. October said. Then he

stopped and laughed drily. "Just joking, In fact, none of it will ever be yours, and most of what you do in this life will go unnoticed. But it's often what's unseen that matters most.

"I've been many things in my time," he went on. "I've traveled far and wide and seen sights beyond your wildest dreams. I've been a teacher, a preacher, a salesman, a doctor, a gravedigger, a circus performer, a master magician, a beggar, and a thief. Everything I've ever done has led me to this. It's all been preparation for nights like tonight. There are great things in store for us, Ben, things we'll never take credit for. But like the atoms in the molecules that make up the tiniest speck of the most infinitesimal part of the smallest bit of your little fingernail, just because you don't see it doesn't mean it doesn't exist."

He waved for me to join him at the edge. The barrier was low, less than waist-high, and I was nervous about moving closer. I took a couple of steps toward him, and he put out a hand to steady me. There was warmth in the wind, but a sudden gust might yank both of us off into space in a flash.

"Take a look at this," he said.

He took out a plain white index card and pressed it into my hand. There was nothing on it except a name, *Marilyn Jasper*, a local address, and below that some kind of reference number: 5821. I handed it back, waiting for an explanation, but he simply tucked it back into his pocket. Then, gripping the barrier with both hands and leaning forward into the wind, he said, "Now listen."

"For what?"

"Just listen."

I half closed my eyes, trying to concentrate.

"Listen harder," he said.

From the dull throb of the city below, I began to pick out separate sounds: a train trundling over a bridge, the blast of a car horn. An aircraft passed over us on its way to Heathrow, drowning everything out for a minute. We waited for it to fade, then listened again.

"Harder," Mr. October said.

The endless hum of traffic. The whoop of emergency vehicles here, there, and everywhere. Drums and bass in a distant park, a baby's cry, the night song of blackbirds, a million or more voices whispering in a hundred languages. Then the sudden shocking screech of metal against metal, and something like a small explosion.

"There," he said, taking my arm. "That's what we were waiting for. By my calculation it's central, not far from Oxford Street."

"What was it?" I said.

"Later. Go call the elevator while I get ready for work."

I ran across the roof, past the black benches and shrubs and plants, and hit the button above the service shaft. The elevator rose with a deep-sea groan.

At the far side of the roof, Mr. October seemed locked in a strange kind of wrestling match with himself, his whole body quaking, his hands pulling at his face. He stood mostly in shadow, but I knew what was happening: He was flipping through personalities the way I might flip through a deck of collectible superhero cards.

The bell pinged. The elevator doors opened wide.

Mr. October caught up, now in the shape of the old man I'd met in Highgate. He wore the same crumpled off-white suit with a red tie and looked every bit as exhausted as he had the first time. Beads of sweat sparkled across his brow.

"Go," he said, ushering me inside. "Go go go!"

"Are you OK?"

"I'll be fine. Sometimes the upheaval of changing takes it out of me."

The elevator dropped us down so fast, my ears were popping before we were halfway to ground level.

"What did I hear up there?" I asked.

"Something bad," he said. "Somebody needs us right away."

"Why the old man?"

"Always the questions. He doesn't look like much, but you'll see why when he goes to work. He's the empathizer, the one who takes the pain away."

"Always the riddles," I muttered. "Never a straight answer to a simple question."

"Some answers to simple questions can be very complex," he said.

"See what I mean? You did it again."

We stepped into the service area in the gray dark underbelly of the high-rise, a hallway filled end to end with carts, packing crates, and cleaning equipment. At one end the words EMERGENCY EXIT glowed red above a large metal door. Mr. October strode toward it, mopping his brow. He grabbed the bar with both hands and pushed. The door scraped open and we tumbled out into the street.

"This way," he said. "We have to hurry before she wanders off."

"Who?"

"Who do you think?"

"Marilyn Jasper, the name on the card?"

"You're learning, young man. See, I don't have to explain *everything*."

As we rounded the base of the building and crossed the parking lot, I noticed him hobbling. Each step seemed a tremendous effort, and the pain showed clearly on his face.

"Curse these old bones," he sighed. Without show or commotion, he reached off to his right, closing his fingers around the shaft of a walking stick that hadn't been there a moment before. The stick was made of polished light wood and had a hooked brass handle. "That's better." He stumbled on.

"Why didn't you change later?" I asked.

"Once we get where we're going, there won't be time to change."

"There'd be time if we got there sooner."

"Smart kid, but lippy," he said irritably. "And there'll be even less time if we spend all evening arguing about it."

We followed the snare of winding backstreets to Oxford Street. The lights there were overpowering, the noise nearly deafening. The traffic crawled past at walking pace.

Pedestrians clogged the sidewalks, gathering around bus stops and bright storefronts. I couldn't see any way we could go from here in a hurry.

"Well, this is no good," Mr. October said. "Looks like we'll need company transport."

His fingers crept to his earlobe and gave it a tweak.

"There's a word for this, Ben," he said, waggling his stick at the traffic. "*Pandemonium*. But get ready now, here comes our ride."

Cutting through the sea of jammed vehicles, easing through the tight gaps between them, a young Chinese woman approached, hauling a rickshaw. It wasn't the usual cycle-driven pedicab you see around town all the time, but the hand-pulled kind with a red and gold canopy over its seat. Ignoring the crowds trying to flag her down from the curb, she cut straight to the corner where we stood, waving us aboard.

"Mr. October," she called above the noise. "Please come."

"With pleasure," he said. "Ben, meet Luna. She also answers to the name of Lu."

"Hello," I said.

She nodded stiffly at each of us in turn as we climbed into the seat. Her small oval face had a set, determined expression, and she wore her hair in a shiny black bun. She looked somewhere in her late teens.

We were still settling in, and I was trying to fathom how the small single-seater took the two of us so easily, when she set off into traffic, ducking between stranded taxis and vans whose drivers were leaning full-time on their horns. Steam rose from the streets as if the city were close to boiling point. The air hung thick with the smells escaping the fast-food stalls tucked between touristy shops and department stores.

The rickshaw girl turned onto a side street, picking up the pace through lighter traffic, legs pumping like pistons, feet slapping the ground with a steady rhythm. From the waist up she looked fixed and still, hardly moving. She faced straight ahead, glancing neither right nor left as she went.

"Almost there," Mr. October said excitedly. "Another two blocks and your education begins."

We were on Wardour Street now, slipping easily between cars, through spaces that even motorcyclists couldn't make.

"When we get to the scene," Mr. October said, "your next task will be to stand and observe. You're likely to see strange and disturbing things, and it won't be easy, it won't be pleasant, but you were made for this, Ben. The Overseers are agreed with me about that."

I heard sirens nearby, and a woman screaming above the street noise. The buildings towered above us on both sides like dark castle walls, the lights of bars and clubs below washing the pavement red and green.

At the head of the rickshaw, Lu ran on. Farther along she began to slow. Crowds were gathering at the four corners of an intersection. Two cars had collided there, by the looks of it at very high speed. A black Mercedes and a blue Volvo were enmeshed, nose to nose, in a tangle of steaming metal and shattered glass, their hoods raised off the ground where they'd met.

A red-haired woman in her thirties staggered around the street, waving her arms and yelling at the crowd.

"Why don't you do something?" she cried. "You saw what happened. Don't just stand there!"

"Here," Mr. October called to Lu. "This is as far as we go."

She stopped a little way short of the accident, and I climbed out first before helping Mr. October down.

"Shall I wait?" Lu asked.

"No, we can take it from here," he said.

With a curt little nod, she maneuvered the empty vehicle back and around and returned up the street the way we'd come.

Mr. October guided me into the crowd of onlookers. The woman was still ranting, still pacing up and down. She wore a dark green dress, torn at the elbows and shoulders, and one of her shoes was missing. Her face and hands were darkly smudged, and blood trickled down her nose from a cut on her forehead.

"Won't any of you speak up?" she said. "It's obvious what happened. He was speeding the wrong way up a one-way street. There was no way I could avoid him."

No one reacted. No one replied. Police and paramedics pushed through the crowd, ignoring the woman's protests and heading straight for the wreck. Stretchers were laid out on the ground, a mangled door was pried open, and the body of a young man was lifted clear by the team.

The man was in bad shape. Blood coated his face and clothes. He moaned and covered his eyes as they lowered him onto a stretcher.

"See him?" the redhead asked no one in particular. "He's at fault. He's probably drunk — you should Breathalyze him before anything else." She stormed to the front of the crowd. "What's wrong with you people? If all you're going to do is gape, why not take a photograph too?"

Some police officers were trying to disperse the crowd. Others were setting up road blocks and diverting traffic. The woman had planted herself in front of us, and her voice was becoming so shrill, I had an urge to cover my ears.

"What about me?" she went on. "I'm the victim here. I'm the victim, but they don't care. I'll get the blame for this too, just you wait. All my life I've been on the wrong end, never had a lucky break. Look, if I'd swerved to get out of his way, I would've taken half of you with me. What then?"

"Marilyn."

Mr. October's voice was practically a whisper, but it was enough to shut the woman up.

"Marilyn, no one's accusing you of anything."

He stepped from the crowd, one hand supporting himself on the stick, the other extended toward her. As he approached, the anger drained from her face, and her eyes filled with confusion and fear.

"How do you know my name?" she asked.

"Come here and I'll explain."

Very slowly she lifted her hand to his. Their fingers were

not quite touching when a tiny bolt of white lightning sparked around and between them. Mr. October craned toward her, whispering something that made her stare at him in shock. She wobbled on her legs, and he took a firm hold of her hand, turning her to face the crash.

The injured man on the stretcher was being hurried away. A twirling ambulance light turned everything blue, then black, then blue. Some of the crowd were drifting away toward Oxford Street or deeper into Soho, so not all of them saw what I saw then — a second body being pulled from the wreckage.

It was the body of the woman with Mr. October — same hair and clothing, identical marks around her hands and face. But unlike the woman with Mr. October, she wasn't moving. Her eyes stared blankly up and she lay very still as they eased her onto a second stretcher and covered her face with a sheet.

"Move along, please," one of the police officers said. "It's over. Nothing else to see."

He never looked at Mr. October or Marilyn Jasper, never gave them the slightest notice, and without really thinking about it, I understood why.

"That can't be me," Marilyn said. "I can think. I can feel. I remember what happened."

"Separation is never easy," he said. "And it's never easy to let it all go."

I thought she might burst into tears; I hoped she wouldn't. Her eyes were brimming, but she didn't break down. Instead she nodded to show him she accepted what he'd told her. Still gripping her hand, he led her away from the scene.

As they passed me on the corner, Mr. October leaned toward me and said, "Tomorrow you'll see all the rest. Get a good night's sleep, Ben; you'll need it. I'll be in touch."

I didn't answer. I wasn't supposed to. I watched them walk up Wardour Street into the darkness past the traffic. Above them, a shooting star crossed the sky.

Then I realized the star was much lower than that. It soared above the street but below the rooftops. For a second or two its brightness was incredible, flaring every which way, leaving trails of light as fine as a spider's thread. Then it dimmed and faded, becoming just another light over the street, and I knew Marilyn was on her way.

# 9

# THE ENEMY

Despite all I'd seen, I slept well that night. I might not have if I'd seen the note Mum had left for me in the kitchen.

It wasn't so much what the note said, but the way she'd written it.

*Hi love,* it began. *Sorry missed you tonight, very tired. If you're up early we'll need milk and bread from the corner shop. Money in sugar bowl. X*

I was still rubbing sleep from my eyes when I found the note, so at first I didn't see what was wrong with it. Pocketing the money and pouring a glass of juice, I read it again.

Mum's handwriting was all wrong. It wasn't her usual careful, looped style. It looked like something she might've scrawled in the pitch dark while drunk.

She wasn't much of a drinker, though. She never even had booze in the house.

I bought the milk and bread, came home to put the kettle on, then carried a coffee upstairs for Mum. But when I heard her snoring lightly behind her door, I decided not to disturb her.

Work was wearing her into the ground. She was exhausted, that was all. She must have scribbled the note last night while half asleep. I made a bacon sandwich and ate it at the breakfast bar, and tried not to give it another thought. But something about it still gnawed at me.

Through the window, I could see the shell of the building across the street, which the council had demolished and were now rebuilding. The side wall facing our maisonette was covered with graffiti, spray-painted signatures and paintings of police in riot gear waving truncheons at thieves with balaclavas covering their heads. A stenciled black cat climbed the right side of the wall in pursuit of a stenciled rat. And running top to bottom down the left was a message in bold, black letters I had to twist sideways to read:

*Regent's Canal Angel Exit*
*See You There 11 a.m.*

I knew right away this was Mr. October's way of getting in touch. I also knew — I couldn't explain how — that because the message had been put there for me, no one else would see it.

By the time I was dressed and ready, Mum still hadn't

made an appearance. I crept to her room to let her know I was leaving.

"I'm off to meet a friend," I whispered.

"Nnn," she replied, not opening her eyes. She was murmuring something else that sounded like "good day" as I closed her door and went downstairs to let myself out.

Broadway Market was the usual Saturday crush. On either side of the green market stalls, the sidewalks were clogged with strollers, bicycles, and coffee shop patrons. I stopped at one stall, which had collectible Marvel comics laid out in clear plastic bags, and skimmed through Tales of Suspense #51.

The comic was in good condition, but I'd never be able to afford it. I was slipping it back in its protective bag when someone grabbed me from behind and turned me all the way around.

A girl with ragged short hair thumped me lightly in the chest with the heel of her hand and glared at me with eyes as keen as a cat's.

"You," she said. "I knew it was you."

"Get away from me. What's that for? What do you want?"

"You know very well," she hissed.

She looked more reptilian than human. There was a coldness and anger about her that made me uncomfortable, and it took a moment before I could place where I'd seen her before. I hadn't recognized her without the sunglasses.

"Yes," she said. "So now you remember. You and him down by the canal. Did you think you could get away with that?"

"We didn't do anything. It was an accident. Could've happened to anyone. You hit a pebble or something."

"Now, you know it wasn't like that."

"Yes, it was."

She bared a set of uneven yellowing teeth. "Stop fighting me, boy. I'll mess you up." She seized my arm, digging her fingernails in. "I'll mess up your friend even worse."

"I'll get help. I know what you are."

"Oh yeah? And what's that?"

"A thief. I'll get you arrested."

"See how far you get. I'll make mincemeat of you before you can say *boo.*"

I looked around the street, hoping someone would see, but no one did, or else no one cared. The crowds streamed around us as if we weren't even there. A procession of couples with strollers pushed their way past us. Farther down the street, a stocky, bearded man was straining to hold back a bull terrier as it tugged at its leash.

"You're in cahoots with him, aren't you?" the girl was saying. "That sad old psychopomp. You'll steer clear of him if you know what's good for you. Don't get involved, kid, if you don't want bad things to happen to you and yours."

"I don't know what you're talking about. Let go of me." I tried edging away along the stall, but she held my arm, digging her nails deeper.

"Stop fighting me or else," she said. "You know exactly

what I'm talking about. Don't go on with this, or I'll have to do something about it."

We both stopped a moment, turning to look at the sound of a man's voice bellowing not far away.

"Bronson, get back here!"

The bull terrier had broken free and came bounding up the street, colliding with a two-seater stroller along the way. Twin girls in the stroller began bawling at the top of their lungs as the dog's owner ran red-faced after it, still yelling. I saw the whites of the dog's eyes just an instant before it leapt, sinking its teeth through the thief's jeans and into her left thigh.

Her scream brought the market to a standstill. She lost her grip on my arm and stumbled back, the terrier hanging on for dear life with its legs paddling clear of the ground.

Others were running to help now, but there wasn't much they could do. The girl wheeled around, screaming, and the dog spun with her at right angles to her thigh, jaw locked in place. She fell aside into a cake stall, knocking over a display of cream horns and vanilla slices, which she then trampled to mush underfoot.

I backed down the street, nursing my arm. It felt like her nails had broken the skin, but my pain couldn't be anywhere near as bad as hers.

The dog's owner fought his way through the crowd and took hold of the snarling animal with both hands, trying to yank it free.

"Don't!" someone yelled. "It'll take half her leg with it."

"Get that thing *off* me," the thief shrieked.

"Easy, easy," someone else called.

The girl was mewling in agony. Her furious eyes found me in the crowd, just for a second, before she spun around again, carrying the dog and the man holding on to it with her. Together they crashed through a burger stall, collapsing in a heap among piles of spilled raw meat patties and linked sausages.

I took off for the bridge, along the clogged street, not looking back until I'd reached the next block. A dark figure wove its way toward me through the crowd, moving so fast between the stalls I couldn't make out its face. It couldn't be the girl — I doubted she could move at all after what had happened — but I wasn't taking chances. By the time I reached the towpath by the canal, I was running full pelt.

It was quieter by the water than it had been last time, and the chaos back on Broadway Market seemed light-years away, but I didn't slow down. I kept going, fast as I could, trying to clear my head of what I'd just seen.

How did the girl know Mr. October, and why had she warned me off? *She isn't what she seems,* he'd said, but I had only the foggiest idea what he meant.

A few minutes along, past the Queensbridge Road bridge, a wave of warm air rushed at me from behind, a breeze out of nowhere. There was a *whoosh-whooshing* noise like steadily beating wings, followed by a piercing cry that ran straight through my bones.

I turned to look just as it crashed straight into me, a huge dark shape that spun me around and down to the ground with one powerful blow.

All the breath was knocked out of me as I landed, scouring my knees and hands on the path. A sharp, searing pain ran through my right shoulder, so intense I thought I might black out. When I reached for it, it felt damp to the touch, coating my fingers in blood. That slow thudding noise came again, soft as a heart trapped underwater, just before I heard something land heavily on the path in front of me.

"Get up, boy. Stand up and see."

The voice sounded suffocated, dry as deadwood.

My eyes were swimming, and the path ahead was awash with multicolored lights, green and blue and white, the sun refracting off the water.

A figure cloaked in darkness stood over me, skinny as a wraith but easily six and a half feet tall from its scuffed boots to the tip of its misshapen head. Its clothing was tattered and black, with tufts of pale straw jutting from tears in its sleeves. At first I thought its face was covered by some kind of gray-brown mask, but that *was* its face, the flesh melted out of shape and held together by crude black stitching. Its eyes were red and glaring, the left half-covered by a permanent lid, the right having no lid at all. Its lips curled into a sneer, exposing rows of discolored, jagged teeth.

A hiss arose from the demon's throat. I cowered down, not daring to look, not daring to look away.

"Harvester," the scarecrow-like thing said. "You're meddling in matters that don't concern you, and the penalty for meddling is pain the like of which you've never known. Some doors should never be opened, lest your house be brought down and your bones ground to dust. Everything you love will be torn apart."

The thing moved closer, extending one three-fingered hand, resting a curved talon against my throat. It felt sharp enough to open me up from ear to ear, but it only gave me a gentle prod, forcing me to look up into those burning red eyes.

"First and last warning," the demon said.

"How . . . ," I began, shaking uncontrollably. "How do you know me?"

"What the Ministry of Pandemonium knows, we also know. Do you understand the warning? Will you forget everything you've seen and swear never to see him again?"

"Who? Mr. October?"

The scarecrow bristled at the very mention of his name. With one hand and one sweeping movement, it took me by my injured shoulder, hoisting me up to my feet, then off my feet and clear of the ground.

"Never," it said. "There are some thoughts too dreadful to think and some words you should never speak aloud. You never met him, are we clear? You never knew him. And you'll never ever speak his name. Understand?"

My shoulder was screaming. I couldn't think clearly enough to reply.

"Speak up!" The voice scraped like claws in the night. "Speak up or I'll leave my mark on you. I'll give you a message to deliver to your leader."

"D-Dunno what you mean," I managed to say. "I don't have a leader. Mr. October said —"

"There you go again."

The scarecrow didn't give me a second chance but set to work at once, scratching one talon in a series of minute crisscross strokes across my cheek. I winced at the slicing sensation and the warmth of my blood running down to my neck. At the same time the pressure of its grip tightened around my shoulder, and everything turned gray for the next few seconds.

I heard the distant roar of an engine and snapped back to my senses in time to see a single dark cloud crossing the sky, lower and blacker than a typical storm cloud. The demon's needle-sharp talon whispered on, back and forth across my cheek.

"There," it said, leaning back to admire its handiwork.

"Please," I whimpered.

Above us, moving at incredible speed, the storm cloud began breaking apart. As it swept toward us, I began to see what it really was. Not a cloud of vapor, but a gathering of angry, black-feathered creatures flying low in a cloud formation.

The urban ravens.

I saw the first of them hurtling our way just an instant before the demon did. The bird struck it beak-first, full force, in the side of the head. A second crashed into it from behind. The next thing I knew, the vicelike grip on my shoulder disappeared and I was back on my feet, back on solid ground, as the rest of the birds attacked all at once.

They tore into the scarecrow in a frenzy, thirty or forty in number, black beaks plunging and tearing like blades. They clung to its clothing in a heaving, flapping mass, pecking and squawking and yanking out mouthfuls of straw. Two large ravens clung to its face, and the chilling scream that followed told me exactly what they were doing. The two birds took to the sky, each carrying a prize in its bill: a bright red orb.

The attack continued. I reeled away, horrified but watching in wonder as the demon blundered off along the bank, hands clamped to its face, carrying the hungry flock with it. For a moment I thought it would topple into the water like the sunglasses thief, but instead it stumbled around a curve in the path that carried it into the darkened archway under a bridge.

I'd only lost sight of it for a second when a roar went up in the tunnel, the cry of something wild and demented. The ravens scattered, some flying north, others west, some rushing past me at head height, following the canal route I'd taken from the market.

Whatever had startled them away was still there, right around the corner and under the bridge. Preparing to come again. If it did, I knew I wouldn't get off so lightly again.

A low growl crept toward me, the sound of a wild beast preparing to strike. I was backing away from it, my heart in my mouth, when I heard something else: the angry grumble of an engine on the canal, then the chime of a familiar voice.

"You rang?" said Lu from the wheel of the white, low-slung motorboat bobbing on the water behind me.

I looked at her, astonished, nearly speechless with relief. "Ring? What did I ring?"

"Never you mind. Get in, get in right now. Time to go."

# 10

# A CRACK IN THE WALL

A s soon as I stepped aboard, Lu pulled the vessel away at an alarming rate, spinning me off my feet. I landed in the back where a blue tarpaulin covered the seat. The tarp appeared to be moving by itself.

Mr. October pushed out his head and slowly sat up, yawning and stretching. He threw the tarp aside and looked at me, watchful as a hawk. His silver tooth blinked in the light.

"You rang?" he said.

"Lu already said that. What does it mean?"

"Wait."

We were passing under the bridge where the creature had hidden. Its growl became a raging howl beneath the arches, following us all the way out. When we were safely on open water again, Mr. October relaxed.

"So what have you been up to since last night?" he asked.

I was excitable and shaken and the words came out in a

breathless muddle. The girl at the market and the demon and the cloud of ravens . . .

"Slow down," he said, passing me a tangerine he seemed surprised to find behind his ear. "What's your understanding of all you've seen today? Think about it. Take your time."

Peeling the fruit with a thumbnail, I said, "Well, when the dog went after the girl, and later when the ravens attacked, I thought . . ."

"Yes, what did you think?"

"I got the feeling I made it happen somehow. I made them attack. But I don't know how." I looked up from peeling the tangerine. "What did you and Lu mean, I rang?"

"A figure of speech. However, our people in the dispatch office received two coded distress calls from you, logged at 10:18 and 10:23 precisely. You called for help and we answered."

I popped a tangerine link into my mouth, bitter and sweet.

"Even born helpers need help sometimes," Mr. October said. "You sent the distress calls without knowing it, but that's only a part of your gift, Ben, the hidden part you're still learning about — it's why we took an interest in you from the start."

"The girl," I said. "She's more than just a thief, isn't she?"

He nodded. "Yes. She's many things."

Lu zipped across the water, churning up a trail of foam past a line of brightly painted moored barges.

Looking back, I saw a slick, dark shape, shiny as an eel, slither into the water near the tunnel.

"What did it look like, your attacker?" Mr. October said. "Did it look anything like this?"

He turned away for a second, then looked at me squarely, making a face. When Mr. October made a face, you sat up and took notice. The scarecrow regarded me blankly with the same misplaced red eyes the birds had gouged out.

"That's it," I said through a shudder. "Exactly like that. Except it had bits of straw sticking out of its clothing and fingers with talons."

"Curse it," he said. "Should've seen this coming. And what did he say?"

"It . . . *he* said I shouldn't meddle in things I don't understand. And he threatened to tear my house down and turn my bones to dust. Oh, and he said never to mention your name — that it was the worst thing of all."

"He always was a pompous so-and-so." Mr. October switched faces again, back to the swarthy pirate, then touched the mark on my cheek. "And I suppose he left this message for me?"

"Yes. What's it say?"

"It's written in a runic alphabet known as Futhorc. It essentially says caution, stay away or face the consequences. The literal translation is, *Those who enter do so at their peril — we own the night.* As I said, pompous."

Next he inspected my damaged shoulder. The nerves sang up and down my arm. Finding bandages and antiseptic lotion in a pocket, he set about tending to the wounds.

"Sorry to see you in the wars," he said. "You'll live, but I should've warned you about them. I just didn't think they'd pick up on you so soon."

"Who are they?"

"The one you met today is known as Synsiter," Mr. October said.

At the controls of the speeding boat, Lu tensed her shoulders and spat in the water.

"Synsiter?" I said.

"Nathan Synsiter, second in command to Lord Randall Cadaverus, one of Cadaverus's messengers. Strictly speaking, Cadaverus is no more a lord than I'm a quantum physicist. He worked at the Ministry until, oh, eleven or twelve centuries ago. In those days he went by the much less grand name of Ben Crawley, a name he changed after he defected."

This new information whirled through my mind. Houseboats and elegant waterside apartments sailed by. A family of mallards huddled on the bank near the exit at Shepherdess Walk.

"One day," Mr. October continued, "it came to the attention of the Overseers that a team of junior clerks, led by Crawley, were misfiling records of the newly deceased. In fact, they were stealing the names of the dead for their own nefarious reasons, working against the salvage department to keep us from carrying out our duties. By the time their plot was uncovered, they'd already formed their splinter group and the damage was done. They were expelled from the Ministry, of course, but they've been making our work harder ever since."

"How so?"

"They're very much like us," he said. "They share many of our powers, including the ability to change appearances. They can manifest themselves at any time, anywhere. Three of their number were there last night in the crowd. They would've stolen Marilyn Jasper away if we hadn't been there, just as they stole the Willow children, who you saw in your classroom."

"Mitch and Molly." A sickly sensation clutched my stomach. "What would they want with them?"

"The same thing they'd want from any other strandeds. The more confusion and tribulation and grief they cause, the better it is for them. They thrive on it. They devour it. It adds to their power and enables them to bring yet more disorder and chaos to the world."

I chewed another segment of tangerine, but the sweetness had gone and I only tasted the bitterness. I threw the rest of it over the side.

"You've seen them at their worst today," Mr. October said. "Loud and bombastic, all bad tidings and bile. But make no mistake, they can be extremely subtle too. They might whisper in your ear and put a thought in your head, a thought you mistake for your own. Why not keep the wallet full of cash you find in the gutter even if it hurts someone else? Why bother to help the poor homeless guy lying in the street?

He's probably an addict who put himself there. You see how it works?"

"Yeah, I think so."

"That's what they did to the Willows on the morning of the fire — just a whisper in the parents' ears as they bought bread at the café. It couldn't hurt to spend another ten minutes over coffee, could it? Which was all the time they needed for the building to go up in flames, giving them an opportunity to steal the children away."

Taking this in, or as much of it as I could, I felt the start of a headache. My brain was overloading.

"I was asked to help those kids," I said.

"Perhaps you still can, but it's harder now. They're not on our radar. They're hidden."

I looked back at the canal, calm and glassy except for the boat's trail, no sign of the slimy beast I'd seen sliding under the surface. It too could be anywhere now.

We were slowing. Lu was steering us to the bank at the Angel exit, clucking her tongue at the conversation she'd overheard. As the boat settled and we began climbing out to the towpath, she tapped my arm.

"The Lords are very bad," she said. Her small face was pinched and deeply serious, her eyes unblinking. "You take great care, Ben Harvester. Stay away from them. Very bad."

"OK."

While Mr. October led me up the steep path from the canal, Lu steered the vessel under the bridge and sped away west. We continued up onto Colebrooke Row, then took another slope toward Upper Street.

"What did she mean?" I asked Mr. October.

"Lu? Ah, she's talking about the Lords of Sundown — Randall Cadaverus's team of outcasts. She lost her entire family to them ten years ago and she's been with our department ever since."

"What happened?"

"Her parents had a small business in Soho, a Chinese apothecary — well established but not terribly successful. They were always in debt, struggling to make ends meet. One night in a fit of desperation, her father gambled away everything they had in a game of mah-jongg — lost the business, the family home, everything. Next day he drove his family through a railway crossing into the path of a speeding train. He was killed instantly; so were his wife and two sons. Lu was the only survivor. She's grown up believing that one of Cadaverus's followers took part in the game that ruined her father. He cheated, of course, the game was rigged, designed to drive the man over the edge. And as Cadaverus well knows, a soul in torment is easily led and easily captured. He scored four souls very cheaply that day."

"But couldn't you have stopped it? Isn't that what you do?"

The Y on Mr. October's forehead deepened. "Let's be clear about this. Lives would've been lost whatever we did. What's written is written. All we can do is provide safe passage, give families their peace, and deliver the lost to their departure point. The names of Lu's family were on our list, but the list was leaked from inside the department — by a mean little weasel named Ethan Hill.

"Hill got his marching orders, but too late to stop Cadaverus getting to Lu's family first, before we could. They're still in the great unknown somewhere; we're still looking for them, and Lu still hasn't had a chance to say her farewells."

"That's awful." I didn't know what else to say. "Just awful."

"Yes. Lu's very strong and courageous, but she carries a great sadness with her."

We turned north onto the noisy hive of Upper Street. It was warmer here than by the canal; I felt the heat rising from the pavement.

"No wonder she warned me about them," I said. "But they warned me about you. Synsiter said I should never see you again."

"Then why are you here?"

"I don't know."

"But I do. You're growing up fast, Ben. You're smart enough to make up your own mind, and you don't need to be told what to do. This war has raged for centuries, and the rules have never changed — you can only be on one side or the other. The choice is yours."

A large woman waddled ahead of us on the street, taking up most of the sidewalk and paddling her arms as if swimming freestyle. We edged around her, me to the left, Mr. October to the right.

"Suppose I don't make a choice?" I said. "Suppose I can't?"

"I'm confident you'll do what's right."

He indicated where we would turn off the main street before stopping me on the corner.

"Very soon you'll see the heart of our operation," he said. "Then you'll decide for yourself. If you're with us, the Lords of Sundown will be up in arms. Randall Cadaverus will take it as a personal slight."

"And if I'm against you?"

"Then I would have to kill you," he said, straight-faced.

His words hung in the air; the street noise seemed to withdraw. For several seconds an emergency siren, streets away, was the only sound. Then Mr. October held his sides and laughed.

"Gotcha," he said.

"I wish you wouldn't do that."

"Sorry, son, but after so long in the field, one's sense of humor does tend toward the morbid. But of course you're smart to question, and there's always a third choice, which is to do nothing at all. But then you'd always know what you're missing — and you'd never take advantage of your natural-born gift."

"Mum always talks about my artwork that way."

"Well, that's a worthy talent too. And like any raw talent you're given, it should be practiced and used. It would be a crime to waste it."

He led me onto Camden Passage, a narrow winding thoroughfare of tiny stalls selling trinkets, bead necklaces, many-colored crystals, vintage hardcover books on fly-fishing and pet care and economics, and piles of magazines from the 1950s and '60s. It was like stepping back in time.

We picked our way through the crowd, past a group of shoeless children playing dice on the cobblestones, past a man selling pink sweet-smelling cotton candy from a steaming machine. At the far end of the passage was an organ grinder with a performing marmoset wearing a bowler hat. The monkey ran among the shoppers, doffing its hat to collect loose change.

There was a narrow inlet between two of the shops, a space so tiny and dark, I would've walked past without seeing it if Mr. October hadn't steered me toward it.

"Quick now," he said. "While no one's looking."

The walls were so close together, we had to edge sideways between them, noses brushing the brickwork in front of us. There was a sound of dripping water somewhere, not loud but noticeable because suddenly the busy trinket stalls were muted and the barrel organ music faint and far away.

The light behind us shrank away too. We'd stepped out of the brightness of day into what felt like a cave. Water squelched underfoot. Cool droplets hit the back of my neck, and I shivered and wiped them away as another droplet hit my nose.

Ahead of me, Mr. October cleared his throat. All I could see of him was a vague silhouette, a shadow among other shadows.

"Not far to go, Ben. Nearly there."

As he spoke, a muddy light bloomed out of the pitch darkness ahead. It appeared artificial, not like daylight at all.

At the end of the claustrophobic passageway, we came out into a cobbled alley lit by a pair of gas-burning streetlamps, one on either side of the steps rising to the dark blue door of the only building in sight. Lu's rickshaw was parked in front.

The house, all solid brown brick, looked old and forgotten, with soft light visible between the shutters at the downstairs windows. The upper windows, like the entire upper half of the building, fell into darkness.

It was nighttime in the alley, and above us the sky was a deep midnight blue with a frosting of stars. A brass plaque above the main door read PANDEMONIUM HOUSE. Another toward one end of the building read EVENTIDE STREET.

"You'll get used to it," Mr. October said. "Things aren't quite the same here as they are elsewhere."

"So this is the Ministry's base," I said, following him to the front door.

"We're based everywhere," he said. "This is only one of a myriad of operations we're running around the planet."

The door opened and three uniformed men filed out. Their serious faces were nearly as gray as their jackets, and each had a silver long-nosed rifle strapped across his chest. They eyed me suspiciously, but saluted when they saw Mr. October.

"Security," Mr. October explained. "They're known as Vigilants here. We've increased their numbers threefold since the last information leak. It's their job to ensure no records of any kind ever leave the premises."

"And the weapons?" I asked. I was fascinated by, if more than a little wary of, those rifles.

"Not really my area of expertise," Mr. October said, "but I understand they're some kind of DEW, directed energy weapons, that fire plasma waves or something of the sort. They could stop a rhino in its tracks at a hundred and fifty feet and put it to sleep for ten minutes. Of course, the Vigilants don't actually kill anyone — that would be against our philosophy. We run a strict shoot-to-stun policy here."

I was only now getting a sense of the scale of the Ministry's operation: There was far more to it than I could've imagined. On the opposite side of the alley, the tight space we'd squeezed through to get here was no longer visible. Facing us across the cobbled ground was a dark, unbroken wall.

"It's there if you look for it," Mr. October said. "That is, if you know how to look. See there, and there? From this angle it resembles a wavy hairline crack."

"How do you get the rickshaw in and out?"

"With some difficulty. It's Lu's responsibility, but she's greatly skilled. She was once a contortionist in a circus side-show — used to fold herself into and out of an overnight bag. One of the strangest sights I ever saw, and I've seen very many strange sights."

At last he led me indoors, through a darkened hall and up a flight of creaky wooden stairs. The place had an ancient, sealed-up smell with an undertone of stale furniture polish that reminded me of Mercy Road School.

The stairs led us to a long candlelit corridor lined with windowless doors, all firmly shut. There was a muffled tapping coming from somewhere and a constant hum of wind, like a draft trapped in the gutters.

"This way," Mr. October said.

The candlelight in the corridor shivered and twisted as we started along it. As we passed the first few doors, I noted the brass nameplates fixed to each one: SALVAGE, DISPATCH, RECORDS, CONFERENCE ROOM, CLEANING UTENSILS, WAITING ROOM.

Mr. October stopped at a door marked RECEIPTS. He turned toward me, his features reshaping themselves in the flickering light.

"Just think," he said. "Little more than a fortnight ago, you hadn't a clue. You were looking for something, but you didn't know what. And see how far you've come now. On the other side of this door are the answers to all your questions, and once we open it, there's no going back. Do you follow?"

"Yes." I swallowed nervously. "Yes I do."

"Then open your eyes, Ben Harvester. Your life is about to change."

And with a flourish, Mr. October opened the door.

# 11

# THE SOON-DEPARTED

The only light source in the room was a candle in an alcove, its shuddery light falling across a small mahogany desk, on which an old typewriter sat, and the swivel chair drawn up in front of it.

I'd seen typewriters in films and photographs, and one in the window of a Stoke Newington thrift shop, but I'd never been up close to one. It was a small but solid-looking model with a pistachio green metal body, glossy black keys, and a single red key on its right-hand side. Above the keypad were the words LETTERA 22. On the desk beside the typewriter was a rack of blank index cards, the same size as the one Mr. October had shown me on the roof garden.

On a shelf near the desk was another ancient metallic machine, even older than the typewriter, with a scratched and battered silver body and sides of burnished brass. A cogwheel at the rear fed paper from a roll down through it and out the front. I was puzzling over what it could be when the contraption sprang to life.

It began with a bang like a muffled gunshot, then rattled and groaned as the paper edged slowly through it and out the front. The machine rocked so violently on its shelf that the entire room trembled with it. There was a burning smell like engine oil, and white smoke puffed from the joints in its casing.

"What's that?" I asked. "And what's it doing?"

"It's delivering a message," Mr. October said, "which means bad news for someone. It only ever brings bad news. It's an 1873 Stern & Grimwald electric telegraph, a relatively primitive form of communication — but this is a telegraph of a very special kind. It delivers the most delicate and important data there is."

I stepped back, afraid it was about to explode.

"It's noisy," I said. "And it looks like it's working too hard."

"You should see it on busier days when it goes into overload."

For all its crashing and moaning, the machine was incredibly slow, pushing out its paper only a fraction at a time. We waited more than a minute for it to finish. Then, with a final loud crack that sent orange and blue sparks leaping around its body, the telegraph came to a grinding halt and sat silent.

Mr. October tore out the sheet and brought it to the desk, spreading it out beside the typewriter.

"There," he said. "The latest list."

I had to strain to see in the candlelight. A column of names ran from top to bottom of the page, each with some kind of coded reference number.

Mr. October ran a hand back through his hair, then tapped the page near the top of the list.

"The names and addresses speak for themselves. These are the soon-departed, the ones who're about to die."

"About to?" I looked at him, openmouthed.

"Some may have an hour or two if they're lucky, but more likely it'll be a matter of minutes or even seconds."

I clasped my hands behind my head, nursing a throbbing pain. "But there's nothing you can do to stop it . . . because it's written."

"Precisely. Their numbers are up. We can't interfere in any way, and we never have long to prepare."

"My Aunt Carrie's name was on a list like this, wasn't it?" I said. "That's how you knew, the first time we met. You knew before the family did because you had the list before she'd even gone."

"Yes."

"And the same thing with Marilyn Jasper last night. You had her name before we went to the roof, before we even heard the crash."

"Yes."

I fell into the chair at the desk, letting it all sink in. Candlelight played across the typewriter's keys, orange and white.

"So what do the reference numbers mean?"

"They describe the exact cause and nature of death. Here, you see . . ." He leaned over the sheet, tracing each record with a forefinger. "Here's reference 5821, the same as Marilyn. Car crash caused by a drunk driver. And this one, 8847, means natural causes: nonspecific. There are three of those here. Very sad, but not as sad as 10176 — run over by an ambulance while returning from a hospital appointment. The patient had just received scan test results after six months of treatment and the prognosis was good."

"God, that's unlucky."

"No, it's written. It's not about luck. And here's another, 43765 — we don't see many of these. Man packages himself up in a cardboard box and mails himself to his fiancée as a surprise birthday present. Fiancée opens it carelessly with a pair of scissors . . . very unpleasant."

"How did he put the stamps on the box?"

Mr. October shrugged. "It doesn't say."

We fell silent a moment out of respect for the soon-departed.

Then Mr. October said, "Now here's what we do. We have to record these details on the cards, two copies of each, one for our files and one for the field."

"The field?"

"That would be me, or any other operative doing what I do. Have you used a typewriter before?"

I shook my head no.

"Then I'll explain," he said, and took me through it step-by-step: what the various parts were called and what they did, which key or lever to press for which function. The black roller thing was a platen. The single red key was for tabs. The two linked keys on the left were for caps and caps lock.

He rolled the first card into the machine.

"Type it exactly as you see it," he said. "Any mistakes and you'll have to start over. Never file a card until you're a hundred percent certain it's accurate, otherwise all bets are off. If the wrong name goes to records, it gets very messy. The telegraph never makes a mistake, but clerks have been known to."

"And where do they come from, these names?" I said.

Mr. October shook his head, a faraway look in his eyes. "Only the Overseers know that."

It gave me a chill to sit there, preparing to add the first name to the first card. But when I hit the first key — nothing happened at all.

"Leverage," Mr. October said. "Elbow grease. You'll get a feel for it with practice."

After mistyping the first card three times, I began to get the hang of it, and the fourth attempt looked passable. I offered it to Mr. October, who compared it to the printed list before giving me an approving nod.

"Fine. Now the rest."

A few minutes later we had two piles of typed cards on the desk, and I was warming to the typewriter's *click-clack* sound and the *ping* of its return carriage bell. Mr. October pocketed one set of cards and handed me the other.

"Whenever you're alone here, this is what you'll do," he said. "Monitor the lists as they arrive, add the names and numbers to the cards, then file one set of cards only. The second set is for me, or for dispatch if I'm away. At other times you'll maintain the telegraph — oil, dry lubricant, and *User's Quick-Start Guide* are all on the shelf. Can you do that?"

"Think so," I said.

But he saw that I still had doubts.

"Something wrong?"

"It's just the thought of sitting here knowing every time the telegraph makes a sound it means someone's about to . . . about to die."

"I know." He ruffled my hair. "It's never easy. It isn't supposed to be."

As we left the room, the telegraph woke again, chugging away behind us. Mr. October shook his head ruefully and closed the door on it, leading me away up the hall.

Next he took me to the records office. The sight of it stole my breath. The space was impossibly huge, far too big for the building to contain it. White walls rose up as far as the eye could see, floor after floor stacked to the heights with towering filing cabinets. A spiral staircase connected the many levels, and on each floor workers in dark blue overalls perched on rolling stepladders as tall as the tallest cabinets. They moved from one cabinet to another, opening drawers, filing cards, then rolling along to the next.

"Like drones," I said.

Mr. October smiled.

If the place had a ceiling, I couldn't see it. All I could see in the rafters, miles above, was a mass of slowly swirling white mist with tiny winged creatures, possibly bats, circling through it. The room seemed to shimmer as I looked, as if everything inside it was constantly moving.

"It's a living thing," Mr. October explained. "The room is actually alive. The names we keep here go back through eternity. There's a record for everyone who ever lived. And new names are being added all the time, so it can never be still — it's always evolving and expanding."

"Amazing. From the outside you'd never expect anything like this."

"Some of us call it the infinite room, even though officially it's 'records.'"

He set off across the white marble floor, heading for a blocky gray rectangular shape in the distance.

"The room's expanding so fast," Mr. October said, "you'll find it takes ten seconds longer to walk back than to walk where we're going. Soon we'll need transportation to cross it. And new floors are being added every day."

We went on, surrounded by the echoes of opening and closing cabinets, rolling ladders, and the endless groaning wind, louder here than elsewhere in the building.

Closer to the far side of the room, I could see where we were heading. A small booth, jammed between two skyscraper cabinets, was occupied by a round-faced elderly woman with a perm and pince-nez spectacles. A thick ledger lay open on the counter in front of her, and her plump fingers held a pencil at the ready. Some of the drones, having filed their cards, were coming down the ladders and lining up at her booth for more. For each in turn, she reached under the counter and brought out a new stack of cards, then recorded the batch in her ledger.

The workers lowered their heads respectfully as Mr. October approached, but the woman looked far from pleased to see him, screwing up her face as if she tasted something bitter. Nearer to the booth I noticed her hair and clothing were covered with cobwebs. A multitude of spiders flitted about her, weaving with impunity. I guessed she hadn't left the booth in some time.

"Afternoon, Miss Webster," Mr. October said brightly. "More soon-departeds for your books. Ben, please give Miss Webster the cards."

I slid them across the counter. Miss Webster glared at them through her thick lenses, her eyes large and owl-like.

"Meet Ben Harvester," Mr. October said. "Our newest recruit and a rare talent. You'll see much more of him from now on."

"Hmm," she murmured. "That's more work for me, then, isn't it? Welcome, young man."

She sounded so disdainful, I looked the other way, saying nothing.

"So I suppose you'll be out in the field together," Miss Webster said. "All right for some. I haven't seen daylight in thirty-six years."

"Nothing we do would be possible without you," Mr. October reassured her.

"Fiddlesticks." She leaned over the counter, signaling the first worker in the queue. "Next!"

"Well, enjoy your day," Mr. October said.

"What's to enjoy? They're all the same."

"Nice meeting you," I said as we started away. "By the way, you've got spiders in your hair."

"I know," she said tiredly, waving us off with the back of her hand. She must've heard it many times before.

"Absolutely hates her job," Mr. October said when we were out of earshot. "But that's understandable. It's thankless work and very long hours. Whereas the workers, the drones, don't even think of it. They're paper chasers and pencil pushers who don't know anything else. Be glad, Ben, you won't go through life like one of them."

We crossed the vast records room, arriving at the exit some time later. I didn't count the steps we took and I couldn't be sure the room had grown while we'd been inside. But when I looked up, the mist seemed slightly higher than before and the flying creatures even tinier, like specks of dust.

Before the afternoon's salvage began, Mr. October took me to the dispatch room, where in the future I'd bring the second set of cards if he wasn't there to collect them.

The cramped room had ten partitioned desks shoehorned together with two officers seated at each. They wore crisp tan uniforms and bulky headphone sets that must've weighed several pounds apiece, and they chattered away like telemarketers into desktop microphones, reading from the stacks of cards in front of them.

"5963 in NW5."

"Do you read me? That's SE6, repeat SE6. 8847."

"11763 in WC1. Urgent. 11763."

None of them paid us any attention. When Mr. October tried to introduce me, two of the staff adjusted their headsets to listen, but they didn't react and quickly went back to work.

"They'll know you next time," Mr. October said, eyeing a muted TV monitor on one wall. "Don't take it personally if they seem to ignore you. They're always this busy. They take calls from all over the city."

The TV was showing news footage. Two buses had collided on Blackfriars Road, and text scrolled across the bottom of the screen describing the damage: twelve injured passengers, one driver in critical condition.

Mr. October checked his pockets for the duplicate cards and showed me the first.

"See here," he said. "7696. Bus crash fatality."

"7696!" a dispatch girl called from the back of the room. "London Bridge Hospital!"

"I'm on it," Mr. October said. "That's us, Ben. Let's get there before Cadaverus's agents do."

# 12

# DAY SHIFT

For our afternoon rounds, Mr. October wore the old man's body in the rumpled white suit as he always did for delicate occasions. We visited the hospital first.

By the time we arrived, the bus driver was in the intensive care unit and his ghost was pacing the waiting area like an expectant father. Mr. October whispered briefly with the receptionist, an elfin woman with white streaks running through her jet-black hair, then he took me aside.

"It's all clear. The Lords of Sundown have agents in every hospital — there's always a wealth of strandeds and newly-departeds in places like this — but we have our own here too. The receptionist is one of ours. She says none of Cadaverus's crew have shown up yet. Keep a lookout while I deal with the driver. He knows what's happened, but he doesn't know where to go from here."

While Mr. October spoke to the man in a consultation

room across the corridor, I watched the comings and goings of hospital staff, patients, and visitors. If the enemy were as good at disguise as Mr. October said, they could be anywhere. A porter went by, pushing a gurney. A team of nurses followed. A man in a wheelchair with one leg in a cast rolled himself out of an elevator.

A blinding white light flashed behind the consultation room door. The receptionist winked at me and touched a finger to her lips, and I knew then that the driver was gone.

The rest of the afternoon was a whistle-stop tour. After the hospital we had a natural causes at a Putney Vale shopping center, then another at a nursing home in Richmond. Both were elderly and well mannered and knew it had been coming for some time.

The man at the nursing home was sitting in a chair by his bedside, staring thoughtfully at his lifeless body under the sheets. Hearing us enter the room, he took to his feet and looked at us calmly.

"Ah, it's you," he said.

"Samuel Garner?" Mr. October said.

"Yes. I've been expecting you. I've been tired for so long."

"That's fine," I said, hoping I wasn't speaking out of turn. "You can rest now."

He gave a sigh of relief. "At last."

Later, we headed north for a 3618 in Wood Green. A forty-four-year-old man named Howard Burke had taken a tumble while performing a bit of DIY tile repair on his roof. The fall hadn't killed him, but the inflatable children's wading pool in the garden where he landed had — 3618 meant drowning.

Then another natural causes at a tapas restaurant opposite Tufnell Park Tube station. After that, close to Highgate Cemetery, we found the ambulance victim, the 10176.

Bob Fletcher, 38, had been struck while crossing the street by an ambulance racing to answer an emergency call. Death had been instantaneous. Fletcher was livid. The scene had already been cleared, his body driven away, and now he sat by the roadside with a girl in a stylish black suit who was doing her best to console him.

"It's not fair," Fletcher was saying. "My appointment with the specialist was such great news, everything I wanted to hear, and then that idiot came out of nowhere — I didn't have a chance. Look at me now — cuts and bruises, dislocated shoulder, and bloody invisible too! I'll sue, that's what. But who'll pick up my kids from school? Who'll tell my wife? She's expecting me home. I just called to say put the kettle on, we've got something to celebrate. . . ."

He hung his head. The girl at his side stroked his hand. Her tan face was fixed and serious, her black hair short-cropped and spiky.

"I know," she said. "I know."

"Who is she?" I asked Mr. October. "And how can she see him?"

"This is how they operate," he said. "This is how subtle they are. It's why we have to keep up this pace. She's one of them, one of Cadaverus's cronies."

He marched straight to them, addressing the girl in a voice that snapped like a whip.

"You. Hey, you. Scat!"

She looked up in alarm, let go of Fletcher's hand, and scrambled to her feet, facing Mr. October with an expression somewhere between fear and contempt.

"No, *you* scat," she hissed. "We were here first."

Mr. October drew a breath, as deep a breath as his body would allow, and as he leveled his walking stick, a strange animal sound crept from his throat.

"*Shallaleiken fsood man-pareth,*" he said. "*Ark fnaark man-pareth malakayenisti!*"

It wasn't like any language I knew and I had no idea what it meant, but it obviously meant something to her. The girl tottered back several steps, rocking on her feet as if she'd been punched. Her eyes rolled back, showing only the whites. A tremor ran through her, causing her arms to shake violently. She began to shrink into herself, sagging inside her suit.

There was an explosion of dark light, the air turning black where she'd been standing, and then she vanished completely. In her place was a feral gray and black cat, teeth bared and back arched. It took one poisonous look at Mr. October before shooting off down the hill.

Mr. October took a step forward, flipped his stick neatly from right hand to left, then flashed out his free arm as if hurling a stone.

A ball of orange-yellow flame leapt from his fingertips

and trundled down the street, gathering speed after the cat. At the end of the block, the cat scaled a high trellis fence and dropped wailing to the other side. The fireball burst against the stone wall below it, scattering smaller balls of flame every which way. A smell of burning cinders crept up the street.

Mr. October leaned on his walking stick, watching the smoke clear.

"What the heck did I just see?" Bob Fletcher demanded. "I mean, what was that and who are you people?"

"Friends," Mr. October said, helping Fletcher's ghost to his feet. The effort of doing that took something out of him, and he took a moment to catch his breath. "Yes, friends. Unlike the rapscallion you were just talking to."

"You're lucky we got here," I said.

"Lucky? You must be joking. How lucky is it to get run over by an ambulance? What did you do to that girl?"

Mr. October wiped his brow. "That was no girl. That was a shape-shifting agent of darkness."

"Nonsense." Fletcher paced the sidewalk, fuming, seemingly unaware of his oddly jutting dislocated shoulder. "Stuff and nonsense. She tried to help, couldn't you see? An agent of what? Get away. You're insane."

"This will be tricky," Mr. October told me. "He's angry and confused and convinced a great injustice has been done, the very qualities — or rather, weaknesses — the enemy look for in a target. They'll be back with reinforcements if we tarry too long."

"What can we do?"

"Let me think."

He stroked his white-whiskered chin, his face inscrutable. I shivered, sensing a change in the air. It was cooler now. The shadows of privet hedges and garden shrubs were stretching across the street.

Were these the reinforcements he meant? If the Lords of Sundown could take any shape, suppose they were inside these shadows, hiding and ready to spring?

"Look there." I gave Mr. October a nudge.

"Shush, I'm still thinking."

"Think faster, then. It looks like they're here."

The black shapes crossing the ground suddenly looked more like spindly fingers than tree branches. One reached for my feet and I jumped across the curb with a yelp. Another twitched toward Mr. October, though he didn't acknowledge it. At the intersection where the fireball had detonated, a host of new shapes squirmed out from the shade beneath the stone wall.

"What will I do?" Bob Fletcher said. "What's the wife gonna do when she finds out she'll never see me again? And the kids . . . oh God, what a mess. What'll I do?"

A light came on in Mr. October's eyes.

"Listen," he said. "Bob, will you trust me?"

"Why should I? I trusted that girl and you blew her to bits."

"Only because I had to. She would've chewed you up and spat you out if you'd gone with her. You'd be a darn sight worse off than you are now."

"You're mad. I'm not listening to you."

"I'm all you've got," Mr. October said. "What happened to you was tragic, but also inevitable. If it hadn't been an ambulance, it would've been something else, a truck or a taxi or falling masonry. Your time is up, and the sooner you let go, the easier it will be."

The shadows were snapping at our heels. I hopped around the pavement, dodging them. All along the street they were tearing themselves from walls and fences, creeping out from under parked cars.

"Mr. October," I said, close to panicking.

But he ignored me, resting a hand on Fletcher's busted shoulder and speaking to him in low, soothing tones.

"Trust me and I'll take the pain away, and the anger too. I'll make sure you see your wife one more time, give you a chance to say what you need to."

Fletcher's anguished face softened. "You can really do that?"

"I really can."

The shadows stopped in their tracks. Very slowly they began to withdraw, snaking back from the pavement where we stood. I watched them shrinking across the street until they were only shadows again, stirring gently over the asphalt in the breeze.

Bob Fletcher never even saw them. He had no idea what he'd done. Now I knew what Mr. October had meant when he'd said they fed on people's grief and rage. The smell of it had lured them out of the dark, but Fletcher's change of mood had sent them straight back.

"I'd give anything for that chance," he said, "even if it's only a few minutes. Sorry for carrying on before. I must be in shock."

"No apology necessary," Mr. October replied. "But we'd best be off. As you say, she's expecting you."

It was a big art deco house on leafy Brim Hill, a pleasant and peaceful place until they broke the news and Mrs. Fletcher began to scream. I had decided to wait outside.

I stood in the driveway, watching the house, tired and hungry, wondering how Mr. October coped with this all the time, every day. The screaming stopped and a silence drew out, and all I heard then was birdsong, a distant lawn mower, an occasional car rushing by.

Finally the thing I'd been waiting for came: an explosion of light behind a downstairs window, startlingly bright as a camera flash. Seconds later, Mr. October came hobbling down the driveway, looking drained but flushing with pride.

"Sometimes I surprise myself, I'm that good," he said. "That was hard work, but rewarding. Anyway, it's over now. He's gone to where Cadaverus can't reach him."

"But Cadaverus nearly did."

"Yes, he came close. You handled yourself very well, young man."

We turned off the driveway and onto the street, heading to our next call in Belsize Park.

"How did you do it?" I had to ask. "The ball of fire was incredible."

"Thought you'd appreciate the fireworks. Actually, it's mostly for show, and the Overseers don't encourage anything that's for show. They frown on pyrotechnics. Still, it does tend to give the enemy a bit of a fright."

"Could I do that?"

"Not yet. Only at the appointed time, and even then only with practice. And please don't try it at home." He checked the next card, the last on our list. "Ah. Another difficult case."

"What language was it that you spoke to the girl?" I asked. It seemed to me the words he'd used had done even more damage than the fire.

"Ministry dialect." He felt around inside his jacket. "Apocalypti slang, a form of ancientspeak only demons and field agents understand. Here, see for yourself."

He took out a pocket-size book, *The Pandemonium Guide to Apocalypti Idioms & Phrases*, a slim volume that felt weightier in my hand than it should.

"Hardly a catchy title," he said, "but its audience is limited because it's a near-impossible language to learn. Look inside and you'll see why."

Opening the book at random, I could see he wasn't kidding. The print quivered around the page like grubs, the letters scurrying in all directions to form new words, then breaking apart to form even newer words.

"Like the records office," Mr. October said. "The book is alive and constantly changing. It takes enormous skill and concentration to master it."

I turned to another page. More moving, scuttling text. It looked like the book had been colonized by ants.

"Don't strain," he said. "You'll never be able to read it until you're ready. And when you're ready, be extremely careful how you use it. There's nothing more destructive than a few choice words of ancientspeak used in the wrong way. You could build new worlds with the right words, or just as easily tear worlds apart."

I closed the phrase book, fascinated but somehow afraid of its power, and offered it back.

"Keep it for that time," he said. "It's yours."

"OK."

I pocketed the book, amazed by the idea that these words could be like guns or bombs in the wrong hands. There was something awesome about that, something scary. Then again, I realized I may never be able to learn it. I couldn't until the words stopped moving, anyway.


The last stop on the shift, at Belsize Grove, proved to be the strangest of all.

In order to give Mr. October's legs a rest, we'd taken the

Tube from East Finchley and twenty minutes later came out onto Haverstock Hill. Now we were standing on a quiet sunlit sidewalk beside an herb garden that overlooked the curved steps leading down to a basement apartment. Mr. October rechecked the name and reference on the card — Andy Cale, 43765 — and I remembered the unusual circumstances of the death.

"It's the parcel bloke," I said. "He mailed himself to his fiancée."

"The very same."

He started down the steps, testing each one with his stick as he went.

"Some people do the oddest things, Ben. In all my time, I've only seen two other cases like this, both equally grim. Why they don't think these things through I'll never know. It beggars belief, it's so idiotic."

"You sound angry."

"Well, some cases break my heart, and then some, like this . . . they're just wasteful. However, it's foretold — it's meant to be — so what can I do?"

At the bottom of the steps, the apartment's front door was slightly ajar. Blue-and-white-check curtains were drawn behind the window beside it, so there wasn't much to see without going inside.

"Anyone home?" Mr. October called, pushing the door all the way open. "Hello there. Coming through."

Ahead of us was a dim hallway and a wash of brighter light farther on. A chilly draft blew through from the far side of the apartment. At the end of the hall, we came to an open-plan living area, all comfy seating and plump cushions, and a small study space with a desk to one side. Sliding patio doors at one end of the room faced out on a long country garden bordered by willowy trees and wispy shrubs.

The doors were wide open; the draft came from there. A woman was leaning against them, looking out. Her back was turned to us, but I could tell by the way her body was shaking that something bad had happened here. Something you could feel in the still of the room.

Hearing us there, she spun around but didn't seem surprised to see us; if anything she looked relieved. Her mousy hair was matted about her forehead and her face had been pulled out of shape by shock. There were red fingerprints like rose petals trailing down the front of her floral print dress, which wafted around her in the breeze.

On the varnished floor at her feet, an open medicine bottle lay among a scattering of tiny white pills. Outside on the pink and white slabs was a pair of scissors and a shredded cardboard box the size of a packing crate. Her fiancé was slumped against it, motionless, his face and clothing spattered with blood.

"What was he thinking?" the woman sobbed. "He must've been out of his mind. He was always a practical joker, a silly little boy, but this is just too much. Why couldn't he have sent flowers instead?"

"It's all right," Mr. October said, though I didn't see how it could be.

She sniffed and wiped her eyes with the back of a hand.

"He didn't think about me, though, did he? It was a gag, a stupid joke. He didn't think how I'd be affected, what it would do to me." She showed us her hands, the tacky red palms. "See what he's done? I know how it looks, but this wasn't my fault."

"He didn't know about your condition," Mr. October said.

"What condition?" I asked, but he lifted a hand, telling me to be quiet.

The woman padded to an armchair and collapsed into it, staring at the floor near the sofa.

"Yes, he did, as a matter of fact. I told him not long after we met. That's the thing I can't forgive. He just didn't think. Anything for a laugh — the big kid."

"What happened?" I said.

The woman didn't look up. "The doorbell rang and there were these two deliverymen waiting outside with the parcel. It took both of them to heft the thing, and I had them take it to the patio where I could get at it — I don't have the floor space in here. It was so well sealed; I suppose he'd had his buddies help him out — one brain between the lot of them. So I brought the scissors and started to open it, and I suppose I must've cut too deeply because I heard this muffled cry from inside, and then I saw the blood, and then Colin came flying out of there like a big red jack-in-the-box."

"Colin?" I said.

Mr. October shushed me. "Let her explain."

"But I thought his name was Andy."

Andy was what the card said, and the telegraph never lied.

I looked out at the man propped against the box. His arms were at his sides and the fingers of his right hand were flexing. Then I looked at the pills and the medicine bottle at my feet.

"I'm Andy," the woman said. "The pills are for my heart condition. I just couldn't get to them in time. I know he didn't mean to scare me, and he had to jump out before I could cut him again, but when he did, the shock was too great. I could see in his eyes he knew what he'd done, what a mistake he'd made, but it was too late to stop it. Now the bloody fool has to live with it, and I suppose I'm going with you."

She was still staring at something on the floor I couldn't see from where we stood. But I already knew what it was before I moved farther inside the room.

Andy Cale's body lay on its side behind the sofa, one hand at her chest, her legs crossed at the ankles. She'd fallen with her back toward us, and I was almost glad about that: I didn't want to see her face. The floor around her sat in deep shadow, but I didn't feel the presence of anything or anyone else. The enemy weren't here.

"Well, there's one birthday I won't forget in a hurry," Andy's ghost said. "So what happens next? Where do we go from here?"

"I'll show you," Mr. October said, offering his hand.

She took it, and fine bolts of light encircled their fingers as he helped her out of the chair. While he walked her from the room, I lingered behind, watching the patio.

Her fiancé had found a cell phone and was speaking into it in a dull monotone that made him sound half asleep. He was on the line to emergency services, trying to explain what had happened. Too late for her, though. They'd patch him up, but it was too late for her.

"Ben?"

I hurried down the hall. Mr. October and Andy were at the door, waiting. He gave me a nod and I fell in behind them, following them up the stone steps toward the light. It was a glorious day up there.

As soon as we finished at Belsize Grove, Mr. October was seized by a coughing fit. The color drained from his cheeks and he sank to his knees, so I caught him under both arms and helped him to a bench on Haverstock Hill.

He held a handkerchief to his mouth until the coughing died down, and we sat quietly watching the traffic and the crowds at the Tube station across the street.

When he felt able to move again, he excused himself to a public phone box, returning a minute later as the ragamuffin, the persona I'd come to think of as the pirate.

"There's a downside to helping people," Mr. October said. "When you truly care, it's like giving parts of yourself away, a little at a time, parts you never get back. I'm tired of that cranky old body, but it's all I have for such occasions."

"Couldn't you go as you are?"

"Not likely." His eyes glinted darkly; his silver tooth sparkled. "Imagine a soul in torment seeing me like this. They'd take one look and run a mile!"

"But the old guy's getting worse," I said. "Carry on like this and you'll need more than a walking stick to get around."

"Well, that's my burden. I'd be better off with a desk job, but that would be wasting my gift, and you know how I feel about that."

"So what happens now?"

"Now you're going home. You've seen enough for one day — more than most mortals could stand. As for me, it's back to HQ for the next list."

"There are always more lists."

"Always."

"OK. Just be careful."

"Of course."

He smiled. He knew what I meant, though. I meant he should watch out for Randall Cadaverus's masses, the demons from the dark. In spite of the sunlight, I felt a chill. If I hadn't already made an enemy of them before today, I surely had now.

# 13

# WHERE THERE'S LIFE

Sunday went the same way. The telegraph worked overtime and we took calls to all quarters of town.

We had our second drowning of the weekend, a fall down stairs, three more natural causes, and a drive-by gangland shooting before lunch. The afternoon brought us cases of liver sclerosis, asphyxiation caused by a faulty gas appliance, a heart attack, another natural causes, then a false alarm when a suicidal man jumped onto railway tracks at Brondesbury Park only to find the line was closed for maintenance.

At least, I thought it was a false alarm. But the telegraph couldn't be wrong.

The man had mangled his legs on the track. As he limped up from the station, he lost his footing at the top of Salusbury Road and stumbled into the path of a driver who'd chosen that exact moment to overtake a slow-moving road sweeper in the brand-new Ford Focus RS he'd stolen five minutes earlier from Paddington Recreation Ground.

When the man wandered into the road in front of him, the driver floored the brakes, tore at the wheel, and went into a swerve, veering across the street and straight through the facade of a small grocery shop. He hadn't been wearing a seat belt. That, explained Mr. October, was why his was the name on the card, not that of the suicide case who'd shuffled away up the street long before the first ambulance came.

"The one who got away, won't he try something else?" I asked.

"Not if he's not on the list."

"And if that man hadn't stolen the car?"

"Lightning strikes wherever it will. It would've found him one way or another." He looked at me, amused. "Always the questions. Don't you ever get tired?"

"Don't you?"

I was sure by now that Mr. October never slept. He never stopped. One case followed the next, day after day, and again he returned to work from Brondesbury Park while I went home shattered.

Before I left, we agreed that I'd join him at the Ministry or in the field every day after school. He wouldn't pressure me, he said. It was up to me. But I knew what I wanted. Life at home and school looked gray and mundane compared to this. Out here with Mr. October, I'd started to see a world of many other colors, a world not many others could see.

I belonged to this world, and it filled my mind whenever I

wasn't taking part in it. What I didn't know, though, standing there on Salusbury Road with Mr. October, was how much I'd been missing while fooling myself I could see everything.

What I'd missed was important, and it had been staring me in the face all along.

As soon as I got home, unlocked the door, and stepped in, Mum appeared at the kitchen door. She looked like a ghost of herself, with sunken eyes and messed-up hair, still in her dressing gown and slippers. Her lower lip puckered.

"Where were you all day?"

"Oh, out and about. With friends."

"New friends from school?"

"New friends not from school."

"That's good. I hardly know what's going on with you lately. I'm almost never here for you."

"That's all right. You've been tired."

She stared at something past my shoulder, not quite able to make eye contact.

"But you're happier now," she said. "You're settling in."

"Yeah. Things are better now."

"See, I should know these things. I shouldn't need to ask. I've been a terrible mother."

"Don't be daft," I said. "You're great."

She threw her arms around me, holding me so tightly, I thought I might suffocate.

"Love you, son," she said, and that was when I knew something was badly wrong.

It wasn't because she didn't say it often, but because of the way it came out, spoken under her breath like a secret.

"Fancy a cuppa?" she said, letting go and straightening herself up.

"Yeah, I could murder one."

I sat in the living room like a visitor, perched forward on an armchair, too anxious to relax. She'd been out when I'd come home the previous night. Exhausted from my first full day with the Ministry, I must've fallen asleep before she came in. I hadn't seen her since Friday night, come to think of it.

She brought the tea and sat facing me across the room. Her cup shook in her hand when she tried to drink and rattled in its saucer when she set it down on her side table.

The note she'd left me, I thought. The way she'd written it. Something about it had bothered me, so I'd pushed it away, tried not to think about it too much.

She was putting off the moment, taking her time. She tried to smile, but seemed to have forgotten how.

"Is this about Dad?" I asked.

"No, nothing like that."

"OK."

"How's your tea?"

"It's fine, Mum."

"You haven't touched it."

"It's hot."

She looked at her cup on the side table, but decided against lifting it again. She held her right hand in her lap and winced.

"It's about your hand, then," I said.

"Yes. I think you should sit down to hear this."

"I'm sitting already."

She nodded. "So you are. I'm sorry. Ben, you should prepare yourself. This isn't good news."

I had a sudden falling sensation, the kind that snaps you out of a dream. Something in my stomach turned slowly around. No, this wasn't good news, and Mum losing the use of her arm was only a part of it, only the beginning.

She talked on but I didn't want to hear any more. I didn't want to know what it meant. Her lips moved but her words sailed over my head, except for a few, and I didn't like the sound of them at all: *specialist, biopsy, lymph nodes.*

Seated with her back to the window, she fell mostly into shade, a frail figure far away and out of reach. And I couldn't reach out, I couldn't go to her, because for the next few minutes I couldn't move. All I could do was sit there and cover my ears.

"Don't worry," she finished. "These things often work out. We'll do what we can. We'll manage. Where there's life, there's hope."

I slept in fits and starts that night. The hands on the bedside clock never changed their position. Darkness filled the room and the hours were long and empty. I lay with my face buried in the hot, damp pillow until gray first light found its way between the curtains.

*Yes, there's hope,* I thought. *There are doctors who know about this and there are treatments that work. Mum will get better. Other people get better. Sick people get better every day.*

I sat up against the headboard, blinking into the light. I felt unrested and scruffy and was still fully dressed except for my sneakers. An object in my jeans pocket was digging into my hip, and I slid it out: the Apocalypti phrase book I'd had on me since Saturday.

The words were still wriggling when I looked inside. *If only they'd settle,* I thought, *there may be something to help Mum.* If words had the power to build up or destroy, it was the building up part that interested me. Could the right combination of words have the power to heal?

But the book was no use yet. I wasn't ready. I slotted it on the shelf next to a DC Comics encyclopedia, then opened the knickknack tin where I kept the four-leaf clover chain. It should've withered and died by now, but the leaves were still fresh and green.

Love and hope and . . . I couldn't remember what the leaves signified. Love and hope and . . . something, something. I closed the tin and placed it back on the shelf next to my Sweeney Todd shaving kit.

Mum was in the kitchen, not dressed for work. She sat at the breakfast bar with a mess of papers and official-looking forms and looked up when she heard me. She seemed brighter than she had yesterday, and her smile came easily, not so strained.

"Does this make sense?" she asked, showing me one of the forms. "I've done it left-handed and I swear I can't read my own writing."

"I can read it. What's it for?"

"To help us get by while I'm unable to work."

She frowned at the form where she'd signed it.

"It's strange not to recognize your own signature. Well, if they can't decipher it and send it back, you can fill it in for me, can't you? Do us a favor, darlin', and seal it up. It's awkward doing it one-handed."

"No probs."

"And pop it in the mail on your way to school."

"I'm not going to school."

"Beg your pardon?"

"Someone has to be here to look after you."

"Don't be daft. Like it or not, you're going." She squeezed my fingers with her good hand. "Yes, there'll be changes around here, and no, it won't be easy. But believe it or not, I still have friends. They'll visit me and a nurse will come once a week. And every other week I'll have an appointment at the hospital, so you might like to help me with that."

"OK."

"But everything else will be exactly the same, understand? Don't think you can skip school that easily. I'm not your excuse."

Fitting the claim form into its envelope, I sealed it and put it aside.

"How long have you known?" I said.

"Since Saturday. Actually, I've known something was wrong for some time, but it was Saturday when I got the . . . when the doctor explained it."

I looked away, chewing my lip. Sunlight crept slowly across the street below. The graffiti-covered building looked somehow different this morning, but I couldn't place how.

"You're going to get better," I said. "People do."

"Yes they do, so we won't get down about it. This won't stop your schooling and it won't stop you from seeing your friends."

"But —"

"No buts. That's the way it will be."

"OK."

After breakfast, I slipped the envelope into my backpack and stood watching her from the kitchen door. Still at the breakfast bar with a memo pad in front of her, she was practicing left-handed writing. She looked peaceful, lost in thought.

"Love you too," I whispered, then turned quickly down the hall and went out. By the time I'd clomped down the stairwell, my eyes were burning. I stood on the path outside wiping them with my sleeve.

Across the street, workmen in hard hats and luminous yellow jackets were setting up around the unfinished building. A regular chip and tumble of bricks sounded somewhere inside its shell. A cement mixer churned away.

The graffiti did look different. Something about it had changed. My eyes cleared, and a numb sinking feeling went through me when I saw what it was.

The stenciled cat and rat were still there, up on the wall's right side. But now the cat's head seemed tilted, and its hungry eyes weren't fixed on the rat just above it. Instead they were staring at me.

Not only staring, but burning right through me. Its face looked weirdly alive. In a speech bubble next to its head were the words:

*We're watching. We can get to you and yours anywhere, any time.*

"Leave me alone!" I yelled. "Leave us alone! She never did anything to you!"

I took off along Middleton Road while, behind me, the workmen stopped what they were doing to stare after me all the way.

# 14

# THE SCAR

As soon as Mercy Road School came into view, I slowed to a standstill and doubled over on a street corner, hands on knees, gasping. The street vibrated with car engines and the voices of kids in the yard.

The warning on the wall had shaken me up. It wasn't just saying don't meddle. It didn't just mean they could get to me whenever they liked. *You and yours.* Had I made a target of Mum as well as myself?

"Behind you," someone whispered.

I swung around and there he was, the raggedy man, the pirate, lolling on the low wall outside the chapel, his face upturned to the sun.

"You," I said, surprised but glad to see him.

"You've been having an emotional ride, I can tell."

"How did you know? Did I call you again?"

"You must've done. I can't answer if you don't call. What's the problem?"

"Mum's very ill. I found out last night. And I don't know what to do. I think it's because of you and the Ministry."

A look of sheer surprise. "Really?"

"Yes, because I've taken sides. I think they're getting to me by getting to Mum."

Across the street, five of the gang of six stepped off a bus and into the gray and maroon mob. In the midst of the crowd, Raymond Blight was picking on a kid half his size, dragging him along by his tie.

"You sometimes appear as a businessman," I said to Mr. October. "Very smart in a suit."

"So I do. Not my alter ego of choice. I'm not exactly the tie-wearing kind, but you have to keep your superiors sweet at board meetings."

"Did you ever dress up like that and go to a café on Mare Street? Did you leave the waitress a massive tip?"

Mr. October frowned. "Why do you ask?"

"Because someone did, and if it wasn't you, it could've been one of them. She made him sound like a charmer, but I bet he put a curse on her or something." I looked at him sharply. "Could they have made her sick?"

He considered this for a moment. "They could, but I doubt they did. It would be a waste of resources. And other things could have made your mum ill. Working too hard, pining for your dad all these years, always worrying about money. Life gets to people in all kinds of ways."

"You sound very sure."

"Well, I noticed her with you at your Aunt Carrie's funeral. I can tell a lot about people at a glance. First impressions aren't always everything, but that's what I saw in her."

"But their warning . . . They left me a message on a wall. Doesn't that mean something?"

"I know these demons," he said. "I know Randall Cadaverus and all his evil hordes. They're basically bullies and, like all bullies, cowards at heart. They know you can harm them by being with us, and they mean to scare you away. That's precisely why you should stay. Always do the thing your enemy would least want you to do."

The first bell sounded across the street.

"Will Mum be all right?" I asked. "Is she safe?"

"Try not to worry. I'll put a watch on your house if you like. But I believe she needs something more than protection and medicine."

He slid off the wall, checking his pockets, and pulled out a fresh set of cards. He made a face as he read the first one.

"Duty calls," he said. "My plate is full again. So will I see you at the office later? I'll understand if you can't come."

"Dunno. I'll try."

"That's all you can do. And now I'd better look lively. There's a 24381 in Bermondsey — very unpleasant indeed."

"Mr. October?"

"Yes?"

"What does she need? If it isn't protection or medicine, then what?"

"Closure," he said mysteriously. "You'll soon understand what I mean." He glanced up and down the street. "I don't suppose there's a phone booth nearby, is there?"

Becky wasn't in homeroom that morning, and by English with Mr. Glover she still hadn't appeared. Although we'd only spoken once, I felt at a loss without her there. She was the only one who'd had anything to do with me so far.

"Listen, everyone," Mr. Glover said as we settled at our desks. "Here's your chance to let those wildly imaginative minds of yours run free . . . as long as you don't let them run freely through the door to the corner store. Today you'll write your very own short stories, on any subject you like. Each of you will produce a masterpiece of at least five hundred words. You have fifty-five minutes from now."

Groans around the room. Much shuffling and fidgeting. Mr. Glover sat behind his desk, grading papers for the first half hour, then patrolled the class, snatching half-written pieces from desks and reading aloud:

"Fascinating, Tommy. 'The creature came into the room looking uncannily like something no one had ever seen before.' I'd have a think about that if I were you."

Muffled snorts and giggles.

"Don't know what you're laughing about, Dan," Mr. Glover said, stopping by the twins' desk. " " "Curse you!" McBride bellowed. "Just for that, I challenge you to a duel at dawn." " "

Even I laughed at that one, but I hadn't fared any better. In fact, I'd barely started. When I closed my eyes, all I could see was my mother holding her pen in the wrong hand. I could see the hungry cat's eyes on the wall. The demon thrashing its arms by the water as the ravens swept down. I had loads of things to write about, but I didn't dare share them with anyone.

At the top of the page, I'd scribbled, *Where there's life, there's hope.*

"Very profound, Ben," Mr. Glover said over my shoulder, making me jump. "So what's the rest of your story about?"

"Dunno," I shrugged. "That's all I've come up with so far, sir."

"Well, you still have twenty minutes to pull something out of your hat. Must try harder."

I didn't get much further. I'd have to do the rest for homework. When the class ended, I started putting away my pens and books, then looked up to find Matthew and Kelly from Becky's gang standing over me.

"You're Becky's pal, yeah?" Kelly said accusingly, her usual stone-cold stare fixed on me.

"Am I?"

"Well, that's what she says. She says there's something she needs to talk to you about. Sounds important, but she wouldn't tell us what it is. Do *you* know what it's about?"

"No idea. Where is she?"

"Dentist," said Matthew. "Having all her teeth out."

"Just a filling," Kelly said. "He's joshing."

"She'll be in about lunchtime," Matthew added. "She asked us to tell you, that's all."

"OK. Thanks."

The conversation ran dry after that and they soon turned away. After break we had Mr. Glover again, this time for English Lit: more readings from *A Tale of Two Cities* followed by half an hour's reading by ourselves while Mr. Glover graded more papers.

Becky came in ten minutes before the end and sat with her friends, but when the bell rang for lunch she stayed at her desk, obviously waiting for me.

"How was the dentist?" I asked.

"Fantastic. Best time of my life," she said.

We started down the corridor.

"Are you going to your usual place?" she asked. "You always chow down at the crypt, dontcha? I'll join you, but I can't eat anything. And remind me not to order hot drinks. I won't feel a thing and it'll run all down my chin."

"Something cold with a straw," I suggested.

At the crypt tea rooms I got a grilled cheese with coffee while she got milk. It was as noisy and echoey as ever, but less busy than usual, so we took a table in an alcove near the entrance, just below the steps. While I stirred my coffee, Becky pulled a newspaper from her bag and opened it on the table to page seven.

"So what've you got to say about this?" she said.

She pointed to a follow-up story on the fire children.

"SOURCE OF FATAL BLAZE STILL UNKNOWN," read the headline. It was too dim in the alcove to read the smaller print, but Becky wasn't showing me that. She wanted me to see the photograph of Mitch and Molly that accompanied the story: Mitch holding a teddy bear, Molly clutching a rag doll to her chest.

"Got your sketch pad?" Becky said. "Let's see it."

She drummed her fingers on the table while I unzipped my backpack.

"By the way, my folks were dead impressed by your portrait. They want to get it framed. They think you're very gifted."

"Tell them thanks."

She flipped through the sketch pad to my drawing of the children. Her gaze skipped between that and the newspaper photograph.

"Yup," she said, "as I thought. Apart from the sooty marks they have in your drawing, they're nearly the same. How do you explain that?"

"I can't."

"Tell the truth, Ben." She sat forward, watching me with impatient eyes. "You saw them after the fire, didn't you, all smoky and dirty, right there in Miss Whatever's class. Why not admit it?"

Part of me wanted to, but if I spoke about the fire children I might be opening a door to everything else. One word about them and I'd soon be chewing her ear off about Mr. October and the Ministry and the rest of it.

Some secrets, I knew, were best kept to yourself and never shared.

"Final answer?" she said, folding the newspaper back into her bag. "Well, if you won't say, then I won't tell you what *I* saw. You're infuriating, Ben, you really are."

She got up in a fluster, with a look that told me I wasn't meant to leave with her.

"Oh, and another thing," she said. "What's that on your face? That pattern? Looks like a scar."

My fingers went to my face. I'd almost forgotten about Nathan Synsiter's "message." Mum hadn't mentioned it. Nor had anyone at school — not the staff, not the other kids in 8C. Perhaps they couldn't see it. But if they couldn't, how could Becky?

I decided to check around class after lunch.

"Nah, there's nothing there," Ryan said when I asked. "Someone's been putting you on, mate."

"Is this a trick question?" Matthew said. "Nope, not a jot. Look in the mirror if you don't believe me."

I asked the same thing of the twins, who both answered at once. "Nothing at all, Ben."

Mel was more amused than anything, grinning at the question.

"This is one of them, like, practical jokes," she said, "like when someone says your laces is undone and you ain't got no laces, innit?"

I spent social studies crouched down at my desk in hiding. We were supposed to have researched our chosen news stories from the previous week, to be ready to discuss with the class. I'd given a lot of thought to the fire children, but I hadn't done any actual work. My classmates got up to speak in turn, but the last bell of the day sounded before Miss Whittaker got to me.

The bell was still screaming through the corridors as I ducked inside the bathroom. In the mirror, the scar on my cheek was clearly visible. I was still examining it when a toilet flushed and Raymond Blight left the stall to wash his hands at the sink next to me.

"What you looking at, fish?" he sneered, catching my eye in the mirror.

"Nothing."

"Fixing your makeup, huh?"

He didn't have many social skills, old Raymond.

"Is there something on my cheek?" I asked, thinking I may as well while we were here.

Raymond shook beads of water from his hands and wiped them with a paper towel. "What, here?" he said. "You mean this?"

Without warning, he jabbed a hand hard into my chest, throwing me back against the sink with enough force to send waves of pain through my hips and legs. He pinned me there, pushing me back until I felt the cold mirror thump the back of my head. At the same time, he brought his free hand to my face, coiling his forefinger against his thumb.

"This here?" he said, flicking my cheek, flicking hard. It stung like a bite. "Got a mark on your face, fish? I'll make you a mark. Where are your poncy friends when you need them?"

Flick flick flick.

"Stop," I said. "I was only asking. And they're not my friends. Ouch! Stop. I don't even know them."

"No, but you'd like to." His fingernail snapped against my cheek again. "I've seen you sucking up to them . . . to Becky. Just 'cause you can draw you think you're something, but you're not, OK? You're not."

"Ouch! OK."

"There's nothing on your face," he said. "I seen you asking the others the same thing. I don't know what your game is, but you're not making an idiot out of me. You're just an attention-seeking mummy's boy."

He flicked me again, this time closer to my eye.

"Don't," I said. "Don't say that."

"What, mummy's boy?"

Somewhere in the center of the pain, with the sink pressing into the small of my back, a white-hot anger came flooding out of me. I took hold of his hand and pushed it away from my face.

"I said *don't*!"

Suddenly he stopped. A look of glazed shock came over him and he whipped back his hand, staring down at it in horror.

The forefinger looked like it had been slammed in a door — not once, but several times. The top joint was a mangled mess and bright blood seeped from the nail — or rather, where the nail used to be. Something had ripped it clean off.

Raymond fell aside, yelping. He set the cold tap running and doused his hand under it, then tore another paper towel from the dispenser and wrapped that around it, pulling it tight. He looked at me then, only a flash and then quickly away, unable to meet my eyes. "What did you do?"

"Nothing," I said. "I don't know. Here, let me look."

He shrank away as if afraid one touch from me would kill him. He tottered backward, flat-footed, bashing into a stall door.

"Don't come near me," he whimpered. "You're a freak. Stay away. Stay away!"

Nursing his injured paw in the crook of his arm, he kicked open the outer door and ran into the hallway, mewling, his cries reverberating through the school.

I stared after him, stunned. I couldn't stop myself from shaking.

*Stay away, enter at your peril. . . .* Mr. October had explained the meaning of the runes, but he hadn't said what it meant to be branded like this, to have to carry the mark wherever I went.

Only Becky had been able to see it. Now I had to know why. I washed and dried my face and collected my backpack from the hook by the mirror, and in the mirror I could still see the mark. If I hurried, I might still catch her. It might not be wise, it might be a terrible mistake, but I ran outside knowing the time had come to tell Becky the truth.

# 15

# BLUE GRANDMA
# AND THE TRAIN WRECK

ecky's gang was already heading up the street on the bus when I got outside. Becky was waiting at the roadside to cross.

"Déjà vu," she said, seeing me.

"Can you still see it?" I said, prodding my cheek.

"Yeah. How'd you get it?"

"Long story. Doesn't matter. But I've been thinking. . . ."

"Oh, have you?"

"You were right about the kids, Becky. I did see them, clear as I'm seeing you."

She all but shrieked with delight, clapping her hands together. Then, suddenly serious, she dropped her voice to a whisper.

"At that desk near the back of the class," she said. "The one where no one ever sits."

"Yes."

"They weren't there today, though."

"No, not today."

"Last week," she confided, "I noticed something too, but I dismissed it, thought I was imagining it. But then you threw a fit, and I knew."

"You saw something too?"

She thought about it. "Not exactly. I felt something there, though, and the light seemed unusual on that side of the room — you know the way it refracts through a prism? And I could've sworn I smelled something too. Something burned."

*She has it too,* I thought. If not the same gift, then something like it. Unlike me, though, Becky seemed happy, even eager to talk about it.

"Do your friends know?" I asked.

"I can't tell them. They don't believe in this kind of thing. Matthew likes ghost stories, but that's all they are to him — stories. Make-believe. I don't have anyone I can talk to about this."

"Me neither."

"So what did the kids do? Did they say anything? And why were they there in the first place?"

"They didn't say much, but I knew they needed help. They're trapped somewhere. Lost. But I haven't seen them since, and I don't know where to start looking."

"Maybe they'll come to you," she said. "They did once before, so maybe they will again."

I hadn't thought of it that way. "Yeah, maybe. In their own time."

"What's up with him?" she said suddenly, staring past me.

Raymond Blight was coming our way up Mercy Road, his face screwed into a rictus of pain. As soon as he saw us, he stepped aside into the road, skirting around us at a safe distance. By the looks of it, he'd come straight from the nurse's office; his finger was wrapped in clean gauze. He scowled but didn't speak as he passed.

Becky turned to me, puzzled, after he'd gone. "Funny, he looked afraid of you. What was that look for?"

"Nothing. He got his finger caught in a door or something and he thinks it's my fault."

"What a dope." She hitched her bag on her shoulder. "Are you going my way? Race you to the nearest caff. I think I can manage a hot chocolate now that the anesthetic's worn off."

I hesitated. I'd be expected at headquarters soon, but now it seemed more important to be at home for Mum.

"Got a phone I can borrow?" I asked. "I'm supposed to be somewhere later, but I'd better call home first. Mum's not well."

"Sorry to hear that." She found her cell phone in the depths of her bag. "It's OK, I've got loads of credit."

Mum sounded upbeat when I called, much brighter than I'd expected.

"Do whatever you like," she said. "I'm fine. I'm not made of glass. Ellie's coming for the evening and we're going to have ourselves a good old heart-to-heart, so you'd only get in the way."

"If you're sure, Mum."

"I'm sure."

"Sounds like good news," Becky said when I handed back her phone.

"It is, in a way." But I didn't want to say more. "Now what about that caff?"

"Last one there can pay." She grinned. "Don't worry. The place is dirt cheap."

And off she ran.


The Portuguese café on the edge of De Beauvoir Square was cramped and dark inside, but there were wobbly tin tables out on the sidewalk, so we took one and sat watching the street. I ordered a Coke, Becky a hot chocolate topped with whipped cream, which gave her a foamy white mustache. She laughed and wiped it away when I pointed it out.

"So you believe me about what I saw," I said.

"Course I do. *I* told *you* what you'd seen, remember? Getting you to admit it was like drawing blood from a stone. Besides," she added, "I don't have a problem with these things — with death and ghosts and all that. I've always taken it for granted. Accepted it."

"Oh?"

"Yeah. Like when I was six, my great-gran passed away. We called her Blue Grandma because of the blue cardigans she always wore — she must've had twenty different ones in different shades of blue. One night my mum came to my room, very weepy and whispering. She said, 'Blue Grandma went to sleep and she's going to sleep for a very long time.' It made me feel very grown up that she'd share this important news with me, and I knew what she was trying to tell me. I said, 'You mean she's dead, dontcha, Mum?' I could be incredibly blunt when I was little."

"Blue Grandma," I said thoughtfully.

"A real sweetie," Becky said. "Plus, I got to see her again at the funeral. I almost expected to. I wasn't surprised. She was standing on the far side of the grave with her sisters on her left and this elderly man in a white suit on her right. Struck me as odd, him wearing white to a funeral. Gran didn't say anything, she just smiled at me like she knew I knew she was there. But I never mentioned it to Mum later on — I thought it'd upset her. In fact, I never told anyone else until now." Becky paused, watching me critically. "Question is, do *you* believe *me*?"

"Why wouldn't I?" I took a sip of my drink before asking, "The man at the funeral . . . Did you know him?"

"Oh, him. No. Never saw him before or since. I just remembered him for his kind eyes and grubby white suit."

She shivered, watching the sky. A cool wind was bringing pale gray clouds.

"Drink up, Ben; it's looking like rain," she said.

I wasn't in a hurry, but I didn't want the rest of the Coke. I was jumpy enough already without the caffeine. We set off along the blustery street.

"Do you see things all the time?" I asked.

"Mostly I sense things. I can't say I've seen that much,

except once a couple of years after Gran. I was nine then, and driving up to the Lake District with my parents for the weekend. They'd offered to bring some of my friends, so Kelly and Ryan came too. There'd been a train crash the week before — really horrendous. Maybe you remember the news."

I didn't offhand.

"Two fast trains on the East Coast line had hit each other head-on and burst into flames. They said you could see the fire for miles. We had relatives who lived close to the scene of the accident, and my folks decided to pay them a visit to break up the drive and recharge their batteries. The back of the house faced a huge field, and across the field you could see the leftover wreckage of the crash. The fronts of the trains were fused together by the heat, so you couldn't tell where one started and the other ended."

She went quiet until we'd crossed the next intersection.

"It was Ryan's idea to investigate the crash site while my folks had tea with my aunt and uncle. The rails were all torn up and that part of the line was closed. It still smelled of diesel and something like burning rubber, and you could see from the way the trains were mangled why so many had been killed and injured."

"That's awful."

"Yeah, it was. Kelly suggested a game of hide-and-seek, 'cause you could still get inside some of the carriages. I wasn't sure because of the people who'd died there, but I went along with it anyway. When it was my turn to hide, I climbed inside a compartment near the front and huddled down between the seats. They'd never find me in there, I thought. The carriage was so dark, they could walk right through and never see me. So I waited, listening to them moving away along the train, slamming doors, and their voices growing fainter all the time.

"It was creepy in there, and I could still smell burning. I thought I'd give it a minute and then go and give myself up. And then I heard something shuffling in the carriage, and this wheezy-sounding breathing. You know, like asthma?"

"God, you must've been scared," I said.

"Petrified. My hands were over my face, but I couldn't help peering through my fingers, and all these shapes were moving around with smoke coming off them. Some were floating high above my head, moving in all directions through the carriage. I was glad of the darkness, glad I couldn't see more. There were so many voices all whispering at once. I wanted to run but I couldn't make my legs work. Then I started to see more detail: badly burned faces and arms and shredded bits of clothing. Just flashes. The smell of smoke became stronger, and I cowered down and shut my eyes, and one of them spoke close to my ear."

We walked to the next block while I digested what she'd just told me. Becky stared into space, reliving the memory.

"Isn't that nuts?" she said.

"No, I don't think so."

"But I never felt like I was in danger. I never thought they meant to hurt me."

"And one spoke to you. What did it say?"

"It sounded like, 'Tell them sorry. I was trying to make it right, but I lost my way.' Four years ago, but I still remember it like it was yesterday. I didn't dream it up, Ben."

"I know."

We stopped under a tree on a corner as the first drops of rain began falling.

"Sometimes I still think about them," Becky said. "I just hope they aren't all still lost, like those children."

"A lot of people are," I said. "That's why I —" But I stopped myself there, watching the raindrops rippling through the leaves. "Well, I have to get going."

"Ah yes, the other place you have to be. Anything exciting?"

"Not really. Just helping someone out."

"Very mysterious. You don't give much away, do you? Well, see ya."

"Yeah."

She set off toward home, breaking into a trot as the rain picked up. I watched her go, glad to have someone to confide in but wary of saying too much. A little knowledge could be dangerous, and it wouldn't be smart to involve her too.

Still, as I started to Islington, I couldn't help wondering how long before I caved in and told her everything else. It wouldn't be easy to keep it to myself. And I wondered what Mr. October would make of Becky, whether he'd see her the way I did, and whether he'd remember her from her great-grandmother's funeral.

# 16

# THE DEATHHEAD

The cold and damp took over the week. Rain fell most nights, and the city streets glittered when I joined Mr. October on his rounds. Ellie had decided to call on Mum every evening, so I was free for the Ministry after school, and when I came home Ellie's umbrella would be propped against the radiator in the hall.

Ellie was a big-boned, good-humored woman with smiling brown eyes and a Mediterranean tan. She'd been a friend of Dad's before Dad met Mum, and she and her boyfriend, Ross, used to join my parents on double dates before they married and I came along.

Ever since Dad left, she and Mum had grown closer, and I knew Mum was in safe hands with her. Not that I was fooling myself — life didn't feel very safe lately and Mum was anything but well — but after Ellie started visiting she seemed more positive, more like her old self.

Ellie couldn't be there all the time, though. On weekends I worked short hours so I could spend most of the day with Mum. She seemed glad to have me around.

On Saturday morning we took a thermos of coffee to a bench in London Fields and sipped the hot liquid and watched dog walkers and cyclists going past. I'd brought my sketch pad and started a portrait of her, hoping to catch her off guard, looking calm and relaxed.

At first she was self-conscious about it, trying to wave me away and cover her face, but by the time I'd finished she was beaming with pride.

"See what I mean?" she said. "Capturing life as you see it, that's what you're good at. I'd rather that than have you keeping the dead company in graveyards."

"It's OK," I said. "I don't go to those places often now."

And I thought, *Because there's no need to. Nowadays the dead come to me.*

Later that day, she had her first hospital appointment, and I took the bus with her. The ride was rocky — you could feel every bump on the road — and Mum couldn't disguise the pain, clutching her arm all the way.

The nurse attending to Mum said it would be best if I waited outside the treatment room. They would be at least an hour. She was settling Mum into a big adjustable chair like a dentist's when they closed the door, locking me out.

Ten patients waited on hard plastic chairs across the ward. Three others waited in wheelchairs. At least half of them looked in much worse shape than Mum, and I hoped she wouldn't become like them if the treatment didn't work.

For a time I wandered from one white ward to another, down one corridor and up the next, the tiled floor squeaking under my sneakers. Everywhere there was a metallic clink of cutlery and surgical instruments, everywhere a sickly smell of disinfectant mixed with blood.

Phones rang around every corner. Porters rumbled gurneys in and out of elevators and operating rooms. I hated hospitals, though I'd never been a patient and I'd only ever visited twice before Mr. October started bringing me. Something about them made me uncomfortable. I'd never known why until Mr. October had explained that eighty percent of the Ministry's cases passed away in places like this.

On Ward 6, a man in his early thirties sat alone outside one of the side rooms. He had a shell-shocked look and his dirty, unshaven face and ragged clothes suggested he'd been living rough. He gave up his seat when an elderly man, not seeing him there, shuffled up with a walker and lowered himself onto it. The younger man stepped away clutching his side, red-fingered from the wound seeping below his ribs.

On Ward 4, in a six-bed unit, two nurses were drawing curtains around the bed nearest the door. A white-haired lady occupied the bed. Her eyes were closed and her lips were smiling. She must've expired in the last few minutes. When the screens were drawn, the nurses' silhouettes moved about her, adjusting pillows and covering her face with a sheet while a third figure much like the old lady's looked on from the foot of the bed, arms crossed on her chest, one foot tapping the floor.

In a waiting area near intensive care, a fuzzy-bearded biker in his fifties nearly barged into me. The bloody scrape marks around his face and neck and his torn leather jacket were typical of road accidents.

"Sorry, mate," he called as he strode away. "Didn't see you there. Just like the truck that hit me."

They were everywhere — on the wards, in the cafeteria, in all the corridors and waiting areas. As I moved through the hospital, I could imagine the telegraph pumping out their names. Sometimes knowing what I knew, seeing what I saw, seemed more like a curse than a gift. There were times when I wished I could shut it all out.

Back on Mum's ward, the clock above the treatment room showed she'd only been inside half an hour. I wished they'd hurry. I was edgy and ready to leave. There were too many strandeds and newly-departeds here, too many voices whispering inside my head.

"How much longer?" I asked the girl at the desk.

She shrugged. "As long as it takes. Why don't you sit with the others, dear, until she's done?"

Past her desk at the far end of the ward, a group of nurses were talking excitedly in quiet voices and nodding vigorously. It must have been a vital medical matter or hot gossip; hard to tell which. A set of double doors swung open behind them as someone else entered the ward, a tall man wearing a black suit and what looked like small round-lensed sunglasses.

But as he moved farther inside, past the nurses, I could tell those weren't sunglasses. They were the dark, sunken sockets of his eyes. His face was little more than a living skull, the flesh as pale as bone. No wonder the nurses didn't see him and no one looked up: It was a Deathhead, one of Cadaverus's agents. One of the enemy.

The eyeless black sockets narrowed when it saw me. Its lipless mouth grinned. Without pause, it made a beeline straight for me, ignoring the treatment room and the other patients waiting outside it.

That told me all I needed to know. It wasn't here for Mum or the others. It was here for me.

I strode past the girl at the desk, then broke into a run along the corridor to another set of doors at the end. I didn't need to look back to know it was following me every step of the way. Turning left past the doors, I legged it along the next corridor, then went left again at the end. My heart slammed inside my chest as hard and fast as my footfalls across the tiled floor. Arrowed signs to other departments and wards rushed past in a blur.

"There's no point in running," the Deathhead called in a scratchy sandpaper voice. "We'll find you wherever you go."

But I didn't care about that. I was more concerned with keeping it as far away from my mother as possible. I ran on, deeper into the maze.

The next corridor I took had a murky, lifeless atmosphere,

as if no one ever set foot there long enough to disturb it. There were no more wards on this part of the floor. There were no more voices or echoes, only a deathly silence. I slowed as I reached a bank of steel-door elevators and hit the nearest call button.

The doors slid open. I jumped inside just as my pursuer rounded the corner behind me. The doors closed an instant before it hit them from the other side, making the steel cage I was standing in tremble. Dry mouthed, I thumbed the button for the next floor down. The elevator simply sat there, thinking it over.

*Come on,* I thought. *Come on. . . .*

It seemed to take forever before it clicked to life and began its descent. I half expected the demon to hammer the door again, but the silence that followed didn't mean it'd given up. It was taking the next elevator down, no doubt.

The doors spilled me out into an even gloomier space than the one upstairs. It was airless and dark with a constant throb of central heating pumps. The smell of disinfectant and blood was stronger, as if this was the source of it and it crept up through the rest of the building from here.

Metal gurneys stacked with black plastic waste bags were shoved haphazardly against the opposite wall. Past them, along to the left, were three closed doors with more loaded trolleys outside. The farthest room had a light on inside. I hurried toward it like a moth drawn by a bulb, stepped inside, and closed the door after me as the second elevator arrived with a crash.

I leaned back against the door, holding my breath, mentally kicking myself for coming this way. From here there was nowhere to go. I'd arrived in the dark bowels of the hospital, exactly where they'd want me to be.

And worse than that, the room I'd ducked inside was the last place I should've chosen. *Of all the rooms in the building,* I thought. Stupidity or just dumb luck?

I was inside the morgue.

A stainless steel counter ran the length of the far wall. At its center were two steel sinks, and between the sinks a length of hose on a spool. A dozen gurneys took up most of the floor space. Three were occupied by bodies draped with clean white sheets.

Their ghosts weren't around, though. If they were, I would have known. By now they'd be wandering freely through the wards upstairs, scared and confused and seeking assistance. In here, though, all I could feel was a cold emptiness. Those three on the gurneys weren't people anymore. They were shells. They were meat.

From the corridor came the sound of footsteps scuffing across the stone floor. Patient, unhurried footsteps. The demon was taking its time. It knew I had nowhere to go from here.

Or maybe I *did.*

My eyes were hazy with fear, and everything in the morgue looked soft at the edges, but to the right of the counter was a concertina screen. And just visible above the screen, the top frame of a door.

As I started toward it, the tiles squeaked loudly beneath my rubber soles. I froze, listening for movement outside. It wasn't easy to hear above the pulse between my ears, but I was sure the footsteps had stopped. They'd stopped right at the door.

My heart skipped a beat.

And then the door was thrown open and in it came, a dark vision with a pale death's-head face. A worm slithered from one of its eyeless sockets; the mouth without lips chanted words I didn't understand and didn't want to. It'd had enough of tiptoeing around, and now it wanted to tear me to pieces.

I jumped back, colliding with the nearest gurney. The gurney, holding one of the bodies, skewed aside and went into a roll. Its wheels hadn't been locked. Running around behind it, I pushed it with all my strength at the demon.

But the gurney passed straight through it, as if it'd dissolved at one end and materialized again at the other. The gurney struck the door behind the demon and rolled back into the room, the impact sending the corpse it carried into a sideways roll off the edge.

"Harvester . . . ," the demon began.

I didn't wait for it to finish. I turned and darted between the other gurneys and around the screen, grasping the door handle and pushing.

The door didn't budge. It wouldn't open outward or inward. I tried again as the demon's footfalls crossed the floor behind me.

Then I saw a metal bolt up near the top of the door, another

171

lower down driven into the floor. The first slid back easily. The second was tougher but gave way when I pulled with both hands. As the demon reached the other side of the screen, I yanked the door open and slammed it behind me and ran on through the next room.

Now I was moving through a cold storage area, a fridge room for bodies. On both sides of the space were the storage units, stacked three-high, gunmetal gray, many of them displaying the names of the departed on their doors. I ran past them toward the murky light farther on, heading for a sign that read PATHOLOGY, FIRE EXIT, STAIRS.

At any second I might feel the Deathhead's cold hand on my shoulder, and it'd drag me back to the morgue or kill me on the spot, if killing was what it had in mind. I kept going, through the next set of doors, across a concrete passageway where my footfalls sounded like shots, then up the first flight of the stairwell.

It was like being in an echo chamber, the bare walls amplifying every slap of my feet on the stone steps. The air was cool and damp as a dungeon's, the light almost nonexistent. I'd taken three turns of the stairs and almost reached the second floor before it dawned on me that the only steps I could hear on the stairwell were my own.

At the top of the next flight, I slowed to listen. In the echoic space below I could've heard a pin drop, but there was nothing. For whatever reason, it must've given up. Perhaps it'd been called away on other business. Or perhaps it'd only intended to scare the daylights out of me, send me a warning shot like the one on the wall back home.

I left the stairwell, following signs to the wards, checking behind me all the way to make sure he wasn't still there. This area of the hospital was quiet except for the kitchen sounds, although the smells coming from there weren't much of an improvement on the ones down below.

Around a corner past the kitchen, I stopped near a private ward. A switchboard phone rang and rang, but the desk was unmanned. A silver-haired man in his sixties paced around the desk in navy silk pajamas, looking flustered and wringing his hands.

"Can you see me?" he said.

"Yes, sir." I took a step into the ward, a fancier ward than the others I'd seen, with soft blue carpeting and classical art on the walls. The lighting wasn't any good, though: a faulty fluorescent strobed on and off, hurting my eyes.

"I can't feel my legs," the man said, blinking in time to the light. "Can't feel anything much. Am I dreaming?"

"No, I'm sure you're not dreaming. Maybe you just woke from a bad sleep."

"I don't know. . . . I don't know. I think they must've drugged me, put something in my food. They gave me something so I couldn't feel my legs. Do you think they might've done that?"

"Who?"

He continued as if I hadn't spoken. "It isn't safe here. I've got to get out before they come again. Will you help? I've got money. I'll pay you to help."

I glanced at the clock above the desk. Still fifteen minutes before the end of Mum's appointment. "People will be here to help soon. Shall I wait with you till they come?"

"Will they help me get away?" He sounded desperate.

"They'll do their best. What's your name, sir?"

"McCready."

"Good. So which one's your room? It's best if we wait there."

"There," he said, pointing.

His door was half open, and through the gap, I could see drawn curtains shutting out the daylight. The stuttering light of a silent TV played around the room and over the figure in the bed. Like those in the morgue, the figure was hidden under clean white sheets.

Seeing that, McCready made a grab for my wrist. His fingers were icy. There was no electric charge, no light show of the kind I'd seen when Mr. October took newly-departeds by the hand.

"That isn't me," he said. "That's my bed, but that isn't me. We can't wait for help. We have to go now."

"Don't worry," I said. "I know it's a shock and a bad way to find out —"

"No! You don't understand!"

He was delirious. He tightened his hold on my wrist. Behind us, the ringing phone stopped abruptly.

"I can't take it back," he said. "Don't you see? It's too late to undo what I've done."

I stared at him in confusion. "What do you mean, sir? What did you do?"

He let go of my wrist and covered his mouth, staring into the room, visibly shaking.

"What is it?" I asked. "What are you seeing?"

And out of the silence inside the room came a sound like a yawning gale. A rustling of sheets as the figure in the bed began to move.

It raised itself up into a sitting position, turning its head slowly toward us. This was no practical joke, no Scooby-Doo ghost draped in bedclothes. I knew that as soon as the sheet fell away, revealing the face underneath.

It was no kind of face at all: no eyes or nose, no features except for the huge red mouth that covered most of its surface. The creature licked its lips, spilling drool on the bed, then wiped its chops with a translucent hand that had seven suckers for fingers. The belch it let out sent a wave of foul air through the doorway.

"You're right," I told McCready. "Time to go."

Whatever the thing on the bed was, it wasn't McCready's body, which meant the man standing next to me wasn't his ghost. Apart from that, I was clueless. The only option I could think of was: Run.

"Come on," I said.

"Too late," McCready said.

He braced himself at the sudden flurry of movement on the bed, as if he already knew what was coming. In the blink of an eye, the creature leapt up and at him, fastening its suckered hands to his face, opening its dreadful red mouth wide as it dragged him inside the room.

The door slammed behind them. McCready started to scream. I covered my ears, not wanting to hear it. But the screams didn't last for long.

# 17

# FALLOUT

A silence emanated from McCready's room. I sagged against the wall by his door, trying to make sense of what had just happened. The screaming had stopped but I still heard it in my mind, and now the strobing light was giving me a headache. Squinting through it, I could make out two figures entering the ward. They seemed to move in slow motion as they rounded the desk toward me.

*The Deathhead came back,* I thought. *It lost me in the basement, but now it's found me again. And this time it's brought a friend. . . .*

They moved nearer, into focus, and I relaxed then, recognizing friendly faces: first Lu, then Mr. October a few paces behind. They were here on official salvage business, I guessed, with Mr. October dressed in the old man's weathered body, feeling his way forward with the walking stick.

"You OK?" Lu asked, looking at me with concern.

"I've been better." I nearly gagged on the words, and my legs were rubbery and weak. "Something in that room . . ."

"We heard," Mr. October said.

"What about him?" I said, gesturing at McCready's door. "Are we too late? He needed help."

"Open the door," Mr. October said.

I hesitated. If that thing was still inside, I didn't want to be anywhere near when it came roaring out.

"It's safe now," he said. "See for yourself."

It took me a moment to pull myself together. Then I made myself twist the handle and give the door a push.

Inside, McCready's corpse lay peaceful and pale among the sheets. His eyes were open, staring up at the ceiling, but he wasn't at home anymore.

The beast was nowhere in sight.

"It returned to where it came from," Mr. October said. "It came and found what it wanted and took him with it."

"What was it?" I asked.

"What did it look like to you?"

*Uncannily like something no one had ever seen before,* I thought, remembering Tommy Farley's English story.

I described it as best I could, as much of it as I could remember, from its nearly transparent, wormy body to its hungry, gaping jaws.

"Mawbreed," said Lu without hesitation.

"Maw-*what?*"

Mr. October agreed. "Sounds very much like one. Some call them Devourers, as that's basically all they do. They're like industrial-strength vacuum cleaners of doom. They come up from the depths to suck out the souls of the living."

I looked at him blankly. "Can they do that? I mean, don't they have to wait until someone passes on? Isn't that how it's supposed to work?"

"There are exceptions." Mr. October closed McCready's door. "The Mawbreed wait for no one. They're a law unto themselves."

"He seemed to know it was coming," I said. "What did he do to deserve that?"

"He sold his soul," Mr. October said with a note of regret. "In return, the Lords of Sundown gave him forty years of prosperity and power, the kind of wealth he could never take with him. He was a banker who foreclosed on many small businesses, refused loan extensions to the needy, and put scores of families out of their homes. Built himself an empire of greed. We can't help him now. The second he signed himself away, he stopped being our responsibility. He wasn't even on our list."

It was a relief to leave the ward behind, to turn away from that room and the stuttering light above the desk. I was jittery on my feet as Lu and Mr. October escorted me back to Mum's ward.

"You're OK?" Lu asked again along the way.

"I will be. Still shaky," I said.

"The Mawbreed are so ugly," she said. "I have nightmares about them sometimes."

I knew what she meant. I'd probably have nightmares about them too from now on.

As we arrived at Mum's ward, I warned them about the demon I'd encountered; it could still be inside the hospital somewhere.

"We'll be on the lookout," Mr. October said, "but frankly, they're ten a penny in places like this. You'd be hard-pressed to turn any corner without coming face-to-face with one."

"But what if I see it again?" I asked. "If I see any more of them?"

"Zap them," Lu said.

"She means use your developing skills," Mr. October said. "You'll be surprised how easily it comes to you."

I looked at him none the wiser.

"You're still growing into the role, Ben," he explained. "So much is happening around you, so many things you can't explain. Things you haven't learned to control yet. Don't question it, don't try to understand it, just try to accept what you're becoming."

"And what's that?"

"One of us. Someone who tries to make a difference."

They didn't wait around once we reached the ward. They had other calls to make, a short list of newly-departeds to visit inside the hospital. Watching them go, I puzzled over what Mr. October had said about my developing skills. Did he mean something else besides the gift of seeing?

Mum came out of her treatment room fifteen minutes late. She looked sickly pale, worse than before she'd gone in.

"A slight reaction to her medicine," the nurse told me. "The first time's always the worst. Also, she told me about your uncomfortable ride here, so I've arranged for a car to take you home. Shouldn't be long."

*I hope not,* I thought. I was anxious to breathe fresh air outdoors, away from this place.

"Sorry to keep you," Mum said, as if it were her fault. "Were you bored waiting?"

"Oh, you know, it wasn't too bad."

We had to wait an hour for the driver, but then the ride took only ten minutes. Mum's head bobbed like a toy dog's in the backseat; she could barely keep her eyes open. She was tired enough to sleep for a week, she said when we got home. She ran a bath and later settled in the living room to watch *Meet Joe Black* on a movie channel.

"After that ordeal, I'm in just the right mood for a good tearjerker," she said.

I brought tea and cookies and sat with her while the film began.

"Is it OK if I go out?" I said. "I mean, I'll stay if you want me to."

"I'm hunky-dory. Run along and get on with your life, darlin'." She kicked off her slippers and spread herself out on the sofa. "Hospitals are no place to spend your Saturdays. I'm glad you came, but now you need to go and do your own thing."

Ten minutes into the film she was already half asleep. I watched her from the doorway, worried by how wiped out she looked. Whatever they'd given her at the hospital hadn't seemed to do her much good.

I slipped quietly away, heading down the stairwell and onto Middleton Road, ignoring the wall across the street. I didn't need to look that way to know the cat was still watching.

Over the next few days, most of my time with the Ministry was spent in receipts. My duties there were light relief after the hospital. There were occasional trips in the field with Mr. October, but I was getting used to the small dark space, just me and the candlelight and the telegraph machine.

On slack nights, when the machine was quiet, I'd sit with my sketch pad, drawing the Mawbreed from memory, or I'd roll paper into the typewriter and tap out my thoughts.

Sometimes I could go as long as an hour without the telegraph springing to life. When it did, I'd drop whatever I was doing, type up the names it spat out, then face the wrath of Miss Webster. Miss Webster was more cobwebbed every time I saw her, the records office continued to grow all around her, and the walks to her booth became longer and longer.

At school, Raymond Blight kept his distance. Whenever I looked at him, he buried his hands deep in his pockets and turned away.

It wasn't just Raymond, either. Rumors about his injury had spread. There were mutters and whispers about me behind my back, and I saw something like fear in the eyes of most classmates I spoke to.

But I still hadn't fathomed what I'd done to Raymond that day; I wasn't sure I'd done anything at all. It concerned me enough to ask Mr. October, who believed it was a sign of those "developing skills." If it was a part of the gift, it scared me more than a little. I wasn't sure how much I wanted a gift like that.

Becky was different from the others, but even she seemed agitated when we went to the crypt on Wednesday.

"What's wrong?" I asked. We were sitting on the outside wall with coffees in paper cups. "It's like my first day all over again. It's like being an outsider."

"You *are* an outsider, in case you haven't noticed," she said. "You'll always be an outsider. It's one thing putting Raymond in his place — who cares what you did, nobody likes him anyway — but it's something else keeping secrets from your mates."

"What secrets?"

"There you go again." She frowned at the curb, scrunching up her dainty freckled nose. "It's been a week and a half now. Ever since we spoke about you-know-what, you've been avoiding me."

"But I haven't. You mean because I haven't walked home with you since?"

"It's not about that." She kicked her heel back against the

wall in a steady rhythm. "OK, yes, it is. Not that I care, but you've always got some excuse, something you have to run off and do."

"I'm not lying about that."

"No, but you're being very secretive about it."

It was true. I was, but only for Becky's own good.

"Sorry," I said.

"No need to be sorry. It's just, I told you something important and secret that happened to me, but you . . . you're all zippered up; you keep everything hidden away."

She set her coffee down on the wall and looked at me searchingly.

"What are you involved in? Where do you go, Ben, every night after school?"

I shuffled on the cold bricks, trapped in the glare of her spotlight.

"Nowhere."

"Bull. You know that's impossible. You have to be somewhere."

"I meant nowhere special."

"If you say so."

One thing I'd learned about Becky: She was like a terrier with a rag in its teeth when she got going — she didn't know how to let go. But now she sat back, deflated.

"Look," I said, "it's not because I don't want to tell you. It's because I don't think I'm supposed to. It could be bad for both of us if I did."

She glared at the pavement, refusing to look at me. "What, so you're working for the secret service now?"

"Not exactly."

"But something like it."

"Don't be daft."

"Something secret," she said. "Something life-or-death important."

I took a deep breath, let it out slowly. "OK. Yes."

A light came on in her eyes. "See, I knew it! Just like I knew about the fire children. You're not as good at hiding things as you think."

"I can't say any more, though," I said.

"I'll keep on at you till you cave in."

"Then I'll have to get used to it. It's like the third degree, talking to you."

"Well, I'll leave you alone if you answer me just one thing. Does it have anything to do with the kids?"

"Yes."

"And with what happened to Raymond Blight."

"That's two things," I said. "Let's change the subject. What are you writing for English this week?"

She rolled her eyes. "A ghost story. What does it matter? I'm trying to talk to you."

"It's not easy, I know."

"*You're* not easy. You're bloody hard work, Ben Harvester. If I'm like the third degree, you're like the *Mona Lisa*."

"I'm what?"

"You know. That enigmatic smile, giving nothing away, keeping it all to yourself."

A silence fell between us. The bell across Mercy Road announced the end of break.

"So what's your ghost story about?" I said.

Becky hopped off the wall, turned, and gave me a look. "Not telling. See how you like it," she said.

She snubbed me after school too, making a big show of chatting and laughing with her friends and not looking at me when I passed them at the bus stop. My punishment for not telling all.

As I did every day now, I called home from a pay phone a few blocks up Mercy Road from the school. I had a cell buried away somewhere in my room, but lately I couldn't afford to buy minutes. The phone booth shuddered around me as the school bus went past. I shoved in a coin and punched out the number.

Mum answered on the third ring, sounding as if she'd just woken.

"Nothing to worry about," she said. "The nurse came to dress my arm an hour ago and it knocked the stuffing out of me. I'm over it now, but my arm looks like an Egyptian mummy's."

"Are you sure you don't need me there?"

"No. Ellie's here now. We're looking through vacation brochures."

"Oh?"

We both knew we couldn't afford minutes for my phone, let alone vacations.

"It's like this," Mum went on. "Ellie's thinking of investing in a condo on Lanzarote. She's brought holiday photos from the last time she went. I'll show you when you get back. She says if she and Ross go ahead with this, we can visit any time for free. We only need to wait for a break in my treatment. Isn't that great?"

"Sounds good to me." A change of climate would surely do her more good than the treatment had so far.

"There's something else," Mum said, and then faltered. "Actually, it's kind of a surprise. I'll leave that until I see you."

"Good or bad surprise?"

"A bit of both, I suppose. How long will you be?"

"A few hours, probably. I'll try not to be late."

"OK." After a pause, she said, "I'm so glad you're making friends now. Things are going to turn out fine, darlin'. You'll see."

I felt a chill as I stood there with the warm telephone receiver pressed to my ear. A shadow flashed past the booth to my right, but there was no one nearby on the street when I turned to look.

After hanging up, I leaned against the glass-paneled door, fighting the huge ball of pressure building in my chest. It took a minute to keep the sobbing at bay. It shouldn't, but it upset me to hear her making future plans when neither of us knew how much of a future she had.

How could she be so positive? How could she be so brave?

The feeling passed. I shouldered the phone booth door open and stepped out. As I did, something flickered at the edge of my vision, a sudden movement farther down the street.

No one there. No one who wanted to be spotted, at least.

I set off for Islington at a jog, not looking back but certain I wasn't alone. If the enemy had sent another agent after me, it would be wiser to keep to the streets, avoiding the canal's quiet corners and dark bridges. Anything might happen down there.

Rush hour was a while off, but the streets past Southgate Road were busy enough to help me relax. At Essex Road I checked behind me for the first time, but by then the follower could've been anywhere in the throng of people and traffic.

Had I imagined someone there? Perhaps all I'd really seen from the corner of my eye was a bird flying by, or its shadow.

I wished I could believe it, but nothing in my world seemed imaginary now. When I woke in the night with cold sweats, I wasn't waking from dreams of imaginary monsters. These were dreams of the Deathhead stepping into the morgue, of the Mawbreed rising from McCready's bed, and the last look on McCready's face before it dragged him inside the room.

Just because I couldn't see it didn't mean it wasn't there. I sprinted the rest of the way to Camden Passage, running to stay ahead of my fears, not slowing until I'd found the damp crevice between the walls and snaked through it again, passing from daylight into dark.

# 18

# THE FOLLOWER

No matter how often I came to the Ministry, that shift from day to dusk never failed to amaze me. A few short paces from daylight, Eventide Street stood secretly under the stars, its streetlamps bathing the cobblestones in amber.

I moved indoors, flustered after the run. Upstairs, along the musty hallway, a dull light shone under the receipts office door. Before I could open the door wide enough to see inside, a small voice chirped, "Oh, hi, Ben. Won't be a min. Just finishing my shift."

A petite girl dressed all in black hunched over the desk — *my* desk, as I'd started to think of it. She looked to be in her midteens and had pale alabaster skin and a wild maze of back-brushed black hair. She didn't look up as I came inside, focusing all her attention on the card in the typewriter.

Her typing, like mine, was basically two-fingered hunting and pecking. Next to the desk, the telegraph machine gave a worn-out sigh after pumping out another list of unfortunates.

"Uh, hi," I replied. "How do you know my name?"

"Everyone knows your name around here," she said. "You're usually in about this time of day, aren't you?"

Finishing typing, she took out the card and compared it with the printed sheet. Satisfied that they matched, she sat back and smiled up at me. A kink in one of her eyes made her seem to be looking in two directions at once, left and right of me.

"I'm Sukie," she said. "Pleased to meetcha. I've heard lots about you, but we keep missing each other coming and going. I usually clock off before three."

I stared at my shoes, not quite able to meet her look.

"Good to meet you too."

"Is it true what they say, that you saw a Mawbreed up close and lived?" she asked.

"Not that close," I said. "But close enough."

"Still, it's astounding. Not many see them and survive to tell the tale. No surprise they're calling you Wonder Boy around here."

I felt myself flush. "I didn't actually do anything, though."

"Modest too. Well, whatever you say."

"I didn't know we had to deal with things like that," I said.

"Well, the minute you take sides against them, the enemy are at you all the time. They'll throw everything they've got at you. You'll always have that feeling — better get used to it."

"What feeling?"

"Of being followed, like just now."

I looked at her, surprised.

"Sorry," she said. "I must stop doing that, looking inside people's minds. It's intrusive and rude of me. But they tell me it's a gift, so I can't deny it."

"It must be hard, though, knowing what everyone's thinking all the time."

"Tell you the truth, it gives me a headache," Sukie said. "All those voices jabbering away at once. And if I'm ever anywhere near a demon, that's the worst. They think thoughts I wouldn't want to repeat. But then, I hear good thoughts too, like the ones you're having about your mum. I'm sorry to hear she's been ill. I hope she'll be well."

There was something creepy but fascinating about this. "Can you tell me what else is on my mind?" I asked.

Sukie answered without hesitation. "'Creepy but fascinating...' and you're also thinking of an address in Dartmouth Park — Spencer Rise, I think — but I can't see the house number. Seems urgent. Am I right?"

I shook my head. "No, I don't know that address. Never been there."

"Oh." She looked momentarily puzzled. "Then someone else is thinking it. I've got a fairly wide radius and pick up things from all over the place. It's probably one of the girls in dispatch."

She rose from the desk, taking one of the two sets of typed cards. "Mr. October's due in soon. Can you see he gets those?"

"OK."

"Uh-oh, here comes another one. I'll leave that to you, if you don't mind."

The telegraph moaned and coughed out a solitary name.

"Time to face the old dragon in records," Sukie said from the door. "Nice talkin', Ben, and apologies for reading your thoughts."

"That's OK. They weren't all mine."

She laughed and slipped away.

After she'd gone, I took the printed sheet to the desk and sat down to type. *Wonder Boy,* I thought. Was that what they really called me here?

Rolling a card into the platen, I set to work.

The next half hour went slowly. I stared at the telegraph, willing it to be still. Not that I minded the work, but as long as the machine kept quiet, the living kept living. I took paper from my backpack and fed it into the typewriter, then stared at the blank page a moment before typing:

*The first time I set eyes on Mr. October, he didn't look like anything special.*

But first impressions weren't everything, and I'd learned so much since this all began. In the receipts office I'd had plenty of time to think over what had taken place since we met, and now I wanted to record it — for myself, if no one else.

I was on my third page when the telegraph drew breath, exhaled a jet of steam, and clattered into action. I snatched the sheet from the typewriter and put it away. As I did, the door flew open. The candle flame shuddered and nearly went out.

"Ah, there you are," Mr. October said, poking his head around the door. "How's it going?"

"Not bad. It's been fairly quiet till now."

He glared at the working telegraph, blew air through his lips. "It's bedlam out there today, and it doesn't look like it's slowing down soon." He came over and perched on the edge of the desk. "My poor old aching dogs."

"Huh?"

"Isn't that slang for *sore feet* in your neck of the woods?"

"Dunno about my neck of the woods. We haven't been there long," I said. "Though I did once hear Dad say 'dog's barking,' and I had to ask what it meant. He said it meant the phone was ringing. Dog and bone, telephone; rhyming slang, you know? I've always remembered that."

Mr. October looked at me, nonplussed. "Never mind. I've been on my feet all day, that's all. Three 6457s and a frankly bizarre 1312633. Hard to explain. Very complicated. So how's my star apprentice today? Do you know what they're calling you around the department now?"

"Yeah, Sukie told me. Oh, and she asked to make sure you got those."

"Did she read your mind?" he asked, collecting the cards.

"Mine and someone else's, she didn't know whose."

"She'll be a major asset in the field one day," he said. "We're still undecided about how to put her talents to best use, but we'll have a better idea when she learns to distinguish one voice from another."

He rifled through the cards, a grave expression deepening the Y on his pirate's brow until his eyebrows met in the middle.

"Not good. Very nasty. Oh dear," he said as he read the last card. "Looks like you'll have to join me tonight, Ben."

"OK. But what about this?"

The telegraph rocked away, spitting out names and smoke.

"We'll draft someone in," he said. "Don't worry about it now. Get yourself ready while I talk to dispatch. I'll meet you outside."

Pushing himself off the desk, he went out.

The noise of the still-working telegraph chased me out a minute later. The smell of stale varnish followed me downstairs. As I stepped outside the main door and started down the steps, a figure moved out of dark cover across the alley, giving me a start when it spoke.

"Ben? Is that you?"

She took one tentative step forward, then hurried toward me. Light from the gas lamps fell across her face, but it still took me a second to place her.

"Becky? What're you doing here?"

"What do you think? I followed you." She looked anxiously around. "Ben, what is this place, and why is it night?"

"There's no time to explain. If they see you . . . I don't know what they'll do. How long have you been here?"

"Seems like ages. I'm not sure. I found my way in, but then couldn't find a way out. Where'd it go, that place between the walls?"

I shook my head, trying to think. Mr. October would be out any minute.

"I'll walk you back," I said. "The entrance is still there. You just have to know how to look." We started across the cobbles to the far wall. "Listen. You've got to promise not to breathe a word of this. You can't tell anyone, not even your friends."

"I won't." She dug in her heels, stopping halfway across the alley. "But I don't want to leave, either. Now that I'm here, I want to know more."

"It isn't up to me," I said.

"Then who?"

"You should be going."

I took her arm, a little more firmly than I meant to. She brushed me away.

"Becky, I'm serious."

"So am I."

"Yeah, but —"

"Why shouldn't I see?" She looked at the starlit sky, then at me. She wasn't afraid; she was about to burst with excitement. "Besides, if I leave now, I won't be able to tell you the news."

"It can wait."

"No, it can't."

"Then hurry. What news?"

"Hold on, it's best if I show you."

She rummaged through her bag, picking out loose papers and tissues, pushing them back.

"Where is it?" she said. "I know it's here somewhere. You won't believe it, Ben. I could've kicked myself when I found out. It's all about —"

The main door thumped behind us. Becky clutched at me, nearly dropping her bag. We turned to see Mr. October coming down the steps, still in the guise of the raggedy man, the pirate.

Nests of shadows swarmed around his head as he strode toward us. His boots clicked and squeaked on the cobbles. With the streetlamps at his back, I was seeing him as I'd never seen him before: a sinister silhouette. Stopping short of us, he craned his upper body closer, then still closer until we were almost nose to nose.

"What's the meaning of this?" he said. His dark gaze skipped between me and Becky. "Shall I call the Vigilants, tell them we have an intruder?"

"I . . . I can explain," I mumbled.

"You'd better. Do you know what happens to uninvited guests here? Can you imagine what happens to those who assist them?"

My mouth went dry. For the first time ever in Mr. October's company, I began to feel something like dread.

Becky shrank from him with a whimper, hiding behind me.

Mr. October's eyes burrowed into us, brimming with darkness, unreadable.

My heart lurched. I tried to inhale but couldn't.

Then he threw back his head and roared with laughter, howling at the moon.

"Gotcha!" he said. "That's four times now, young man. You fall for it every time, hook, line, and sinker. That's why it's so irresistible."

"Do that again and I'll walk. I'll quit."

"That'll be the day." Now he turned his eyes on Becky, studying her as if she were some strange undiscovered species. "So who've we got here?"

"It's my fault," I interrupted. "Don't be angry with her."

"Have you ever seen me angry?" He still looked more amused than anything. "Well, yes, fair enough, there are times when the work's so intense I lose my temper. I've been known to hurl the odd fireball in anger . . . but my argument's with others, not you."

"I know this man," Becky whispered. Slowly loosening her hold on my arm, she straightened herself up to face him. "I've seen him before. I'd know him anywhere." She was watching him with bewildered eyes. "But he didn't look anything like this last time. He looked like . . ."

"Very perceptive," Mr. October said. "My, Ben, there's so much talent at your school."

"You remember him from your great-gran's funeral?" I said to Becky. "How come?"

"Her gift isn't like yours," Mr. October said. "She senses but doesn't see so clearly." To Becky, he said, "It was a long time ago. In your case half a lifetime ago, in mine just a heartbeat. I stood with your grandmother at her burial service. And yes, I looked different then. I had on my mourning clothes."

"How . . . I mean, why . . ." Becky looked at me for answers, but she hadn't fathomed the questions yet. "I mean . . . what were you doing there with my great-gran?"

"Helping," I said. "This is Mr. October, and that's what he does. He helps — we help — the dead."

It took her a moment to absorb what I'd said. She fell back a couple of paces, openmouthed, and I could all but see the cogs turning behind her eyes.

She recovered quickly, though, taking a breath before she spoke. "So you help them how?"

"We provide for them, help them along to the next stage," Mr. October said. "Some are ready as soon as the life force leaves them. Others, like your great-grandmother and Ben's aunt, hide away and don't come out until the very last minute. In fact, your great-gran was so late, she only just made the funeral, but it ended well."

The stunned look faded from Becky's face. She nodded to herself, as if weighing everything up, coming to a decision.

"OK," she said, reaching back inside her bag. "In that case, if that's the truth about what you do, you really have to see this."

"Sorry, there's no time," Mr. October said. "We're already behind schedule. You'll have to wait till later. Lu, where's our transport?"

I hadn't seen Lu follow him out, but now she appeared behind him, hauling her rickshaw from its cover of shadows in front of HQ and pulling up alongside us.

"Hi, Lu," I said.

"Hi, Wonder Boy."

"Is there room for three inside?"

"Room for as many as you like," she said. "Bigger, smaller, any size."

Becky looked at me askance. "What's going on? What's she mean?"

"You'll see. Lu used to be a contortionist. This vehicle was part of her act."

We scrambled inside under the canopy and squeezed shoulder to shoulder, Mr. October to my right and Becky to my left.

"Wait a minute," Becky said. "How's this possible? It's a single-seater, isn't it? And what am I doing sitting in a rickshaw, anyway?"

"Watch," I said. "You wanted to know everything, so here's your chance. Just wait till she gets going — it's a sight to see."

"Ready?" Mr. October called.

"Ready," Lu answered.

"Then take it away!"

And, gathering speed as she went, Lu ran straight for the wall, steering us toward the invisible gap.

# 19

# THE NEW RECRUIT

W ell ... if moving from daylight into night-time in just a few steps seemed incredible, what happened next boggled my mind. It always did.

"Oh my God," Becky gasped, squashed tightly against me.

It wasn't the first time Lu had taken us from HQ. Mr. October called on her whenever the workload grew heavy, so I knew what to expect. But each time was as thrilling as the first, and when she hit the gap at full speed, I couldn't help punching my knee and stifling a cry: *Geronimo!*

From the alley, viewed from a certain angle, the space between the walls appeared nothing more than a paper-thin slit. From other angles you couldn't see it at all. For the next few seconds it was like passing through the cool brickwork itself. There was only a *drip-drip-drip* and its echo and a narrow slice of brightness waiting straight ahead.

The pressure dropped, making my ears pop the way they might on a train speeding through a tunnel, and then the light flooded over us. We were back in the midafternoon, serpentining between trinket and book stalls and street musicians.

"What did I just see?" Becky said incredulously. "Did we really shoot through that tiny space at twenty-odd miles an hour?"

Mr. October nudged my elbow, speaking quietly, for my ears only.

"What do you think, Ben? Can you vouch for your friend? If not, I can wipe her memory. She'll forget everything she's seen and we can drop her off right here."

"She's fine," I said. "Just think: She found her own way to HQ, and not everyone can do that. And she remembered you from the funeral even though you had a different appearance then. She's gifted that way. She's OK, really she is."

That seemed to satisfy him and he settled back for the journey. Lu slowed as she turned onto Upper Street, awaiting instructions.

"It's a 19127, Lu," he called. "Camden, and sharpish."

"OK!"


A 19127, as Mr. October often said, wasn't good. None of the numbers were good, exactly, but this wasn't the easiest way to introduce Becky to the team, if she was going to be a part of the team from now on.

At Chalk Farm underground station, Paul Butler, 34, had

been hit by an approaching train after dropping his phone on the tracks and jumping down to retrieve it.

Mr. October made us stay back from the platform edge — "A bit messy down there, don't look" — while he entered the tunnel in search of Butler. Butler had actually died of shock, but no one besides us would ever know. When he'd seen the lights racing toward him, his heart gave out on the spot. His ghost had leapt clean out of his body and set off running before the train hit his still-standing corpse.

Two minutes after Mr. October went looking for him, a bright light bloomed in the tunnel, and it wasn't the light of another incoming train.

"That means he found him," I told Becky. "It means he's OK. You'll figure it out as you go."

The next stop was a nursing home, the first of two natural causes on our shift. Lottie Fraser, 86, had passed away peacefully in her sleep, but you never would've guessed by the way her angry soul was carrying on when we got there. She refused to believe it, refused to leave, and had taken to the TV lounge in protest.

The lounge was as large as a tennis court. All around it, elderly guests slumbered in armchairs with their mouths wide open or nodded in front of game shows while Lottie besieged the place.

Charging from chair to chair, she scattered magazines and newspapers to the floor, swatted teacups from saucers, tugged at the curtains and switched TV channels, which brought moans of protest from anyone still awake enough to notice. Nurses chased the trail of disorder back and forth, unable to fathom what was happening or where the poltergeist would strike next.

"I ain't going," Lottie said fiercely to Mr. October. "I ain't ready. My family's visiting Sunday and I ain't seen my granddaughter yet. Can I have one more week?"

"You could if it were up to me," Mr. October said. "Unfortunately, it's not up to me. Let's have a little chat about this, shall we?"

While he escorted Lottie back to her room, I took Becky to wait outside where we wouldn't attract attention.

"He's changed," she said. "Now he looks like the old guy I remember with Gran. He's got the same shabby suit and everything. What is he, a master of disguise?"

"You'll get used to that too. He changes all the time. Different personas for different occasions."

"So this is what you've been doing all this time?" She looked back at the home. "Can't say I saw the old woman too clearly. I could see what she was doing in the lounge and I heard her well enough, but she looked a bit fuzzy round the edges."

"Things make more sense over time," I said. "I didn't see much myself until I met Mr. October. This probably seems a bit freaky to you."

"Not freaky exactly. It's sad when people don't know how to let go. Makes you want to help, and I can see why you do.

You could've told me, though. I would've understood. You could've trusted me."

I knew that now even if I hadn't before. "About this news you wanted to tell me . . ."

"Oh yeah, hang on to your hat. You'll never believe it, but —"

She was interrupted by Mr. October bursting out through the doors, rubbing his hands together.

"No dillydallying, you two. Took me so long to make the old girl see sense that we're even further behind schedule now. All aboard the rickshaw!"

"Later," Becky said as we ran for our seats.

Our next stop was Hyde Park.

The homeless man had been dead a few minutes when we found him. Even when you had a name and reference number, tracking people of no fixed abode was never easy. They didn't often show up in hospitals — most often we found them under bridges and inside shop doorways.

His scraggy hair was plastered across his face and there were holes in the knees and elbows of his clothes. He wore one black shoe, one brown, and no socks. A yellow dog ran around the body, yapping at his ghost, which sat on the backrest of a bench, looking down.

"8364, hypothermia," Mr. October read from his card. "Are you Judd Gardner, sir?"

The man didn't look up when he answered. "I used to be, mate, but that was a long time ago."

In Hampstead we visited the home of a former TV personality, a stocky man with a chubby joker's face and a badly fitting toupee. You got the impression he meant everything he said to be funny. He'd spent the afternoon drinking alone, and after one martini too many he'd decided to take a dip in his swimming pool, climbing the high diving board fully clothed, forgetting the pool had been drained for cleaning.

He was in a quandary when we turned up, unable to believe what he'd done. He'd had a comeback planned for next year, a stand-up tour and a new game show. He insisted on showing us highlights from the TV programs that had made him famous. He had them all on DVD, but his disembodied hands couldn't pick up the remote.

It took all of Mr. October's powers of persuasion to convince the man his career was over. There'd be no show and no tour dates next year after all. While they talked things over in the space-age kitchen of his luxury house, Lu and Becky and I flopped on the sofa in his living room and watched his old programs. They were pretty good all in all, but some of his jokes weren't as funny as he seemed to think, and Lu didn't get them at all.

After ten minutes, a wave of phosphorescence flashed down the hall, startling Becky out of her seat and prompting Lu to run out to ready the transport.

"I suppose he'll be in all the papers tomorrow," Becky said as we settled into the rickshaw again. "Maybe even on the news tonight."

"He lived alone and didn't have many visitors," Mr. October said. "He won't be found for another three days when they come to clean the pool."

Becky was horrified. "Shouldn't we call and report it?"

"I'm afraid we can't. We're not allowed to interfere with what's written."

"But that's terrible. . . ."

She stared straight ahead as Lu steered us up the driveway and out into traffic. Not everything about the job sat easily with her, then. She didn't speak for a long while after that.

When we answered a 3626 on Edgware Road, she remained seated while we ran inside an Indian restaurant off the main street. Darren Hayes, 23, had staggered inside clutching his chest after an incident with a knife two blocks away. We led him quietly through the kitchen and out to the alley while the team of paramedics who'd arrived just after us went to work on his body on the restaurant floor.

After that, a natural causes in Stepney, another at Homerton Hospital (technically speaking, a disconnected life support machine), and an incident in Walthamstow involving a burglar, a rottweiler, a rolling pin, a frying pan, and a marble chopping board.

We were nearing the end of the shift now. Darkness had settled over the city. After our last call, a 7325 in Hoxton, Lu pulled to the curb alongside a brightly lit grocery store on Essex Road. They were dropping us off before returning to HQ, and I was climbing out when Becky pulled me back.

"Hang on a minute," she said. "Can I have my say now?

I've been trying to tell you since before we set off. Will you listen this time?"

She took a newspaper clipping from her bag and smoothed it out on her knee.

"I don't know how I missed this," Becky said. "It's been under our noses all this time." Her urgent look traveled back and forth between Mr. October and me. "Ben, it's about Mitch and Molly, the fire children. I think I know where they are."

# 20

# THE SHIFTERS

The clipping came from the paper she'd shown me at the crypt the previous week. Molly and Mitch stared out from the photograph, and beneath the headline, the story ran:

A house fire in Hackney in which two young children died is not being treated as suspicious, police have confirmed.

Molly Willow, 6, and Mitch Willow, 4, died in their home on Henryd Street two weeks ago this Friday.

Firefighters attempted to rescue them from the second-story bedroom where they were trapped, but their deaths were confirmed on arrival at the hospital. The cause of death was given as smoke inhalation. The children's parents were not in the property at the time the fire broke out.

A police spokesperson said the fire was not arson. The matter is still under investigation, with an electrical fault in the building suspected of being the most likely cause.

Though the Willows were unavailable for comment as we went to press, a family friend told the *Standard*, "Words can't describe what they're going through now. It's unbearable — they were still settling in to their new home when this happened. They can never go back to live there now."

It is understood that the Willow family moved to Henryd Street in late August. Their previous address on Spencer Rise, Dartmouth Park, had been their home for more than eight years. The Henryd Street property is earmarked for demolition after the investigation concludes.

"So what do you think?" Becky asked as I finished reading and passed the clipping to Mr. October. "I've looked at it a dozen times. The kids were too young to call the new house a home. All they ever knew in their short little lives was the other place."

"Lu," Mr. October said suddenly. "Turn this crate around, please, and take us to Dartmouth Park."

Lu nodded. She waited for a break in the traffic, then moved out.

"Sukie," I murmured. "That's the address she mentioned to me."

"Who?" Becky said.

"Someone I met at the Ministry today. She's clairvoyant. You must've been outside at the time, and she tapped into your mind. That's where she got the address."

My lips were dry by the time Lu led us up the slope onto Spencer Rise. The street was drenched in darkness, silent and still. You could easily forget you were just a few beats away from the city's thudding heart.

"Which number?" I asked.

We were slowing, moving uphill at close to walking pace.

"Somewhere near here . . . no, farther up on the left . . . in the twenties," Becky said.

She closed her eyes and concentrated. Even if she couldn't yet see the dead, she could feel them nearby. When she gasped and opened her eyes again, Lu immediately came to a standstill.

"They're here," Becky said. "I'm sure of it."

It wasn't the only house on the street with a FOR SALE sign outside, but she didn't pay any attention to the others. She'd hopped clear of the rickshaw and hurried through the creaky iron gate before I could read the number on the door. I was about to follow her when Mr. October caught my arm.

"Wait."

"What's wrong?"

"They may not be alone," he said. "If the enemy found the children first and are keeping them here, they won't give them up easily. Best be prepared." He leaned to one side, into shadow, emerging in a different guise, that of the swarthy pirate. "In case of trouble. That old body isn't up to the task."

Becky was at the front door now, jiggling the handle as if she thought brute force would unlock it. I ran up the path to her.

"It might be better if you wait out here," I said.

"Why should I?"

"There are things I haven't had time to tell you yet. It could be dangerous."

"You're full of surprises. What next — monsters and bogeymen?"

"Something like that."

She looked at me in disbelief.

"At least wait till we've checked it out," I said. "If it's all clear, I'll call you."

"But I followed you all that way just to tell you. I brought you to their door. You wouldn't be here without me."

"That's teamwork," Mr. October said. "It doesn't matter who plays what part, as long as the job gets done." He edged toward us on the path, the Y standing out on his forehead. "Are we agreed?"

"Agreed," Becky said reluctantly. "I suppose."

"Good. Then I'll proceed."

He lifted a hand to the door and pressed his palm against it, bowing his head as if in deep thought.

"Now," he said.

*Thud.* The tumbler lock clicked open.

*Clink-clank.* Then the two dead bolts below it.

He gave the handle a sharp turn and push. The door swung open a fraction, then jarred and held fast.

"Security chain on the inside," he said. "Then they're not alone. They have watchers. Lu?"

I pulled Becky aside as Lu advanced up the path, swiveled back on one heel, and aimed a high kick at the door. The door flew open with a crunch of splintering wood.

"Remember what I said," I told Becky.

She nodded, clearly unhappy, and stood back as I followed the others inside.

Apart from the cold — and it was freezing in there — the first thing I noticed was a weird indoor mist. It covered the floor like fog from dry ice, swirling around us up to our shins. There were several points of glowing light inside it, beams skipping to and fro like searchlights.

We waded through the mist along a darkened hall, passing a set of stairs on the right. At the far end, an arched doorway framed a view of the moonlit kitchen.

Everything in the kitchen had a silvery sheen. To the left, the back door's glass panels hinted at the shadowy garden outside. The door had a cat flap set into its base, barely visible through the mist. Off to the right, outside the main window, a black skeletal tree swayed in the night air, the tip of its longest limb scraping the glass.

"Nothing down here," I said, testing a light switch. The electricity must have been cut off.

"Don't be so certain," Mr. October said.

He stood inside the archway, listening.

Silence — no, not quite silence. Apart from the familiar noises of a house settling by night — ticking beams and joists and floorboards — there was a deep, slow-building rumble, more a vibration than a sound, like that of an underground train passing directly under us.

"Shifters," Lu whispered.

"Shifters," Mr. October agreed.

Past him I could see Becky at the front door, half inside and half out, straining to hold herself back. Some of the mist was escaping the house, flowing around her ankles.

"Upstairs," she called, skipping away from it. "I think they're up there. Check there first . . . but wait."

"What for?" I asked.

"Careful. There's something inside the mist."

She'd only just spoken when a slick, dark shape fluttered past my feet, crossing between two points of light. It looked more like a tadpole than anything, and was followed by another, larger dark form roughly the size of an eel. I stepped aside from it, remembering the creature sliding into the canal near the bridge.

The tree scraped the kitchen window, sounding like claws

feeling for a way in. The cat flap opened and closed with a dull thump. What I saw coming through it made the breath seize up in my chest. First one, then another, then a whole torrent, more than sixty of them before I lost count. To anyone else they might've looked like ordinary cats, but to me they were more like the thing that turned itself into a cat seconds before Mr. October threw the fireball. They moved silently and gracefully, as if their bodies were boneless. One by one they shot indoors, landed without a sound, and slid headlong into the mist, out of sight.

"Shifters," Lu repeated. "Watchers. Demons."

"Go to Becky," Mr. October ordered me. "You're not ready for this yet."

He pushed me away from the kitchen into the hall. The mist swept around our legs, alive with darting eel-shaped shadows under its frosty pale surface. The Shifters had entered the kitchen in feline form but now they'd become something else.

"Lu, mind the door," Mr. October said. "Any others you see coming in, zap them. Ben, what did I tell you? Go to the front."

He sounded calm, fully in control, and I was glad to think that someone was. My nerves were squirming like rats in a sack.

As I started back along the hall, the first of the Shifters leapt from its cover of mist and straight at Mr. October. He caught it one-handed in midflight. It twisted, shiny and glistening in his grasp, its black stubby head snapping at him.

Then it suddenly stopped moving, stiffening as if turning to stone. Bracing his shoulder, Mr. October brought it back in a wide arc and hurled it at the wall above the sink where it hit the tiles, shattering into a thousand pieces.

Another one surfaced nearer the back door where Lu had positioned herself. It reared up above her and tilted back its head, glaring down at her with six dead, black eyes, forked tongue flicking. Lu made a very slight but intricate movement with her hand, just an upward flick of the wrist. As she did, the creature's head parted company with its stalk-like neck, sliced away with one clean sweep of Lu's invisible weapon. The head flopped back into the mist; the body sank lifelessly after it.

"Ben, watch out!" Becky called from the front door.

A third creature had broken cover, rearing up right behind me. I bolted away down the hall, sidestepping the growing number of shapes flitting around my ankles. The rumbling sound was louder now; the house was shaking around us. I heard Becky's voice reach toward me through the dark, a small surprised gasp followed by the slam of the front door blowing shut.

She'd tumbled inside just in time.

"I'm OK," she said. "The children . . . Let's go for them now. It's our best chance, while those things are being kept busy in there."

She nodded toward the kitchen, where Mr. October was aiming a forefinger at a creature snaking up one wall, readying himself to launch another fireball.

"Well, are you coming?" she said indignantly, already on her way upstairs.

The mist followed us all the way up, brushing our heels. At the top, moonlight flooded the landing from the open bathroom door. Two other doors faced each other from opposite ends of the landing, both closed. The children had to be behind one of them.

"The one on the left?" I guessed.

"No, the one on the right," Becky said, starting toward it.

She arrived ahead of me but waited until I caught up. She gave me a nod that seemed to say yes, she was sure. I threw the door open and we peered inside.

On a single bed in the corner, Molly and Mitch huddled together among a mound of quilted pillows and throws. There was nothing else in the room. The air had a hazy look and smelled faintly of soot. The children looked up, trembling, their faces and nightclothes darkly smudged. Mitch still held his teddy bear, and for the first time I noticed one of its ears was missing. As he sat up, the bear fell upside down at his side, giving out a gentle rattling growl.

"Do you know where you are?" I asked them.

"It's not our house anymore," Molly said. "They're making us stay but we don't want to be here."

A confusion of shouts and crashes traveled up from downstairs. Something exploded against a wall.

"Can you see them?" I asked Becky.

She nodded. "Sort of. Not too well. I see traces of light and I hear them, though."

"Would you like to come with us?" I asked the kids. "We'll take you away from here if you like."

Mitch rolled off the bed and came forward first, rubbing his eyes. "I'll go."

After a brief hesitation, Molly followed. They stood before us, grubby and forlorn, flinching at a sudden caterwaul from the kitchen.

"We won't see Mummy and Daddy again, will we?" Molly said. "It's all right, though; we know what happened."

"You'll see them, you just won't be able to stay with them like before," Becky said. "Do you know who's been keeping you here?"

Molly studied the bare wooden boards under her feet. "They're not nice to us. We don't know their names, and their faces keep changing."

"Don't let them come back," Mitch pleaded.

The mayhem downstairs — a series of crashes, a piercing scream — threw an urgent note into Becky's voice. "You're safe with us, but we have to go now."

"Follow her," I said, ushering them past me. "Just stay with her. I'll be behind you all the way."

They hesitated at the doorway, looking out. Becky moved to the stairs, waving them to her.

"It's all right," she said. "It'll be fine now. Just come this way."

The children exchanged a glance, nodded in silent agreement, then started along the landing together, Mitch dragging the bear behind him by its one ear.

"That's good," I said, but I didn't like the look of the mist. There were rapid movements close to its surface, and something cold and jellylike slid past my shin. "Don't even look, kids. Only a few steps down and you're out of here."

By the time I reached the stairs, Becky was three-quarters of the way down with the Willow children close behind. A smell of burning and something else, something rotten and poisonous, drifted toward me. It took me a few seconds to realize the house had fallen silent.

"Mr. October?" I called. "Everything OK down there?"

His reply was a long time coming. "It's all clear, but keep your eyes open. There may be others. And if you're coming down, I suggest you avert your eyes. It's a wee bit messy in here. What about the children?"

"We've got them," Becky called from the front door, the children at her heels. "They're fine. I'm taking them out."

"Oh." He sounded surprised, even impressed. "Good work. You do that. We'll follow."

"Hurry, don't look back," Becky told them, ushering them out to the moonlit path. Then she turned and glanced up at me with anxious eyes. "Will you get a move on? Ben . . . Oh my God, what's that?"

I was halfway downstairs when something snared my ankle, tightening around it like a noose. A gray-gloved hand cut above the mist's pale surface, holding me fast, yanking me down. As I tried to kick it loose, a foul earthy scent rushed up at me, and I saw that the hand holding on to me wasn't gloved at all — it was covered with gray, decaying flesh.

The dead, old smell of it made everything inside me go loose. A blind panic seized me as the demon shot up to full height, transferring its grip from my ankle to my throat and slamming me back against the wall.

Its face was familiar. I'd seen it — or one like it — only a few days before. Beetles scuttled around its pale dead flesh. The scent of the grave clogged my nostrils as its breath wafted over me. If a face without eyes could express anything, the Deathhead was expressing triumph. Delicious victory. Its mouth, with shorn-off lips, was as close as it could get to a smile.

"Feeding time," the demon whispered, squeezing my throat. "You stole two souls from us; now I have to steal something back."

*Please,* I tried to say, but I couldn't make a sound.

I heard Becky screaming below me and Mr. October barking instructions, but I couldn't tell what he was saying. Everything around me was blurring and turning soft. The world was slowing to a standstill.

*Raymond,* I thought — a thought out of nowhere. Raymond had had ahold of me, and so had Synsiter, that morning by the canal. Things had a way of happening when bullies came after me, but how? What had I done?

But I was drowsier now, couldn't recall, couldn't think.

*Let me sleep,* I thought. *Let it stop.*

The demon's grip tightened, lifting me up off my feet and clear of the stairs. My body fell slack and a thick gray fog came rolling in. There were footfalls on the stairs not far below me, and somewhere in the gray I heard Lu yelling: "See what you want, Ben. *Try* to see it. If you can think it, you can do it!"

And I did. It was only a simple thought — for all I knew it might be the last thought I'd ever have — and if I'd been able to make a sound I would've screamed it out loud: *Enough.*

That was all. *Enough.*

The Deathhead suddenly relaxed its choke hold on my throat, then dropped me altogether, whipping its hands clear and staring down at them in empty-eyed terror. The strong fingers were withering to stumps, dissolving away as if they'd been soaked in acid, drooping boneless from what was left of its hands.

The demon howled and tottered across the stairs, thumped against the banister, then turned to face me, hissing between its teeth. As it did, my vision cleared just enough to see Lu running up toward it, making that quick-fire motion with her wrist. Seeing her coming, probably knowing what she meant to do, the Deathhead didn't waste another second. It plunged back inside the mist, becoming just another dark shape swimming beneath the surface.

Lu had ahold of my hand now. "Come on, you come with me, Wonder Boy."

Before I could catch a breath, she'd half dragged, half carried me the rest of the way downstairs and out the front door to where the others were waiting on the path. The fire children stood on either side of Becky. Mr. October was nodding appreciatively. Lu slammed the door behind us, sealing the mist inside.

It took some time for my head to clear. I stood inside the gate, nursing my throat, croaking when I spoke.

"Thanks, Lu. Thanks, Becky. You were great in there. Fearless."

"So you all were," Mr. October said, "but we have to keep moving. They'll be furious about what we just did, and we have to attend to these two before they come after us again. Lu? Our transport!"

Soon we were rolling again, the three of us together on the seat with the children at our knees and the house falling back into shadow up the slope behind us. A mournful cry followed us on the air, a hollow call that seemed to rise up from the depths.

Mr. October puffed air from his cheeks and changed his appearance to the old man in readiness for what would come next. "Deary me, I could do with a holiday," he said.

"Is it like this all the time?" Becky asked.

"Sometimes it's worse," he said. "It could get worse yet tonight, now that we've rattled their cage. And I still have more rounds after we've seen the children off safely. Lu, would you call dispatch and see what they've got?"

"Just did," Lu answered, accelerating down Chetwynd Road. "One natural causes, one hit-and-run, one DIY accident with a drill."

"Are you taking us home now?" mewled Molly.

"We only want to sleep," said Mitch.

"It'll be over very soon," Mr. October said in his softest, most compassionate voice. "And then you'll be safe again. And then you can rest."

And it was. And they were. And they did.

# 21

# THE SURPRISE

From our position on the rickshaw, there wasn't much to see. The door in space on the edge of the heath was as hard to distinguish as the fine-line crack between the walls across from HQ.

Mr. October stood to one side of it, stooping and slowly turning its handle like a mime with an invisible prop. Then the door opened, at first revealing a narrow slit, then a dizzying rectangle of golden yellow light standing against the darkness — an entry point into the beyond.

Without hesitation, Mitch and Molly marched hand in hand toward it.

"Now I see them," Becky said tearfully. "They're not looking back. How do they know what to do and where to go from here?"

"That's a mystery," I said. "I'm not even sure Mr. October knows. All he can do is show them the way."

We watched in silence. Whatever lay beyond the doorway blazed like fire, but a welcoming, smokeless fire the children were glad to enter. As they moved inside, their shapes became less distinct. Then they were part of the light itself. We lost sight of them just before Mr. October closed the door, leaving us staring into shadows again.

"Blimey, I can't explain a thing I've seen tonight," Becky said as we walked home through De Beauvoir Square. "But I don't doubt any of it. I feel like laughing or crying, I don't know which. I'm all shaken up."

We walked along, lost in our own separate thoughts, until Becky stopped me on a street corner. "We can't afford to tell anyone, Ben, can we?"

I shook my head. "It's best if we don't."

"We'd be a laughing stock. They'd think we're weird, like I used to think you were weird."

"Yeah, they would."

"What have you gotten me into?" she said. "I feel all funny inside. And now I want to shout about it, but I know I can't. I won't sleep a wink tonight after this."

"You'll get used to it, though. It's the same thing every night of the week."

"What, with the monsters too?"

"Not every night. Just sometimes."

"Did you really melt off that thing's hands?"

"Dunno," I said. "I'm not sure what I did."

"But we saved them, didn't we? We really did."

"Yes, we did."

As she set off toward home along Kingsland Road, I felt a swell of pride over what we'd achieved, but also a nagging fear of what was to come. The war of souls may have raged for centuries, but for us it was only beginning.

It was after ten when I got home. Seven hours on the job, I suddenly realized — so much for part-time work.

Mum was still up and about. "Ah, there he is," she called from the living room. "The wanderer returns."

"Sorry I'm late." I lingered in the hall, afraid she'd see the evening's drama written across my face like the runes. "Everything OK, Mum? Did Ellie stay long?"

"She left half an hour ago. And I'll tell you what, we're really going for that vacation. I have a good feeling about Lanzarote, and as soon as we can get away, we will."

"That's great," I said. "You sound good."

"Do I? Well, it helps to have something to look forward to." She patted the cushion next to her on the sofa. "Are you planning to stand there all night? Come here and tell me about your day and I'll tell you about mine."

It wasn't until then that I remembered she had news, a surprise. Whatever it was, it couldn't be anywhere near as explosive as the news I could've shared with her if I'd dared.

She'd positioned herself so I had to sit on her good side. Her bandaged hand lay slack on her lap. Her left hand ruffled my hair when I settled down beside her.

"So, how was it?" she said.

"Oh, today was OK, just fine, you know."

"That's not very informative."

"Well, it's school," I said. "And mucking around with friends after school. Not much to tell."

"If that's the best you can do . . ."

"You had a surprise for me," I reminded her.

"Yes."

"You said both good and bad, a bit of each."

She nodded. "It's sad news, actually, but good for us in some ways. Would you mind grabbing that envelope, darlin'?"

The envelope on the side table looked official, with the name of a law firm printed across the top — ROSSITER & ALLEN, LTD. It felt thick enough to contain more than just a letter.

"Open it," Mum said. "Read it, and then I'll answer any questions you have."

I emptied the envelope, shaking out a cover letter with a slip of paper stapled to the back of it and another, smaller envelope with Mum's name handwritten on the front. The letter began:

Dear Mrs. Harvester,

Our deepest sympathies at this most difficult time for you and your family. We write in accordance with

the wishes of your sister, Carrie Williams. As execu-
tors of Miss Williams's estate, we herewith enclose the
sum bequeathed to you in her will, a check for £10,000,
and a personal letter which Miss Williams wished us to
forward.

I broke off there, looking at Mum in astonishment. She
pinched her lips and didn't say anything. The check attached
to the letter was signed in a hand as illegible as a doctor's, but
the figures printed across it were clear to see.

Ten. Thousand. Pounds.

My jaw hung open. "Aunt Carrie . . . ," I said. "Aunt Carrie
left you all this?"

She sniffed. "That's right."

"But you hadn't spoken for ages. You had nothing to do
with each other. I don't get it. Why would she —"

"Read the other letter," she said. "That's the hardest part,
but it's the part that explains it all. I should've spoken to you
sooner about this. I never expected it to come out this way."

"Ten thousand quid," I murmured.

I was wary about knowing anything more. Over the years
I'd gotten used to family secrets. Mum had locked all those
stories away like precious stones in a box, but this letter had
changed all that, and now she was handing me the key.

"Turn to the last two pages," Mum said. "Everything you
need to know is there. Start there, third paragraph down."

Aunt Carrie's writing wasn't much easier to decode than
Mum's new wrong-handed scrawl. It slanted both ways, up

and down, all knotty and tangled, and some parts I had to read twice to decipher. Other parts I had to read several times before I could believe what I was seeing.

*It's only money, though, and I know money can't begin to make up for the hurt I've caused. But I also know (a little bird told me) you've had a lean time of it lately, and I hope this will go some way toward helping. It won't make things right, it won't ease the pain any more than a Band-Aid would, but please accept it for Ben if not for yourself.*

*Time's a great healer, they say, and I hope one day you'll find it in your heart to forgive and forget our stupid mistake. I've always regretted the rift it caused, and I've practiced this apology many times. I've picked up the phone but not dialed, or dialed but hung up before it could ring. If only I'd had the nerve, who knows? We may have been best of friends again. We may have had a chance to catch up and make up before this wretched illness wrecked all my plans.*

*I'm not angry or bitter about it. I've accepted it for what it is and for what it's doing to me. It's only another life-form trying to survive any way it can, and it's my bad luck that it's stronger than me now. The great sadness is that it never slows down, won't wait for me to see you face-to-face.*

*So if we never speak again, my love, try not to be angry when you think of me. Try to forgive me for what I did. Be good to yourself and take care of Ben, and if Jim ever comes knocking at your door, simply tell him I'm sorry — before you slap him.*

*All my love, C. xxx*

For long seconds I was dumbstruck, floating, staring at the page in confusion.

Mum wiped her eyes and said, "She always was a drama queen. There's nothing to bloody forgive. Silly woman."

"She should've called," I said.

"So should I have. We were equally at fault there."

"But what was she so sorry for? And what did she mean about slapping Dad?"

I had a feeling about that, perhaps I always had, and in some ways I didn't want to know. I carefully folded the papers back inside the lawyer's envelope, waiting for Mum to reply.

"It's like this," she said. "You know how we all got together one afternoon at the old house, you and me and Dad, and we had this very important announcement to make. . . ."

"Yes."

Not only did I remember it, I could still see it clearly, every detail, from the color of Mum's mauve top to the way she and Dad sat together on the sofa but never looked at each other, from the arrangement of furniture in the room to the thrush hopping on the lawn outside the window. I could feel the awkwardness in the air, and the sadness.

"We said we needed a break from each other," Mum said. "We hadn't been getting along too well for a while, and we'd come up with this new arrangement — maybe for a short time, maybe longer."

"Yes," I said. "You can tell it to me straight, Mum. I know Dad left and didn't come back. I never knew why, though."

"I'm sorry, I was getting to it."

"Dad cried, didn't he?"

"Did he? I don't remember that."

"The night he left. I heard him from my room. Then later I saw him from my window going up the path. He looked back once but my light was out and I don't think he saw me. Later, I thought if he had, he might've changed his mind and come back."

Mum hung her head, settling her left hand over her bandaged right. "He never wanted to leave. He certainly never wanted to leave *you*. We didn't think it would be forever at the time."

"A few years isn't forever. He might still come home," I said. "If he knew you were in poor shape, he'd come back."

"You think so?"

"I know he would."

"Still, he hasn't picked up the phone in all this time. He hasn't written. He might've vanished off the face of the earth for all anyone knows."

"But why?" I said. "Why'd he have to go in the first place?"

Somehow I knew what was coming and what she'd say, but that didn't make it any easier to hear it.

"Because of what happened between him and Aunt Carrie."

It felt like a slap. I turned away, then looked sharply back at her. "How long?"

"Not long at all. It was over before it started, but then it was weeks before I found out, before he broke down and told me. The irony is, I was the one who put them together. I made it possible."

She could see I wasn't following, so she went on.

"It was while he was working all-out on his business, trying to keep it afloat, before they refused the loan that broke his heart. He was traveling up and down the country to meetings and conferences all over the place. You'll remember how it used to keep him away from home four or five nights a week."

"Yes."

"Well, one of those conferences took him close to Carrie's. She had a big old drafty house in the north, near Ilkley, the year before she moved back to the coast. I called and arranged for your dad to stay a couple of nights. The rest you can probably work out for yourself."

I could, but I didn't want to. What with the day's shift for the Ministry and now this, I wasn't sure how much more my head could take.

"As Carrie said," Mum went on, "they made a stupid mistake." Maybe I made a bigger mistake putting them together in the first place.

No wonder Mum had been so low for so long. I'd only had the vaguest idea until now. One mistake, and she'd lost her sister forever. Maybe Dad too.

I turned the envelope around in my hands. The check would help, but Carrie had been right: It couldn't make up for what had gone wrong.

"So that's how it was," Mum said. "The truth came out and I asked for time to think things through. He went to Newcastle, stayed there with friends for a while, but then he moved somewhere else and no one knew where."

"And you haven't heard from him since?"

"No, not once. Seems he's vanished into thin air."

"I miss him," I said.

"Me too, darlin'."

She forced a smile, brightening slightly. "It would be nice to know where he is, at least. Even if he's living a new life in the sun, it would help to know. You never know: We could take our holiday with Ellie and find him living it up in the first bar we pass."

"But we won't," I said.

"No, we won't, because whatever else he did wrong, that's not Jim, that's not your dad. Oh, that's terrible," she said suddenly, leaning around me for a view of the TV.

A light aircraft had lost control and smashed into an apartment building on the south side of the Thames. The breaking news showed a tower of fire captured on camera from a helicopter.

As the story unfolded, I wondered how many seconds or minutes ago the telegraph machine had woken with a start and how many names were on this list. And I wondered if Becky might be seeing this now, knowing Mr. October and Lu and others from the Ministry were on their way even as we watched.

"They're going to have their hands full tonight," I said quietly, more to myself than to Mum.

Mum looked at me askance. "Pardon? Who?"

"The emergency services," I said as the camera zoomed in and the building began to collapse.

# 22

# THE NEXT IN LINE

I had a terrible sleep, the kind where you spend the night dreaming you're wide awake. At one point, about three in the morning, Dad came into the room and sat on the bed, stroking my forehead.

I could barely make out his outline in the inky darkness, but I recognized his voice as soon as he spoke.

"Remember when we were at the old house and you still believed in Santa Claus?" he said. "And you stayed awake one Christmas Eve, waiting to hear him come and start unloading presents around the living room?"

I nodded but, being asleep, didn't reply. I may have moaned and murmured a little.

"You wanted to sneak downstairs and catch him in the act," Dad continued, "so you could tell your friends at school, the ones who didn't believe, that you'd seen him. Just before midnight you heard footsteps and papers rustling in the living room, so you crept down and peeked around the corner. And there I was, rolling up newspapers and laying them in the fireplace so that we could have a fire in the morning. But there were no presents to see. I hadn't put them out yet."

I groaned, tossing and turning. He rested a strong hand on my shoulder to settle me.

"You weren't disappointed to see me instead of him," he said. "You were *angry*. I'd never seen you so angry. Remember?"

Somewhere between sleep and consciousness I shook my head. Angry? I couldn't recall that at all.

"You said, 'Why are you still up, Dad? Why don't you go to bed? If he sees you, he won't come. What're you thinking?' Makes me laugh to think of it now. You always were a dreamer. You always needed something to believe in, like the business you're involved in now."

He stroked my cheek, and his fingers felt soft and clammy against my skin.

"Do you still believe in me, Ben?" he asked.

*Dad,* I thought, *would you mind not doing that? Your hand is so cold.*

"Do you?" he asked.

*Of course I do,* I thought.

A car passed outside, its booming sound system rattling the walls. Its headlights streamed across the window, throwing into sharp relief the figure perched on the bed, stroking my cheek.

It wasn't my father.

That wasn't his face and those weren't his hands. The last time I'd seen this visitor, it'd been at my throat, those hollowed-out eyes just fractions away from mine, the scent of the grave whispering off it.

"We can get to you anywhere, any time," it said.

A gargling sound wormed out of its throat. The lipless mouth opened wide and rushed at me, closing over my face.

With a shout, I wriggled out from under the duvet and threw myself across the room, thumping against the wall and sliding down to my haunches on the carpet.

*It's all right,* I thought. *Deep breaths. No one there. Only me down here on the floor and my sleeping self in the bed, turning over with a sigh and a swish of bedclothes. I'm still asleep. There's nothing to fear.*

*We can get to you anywhere, any time.*

I slept on, dreaming of being awake watching myself sleep. Perhaps this was how newly-departeds felt, displaced and outside themselves, looking in.

My shoulders rose and fell with each breath, and now and again I shivered and moaned. My fists drew into white-knuckled bundles at my chin, clenched so tightly that by morning my nails had cut red half-moon shapes in my palms.

"'All that we see or seem is but a dream within a dream,' innit?" read Mel.

Mr. Glover winced and shook his world-weary head.

"*What?*" said Mel.

"Nothing," he sighed. "Please continue."

"He can't win," Becky whispered. "He's going to break down and cry if she keeps this up."

It created quite a stir when Becky chose to sit with me during English. The others in her gang stared at her as if she'd lost her marbles. The twins said nothing, but I had a good idea what they were thinking. Only Raymond Blight looked the other way, disinterested.

"Did you catch the news?" Becky said.

I nodded. We weren't supposed to discuss it in school, but she was finding it hard to keep quiet.

"I saw him," she said.

"Who?"

She checked around — no one watching — and mouthed the words *Mr. October.*

"On the news report," she said. "After the building came down, he went inside, into the ruins. No one commented or tried to stop him. And when he came out again, a whole train of people were following. Couldn't anyone else see him?"

Mr. Glover's glare cut short our conversation.

"Sorry, sir," Becky said.

"Sorry," I echoed.

"Later," she whispered as Mel returned to reading. "I can't wait for tonight. I'm all jittery. It's like being part of a secret society."

"That's exactly what it is. Let's try to keep it secret."

*     *     *

From that day on, we walked to the Ministry together after school. At HQ I took her through the duties she'd soon be performing, showing her the telegraph and the typewriter and explaining the importance of transcribing each list accurately.

I introduced her to the dispatch workers, who by now were calling me by my name. Becky was impressed by that, but not as impressed as she was by the ever-expanding records office with its miles-apart walls and infinite ceiling.

"How can that be? You mean every single day it grows larger?"

"Every hour, every minute. It never stops."

"So who are the armed guards I keep seeing? And who's the grumpy old woman in the booth? Is she always so disagreeable? And has anyone ever told her she has spiders in her hair?"

"I did once. It wasn't a great idea."

She soon grew into the part, sometimes joining Lu and Mr. October in the field while I stayed behind to file paperwork. On Saturdays she even offered to cover for me while I took Mum to her weekly hospital appointment.

At the hospital I kept to the waiting area outside Mum's treatment room. It seemed wiser not to go wandering. Now and then I saw agents from the Ministry come and go from the ward. I didn't know them all by sight, but with a look and a nod they quickly told me who they were. It was reassuring to know they were around and on my side.

After the hospital, once Mum was home and resting, I'd return to the Ministry and Becky would tell me excitedly about the dramas I'd missed during the day.

The month sped past. Halloween was approaching. The shops filled with broomsticks, pointy black hats, and green, glowing goblin masks. We all brought pumpkins to school, where we scooped out the soggy pulp and seeds to make jack-o'-lanterns. Becky brought an extra, using it to bake pumpkin bread in home ec. It tasted more like cake than bread, with a sweet cinnamon flavor.

In art, the rest of the class volunteered me to take charge of decorations. I painted a scarecrow creature and a Michael Myers mask from the film Dad used to play every Halloween night when I was too young to stay up and watch.

By the time we were done, the art room looked like a haunted house, and the school's corridors resembled the walls of a ghost train ride. Grinning skulls and phosphorescent masks, werewolves and vampires and Frankenstein monsters looked down with eyes that followed you wherever you went.

After Mr. Redfern's class, the last of the day, I was clearing my desk when I heard voices outside the room — Becky and Kelly talking out in the hall.

"But you always have before," Kelly was saying. "What's the problem? It's only for a few hours."

"I know," Becky said. "But I forgot, and now I've got other plans."

"Well, the rest of us are going. It won't be the same without you."

"I'm sorry."

"You're no fun anymore. You're becoming dead boring, actually. You've been boring ever since you made friends with *him*."

I wondered if Kelly knew I was in hearing range. Something in her tone told me she knew very well.

"Don't be like that," Becky said patiently. "Look, if you like, we'll do something this weekend instead."

"Nah, forget it. You do what you like."

"But, Kelly . . ."

Kelly's voice faded as she flounced down the hallway. "And don't bother seeing us off at the bus stop, either. Wouldn't want to keep you from your new best friend."

She stomped angrily down the stairs.

Becky was leaning against the wall looking flushed when I came out of the classroom. She answered without my needing to ask.

"It's nothing. They're trick-or-treating, and they expect me to go because I always have. How can I tell them we have matters of life and death — well, death — to deal with?"

"You can't."

"No, I can't. I'm all right, though. I'm not upset. Kelly's never spoken to me like that before, but I know she's only jealous."

"You could still go if you wanted. They're your friends. You don't have to come every night."

"But I do," Becky said. "I've waited years for this, ever since my Blue Grandma's funeral. Mr. October calls it my true calling."

"I know."

"And if you're lucky enough to find it, or for it to find you, you have to grab the chance with both hands, don't you?"

"Even if it's dangerous?"

"Even then."

At first I'd wanted to warn her about the enemy and the risk of taking sides against them, but after she rescued the fire children I'd never brought it up. She'd seen what was at stake, and she'd never backed down. If anything, the risk was what attracted her. It made her tick.

The clocks had gone back an hour over the weekend, and when we arrived in Islington the sky was showing the first signs of dark. A biting wind swept along the streets, hurrying us on toward the Ministry. Gangs of witches ran up to complete strangers carrying lanterns and shaking buckets of change, stamping their feet against the cold, unaware of the dead man watching from an antique shop doorway.

A field agent I'd seen once or twice before, Joe Mort, had joined the dead man to lead him away. Joe had the wiry frame of a bantamweight boxer, crew-cut black hair, and a thousand-yard stare. He winked at us as we passed and said, "Almost got away, this one. A 1742, dropped stone dead during a horror double bill at the cinema round the corner and ran out screaming."

"Good thing you found him," I said. "Is there much else going on tonight?"

Joe made a face. "It's Halloween. What do you think?"

We were early for work, and when we walked in, Sukie was finishing her stint in receipts, tapping out the last of a tall stack of cards.

"Oh, hi," she said, not looking up.

"This is Becky," I said.

"I know."

Of course she did.

"He's busy," she said before I could ask where Mr. October was. "Sorry, must stop doing that. Last I saw of him, he was running round the building in a fit. One of our operatives spotted a lost soul by the canal just east of here. We've been looking for this one for ages."

"Busy night," Becky said.

"Aren't they all?" Sukie's kinked eyes took us both in with one look. "But yeah, especially when the short days come and seasonal affective disorder kicks in. We've had two 3624s on the Northern Line already today."

"What're they?" Becky asked.

"A bit like the first case you saw," I reminded her. "But intentional."

"Jumpers," said Sukie. "Fatalities on the underground. There must be something about the Northern Line. It's the most popular departure point for suicidals."

"What about the lost soul?" I said.

"Yeah," Sukie said. "A matter of some urgency. Mr. October's all worked up about it. Obviously we need to track it before the enemy do, because as you know Samhain is their special night of the year — they'll be out in force until dawn."

"A matter of some urgency," Mr. October said, sneaking his head around the door. He hadn't yet changed for the evening's duties. His dark pirate persona alternated with the frail old man's, morphing back and forth between them. "There's a lost soul out there we need to track before the enemy do, because as you know Samhain —"

"We do know," I said. "Sukie just told us."

"Ah. Of course. In that case, may I just say 'happy All Hallows'? Here, have a candy apple."

He plucked one from behind his back and tossed it to me, then found another for Becky in the empty space above the door.

"Not for me, thanks; they hurt my teeth," Sukie said, adding her last card to the stack.

"Leave the cards for Ben," Mr. October told her. "I'll need your talents in the field if we're going to find this lost soul. Yours too, Becky. Ben, would you mind holding the fort while we're gone? Shouldn't take more than an hour if we're lucky."

"OK," I said, feeling excluded. Whatever was in the air tonight sounded like something I wouldn't want to miss.

"You won't miss a thing," Sukie reassured me. "We'll call you as soon as you're needed."

"Took the words right out of my mouth," Mr. October said. "Sukie, where's —"

"Already on it," Sukie said. "She's outside bringing the rickshaw."

"Be careful," I said to Becky as they filed from the room. "You don't know what's out there yet."

She smiled back from the doorway, her face patterned orange-black in the candlelight. "I've a fairly good idea, Ben. It's Halloween."

The time dragged after they'd gone. Why would Mr. October require their services but not mine? If this was such a big night for the enemy, shouldn't I be out there doing whatever I could?

I took the cards to sullen Miss Webster in records, then sat at the desk studying the ancientspeak phrase book. The words still wouldn't settle on the page, and my head swam after a few minutes, so I rolled paper into the typewriter and went to work on my journal instead.

As I typed, the wind groaned through the building, and the shivering candle flame sent strange light across the page. Something was coming — I felt it in my bones. As I pulled the first sheet from the typewriter, the telegraph machine sputtered and choked out smoke.

It stopped almost as soon as it started. With a gasp the machine fell silent. I stared at it, expecting more. This happened all the time, though — nothing for hours, then one solitary name, then a whole slew of names sending the machine into rumbling overload. But nothing more came. That was all for now.

With a sigh, not fancying the trek to Miss Webster's booth for just this, I brought the new list to the desk. The reference number 4837 didn't mean much to me, but the name and address were familiar — *very* familiar. My insides turned over; the room darkened around me as I fell into the chair to read it again, then again to be sure.

Perhaps deep down I'd known it was coming. I'd known but kept the thought hidden away where it wouldn't hurt. It wasn't a surprise so much as a shock to find out like this, to see that single name recorded there in stark black and white.

*Mum.*

# 23

# ON THE RUN

A screaming in my head blotted everything out, growing louder and deadlier by the second, like a train fast approaching through a tunnel — a train heading directly at me.

My eyes were hot and streaming, turning the words and numbers on the paper watery. I heard myself speak, or try to, but I hardly knew what was coming out of my mouth.

"Not fair. Not fair. *Notfairnotfairnotfair . . .*"

And then I did something I've been trying to live down ever since. Something that broke every rule in the Ministry's book. Something I never would've done if the telegraph hadn't said what it said.

I got up, shaky-legged, crushing the sheet into a tight ball between my fists, stuffing it into my hip pocket. This was one name I wouldn't, couldn't transcribe. No way could I make myself type it. The telegraph never lied, but so what? That didn't mean I had to go along with it. Not this time.

I turned and fled from the room.

A siren went up around the building the second I stepped into the corridor. It drilled through my ears as I legged it past the other offices, downstairs and out to the moonlit alley.

Mr. October had warned me what might happen if lists were badly transcribed, mistyped, misfiled. The consequences could be dire. The natural order of things could change. But what if the cards were never typed at all, if the names were never filed, but stolen?

If the siren ringing in my ears was any indication, I'd done the worst thing, the most unforgivable thing an operative could do. Until now, no one but the Lords of Sundown had stolen from the Ministry. I'd landed myself in a world of trouble.

My sneakers screeched across the cobblestones as I ran for the invisible gap. A searchlight snapped on somewhere above the dark building, its icy beam falling on the wall ahead of me.

The crevice between the walls felt narrower than ever as I slid sideways into it. For a moment I feared the walls might seal up completely, trapping me there, crushing me to dust where I'd never be found. But the alarm continued to rise and fall, and I heard the slap and thunder of boots in the alley behind me.

Pandemonium security. The Vigilants.

I froze, but only for a second. It sounded like a multitude, uniformed and fully armed and dangerous. The Vigilants had been set on my tail.

Edging between the cold, dank bricks, I came out onto Camden Passage, where covens of witches were still trick-or-treating, and a child-size ghost flapped its arms and yelled "Boo!" as I passed. When I rounded the corner onto Upper Street, the glare of shop windows and car headlights nearly blinded me. Above the rush-hour clamor I could still hear the siren and, closer, the clatter of Vigilant boots.

I tore across the intersection, turning left onto a quieter, darker street. A posse of guards stormed past the top of the street a few meters away, swinging powerful flashlights in my direction. I jumped inside the nearest doorway and shrank back as far as I could, listening to the crackle of their walkie-talkies.

Whatever happened, I couldn't get caught. I had to keep Mum safe, do whatever I could to protect her. But how much time did she have? Minutes or hours? The telegraph was never clear about things like that.

The walkie-talkies faded into traffic noise. I waited a minute in case the Vigilants came back. When I was sure they had moved on, I set off downhill, cutting from one street to the next in search of the canal.

It had to be somewhere nearby. If I could find it, the darkness by the water would give me cover. But suppose the enemy were down there too? Suppose they were already waiting at home? It was a chance I had to take. Breathless, I ran deeper into the night.

I kept to the shadows the whole way, trying not to think about what might be inside them. But if the enemy were out in force tonight — Samhain, their special night, Sukie had called it — then so were the Ministry. Their security forces were everywhere.

The Vigilants patrolled every other street, flashlights scanning doorways and dipping over garden walls. At one point I had to dive behind a mountain of black trash bags and wait there, not moving, until they turned the corner. On another street I hid inside a Dumpster filled with bricks and soggy, splintery lengths of timber, huddling under a muddy tarp that smelled of cat pee.

By the time I scrambled out and got moving again, all the streets were beginning to look alike. I had a sinking feeling I'd lost my way. I'd traveled to and from the Ministry too many times to count, I knew the route by heart, but nowhere I turned looked familiar now.

Mum needed me. I couldn't waste time. But I couldn't afford to panic, either. All I had to do was find a way back to Upper Street, avoiding the Vigilants, and start over again from there.

The breeze whipped up piles of dead leaves from the road-side as I ran. They swirled around me, scraping my face. Jack-o'-lanterns grinned from every other window I passed. The streets were all the same, silent and empty and foreign. I couldn't be far from where I needed to be, but the canal may as well have been miles away.

The next intersection rushed at me up a steep slope. I couldn't decide whether to turn right or left at the end. All I could see stretching in front of me was darkness, more darkness, and the faintest ripple of light.

I screeched to a halt, almost cartoon-style, at the junction. At the far side of the road was a low-walled bridge, and a short distance along the bridge the top of the steep path leading down to the canal. I'd found my route home.

The road was clear. I started across it, readying myself to start running again. Everything ached and my head was throbbing. The shivering light on the dark water's surface made me dizzy. But I had to keep going, I had to believe Mum would be OK when I got there. *Don't give up. Don't let the fear take over.*

I hadn't reached the curb on the other side when the light hit me — a huge light, the blaze of fifty or sixty flashlights snapping on at once, burning out of the darkness from both sides.

I could almost feel heat in those lights. I froze in my tracks, closing my eyes against the brightness as the Vigilants tramped nearer. The clatter of their boots on the cold ground sounded like volleys of gunshots.

"There he is," a voice barked somewhere in the light.

"The thief," said another.

"Hands in the air," a third voice ordered. "Don't do anything stupid, kid. Don't even twitch."

"You don't understand," I said shakily. "Someone needs my help. . . ."

"Don't speak. Don't make a sound."

The command was accompanied by the ratcheting lock and load of rifles.

They didn't kill, I remembered. They were defenders, only licensed to stun. All the same, the cold edge in their voices told a different story — if they could, they would. Whatever it took to preserve the natural order.

Peering through the dazzling haze, I could just pick out the bridge fifteen, maybe twenty paces away. I might make it before they had time to react. And if I could reach the towpath, leg it as far as the first bend . . . I knew the way after that very well.

*Do it,* I thought. *Do it for Mum. If you don't, you'll never see her again. If you never take another chance, take this one.*

I took off. A snarl of mob voices followed me. Flashlight beams swished through the dark in confusion, twisting in all directions.

"Stop now, stop where you are!" someone called.

But I couldn't. The top of the steep sloping path was in range. Another few paces, then down to the water and —

It felt like a punch from a soft-gloved hand. Something hit me between the shoulder blades, knocking me out of my stride. A numb coldness spread through me, turning my legs to jelly and skewing them out from under me. I toppled forward into a fog as my mind went blank, wiped clean.

I passed out before I hit the ground.

\*　　\*　　\*

The next ten minutes are gone. I'll never get them back. The first thing I was aware of, coming around, was the sound of dripping water and gritty footsteps trapped between dark, damp walls.

We were inside the access space between Camden Passage and Eventide Street. Two Vigilants were dragging me through the dark, the toes of my shoes scraping the ground as we went.

"You'll be OK," said the one on the left. A gentler, more patient voice than those back on the bridge. "It usually takes half an hour to recover. You'll feel dreamy for a while, but that's all."

We exited the gap and crossed the alley. I could feel Mum slipping away from me, impossibly out of reach. It was too late now. Above us, the moon shone out of a clear starry sky. The searchlight was still swooping around, giving me a shock as it crossed my eyes, but at least the siren had stopped.

The main door was open at Pandemonium House, and an unsteady yellowish light burned inside. A handful of other security guards filed into the building. Two more were posted outside, standing on either side of the entrance, staring at me with deadpan eyes.

My strength was returning. I could walk by myself now, or I could have if they'd let me. The Vigilants clamped my arms, hoisting me up the first steps.

"Everyone knows what you've done," said the one on my left. "And why you did it. But a crime is a crime, and now you'll have to answer for it."

"I'm not sorry," I said.

"You will be," said the one to my right.

At the top of the steps, they paused to let me rest. Apart from the pins and needles in my fingers and my dull thudding head, I could've fared worse. I'd survived, except I didn't know for how long. What was the Ministry's punishment for people like me?

A sudden commotion across the alley made everyone turn. A clatter of wheels and a *slip-slap* of running feet came from the crack between the walls. Seconds later Lu appeared, rickshaw in tow, passing through the walls and into the glare of the searchlight beam.

"Get that thing out of my eyes," she complained. She brought the vehicle to rest below the steps and dusted off her hands, giving a nervous half smile when she saw me.

Three figures were seated in the shade beneath the rickshaw's canopy, but from where I stood I couldn't tell who they were. The first to move was Sukie, who acknowledged me with a nod as she jumped down. Then Becky sat forward into the light, reaching across the seat to help the third passenger out. When I saw who it was, I nearly cried out with relief, but then a feeling of cold dread took over. Why had they brought her here?

"Mum . . ."

I made a move for the steps. The Vigilants held me back.

With Becky supporting her, Mum climbed gingerly down from the rickshaw and looked around, up at the stars, then at me with mystified eyes.

"Ben . . . is that you? What is this place and what's happening? Am I dreaming?"

I wished she were. I wished we both were, but I was becoming more awake by the second.

"Lu," I said, but she didn't let me finish.

"Sorry, Ben. Orders. The numbers are wrong. They have to balance the books."

My insides lurched. It felt like a jolt from a cattle prod, hearing that.

"Ben, would you mind explaining —" Mum began.

The guard at my right put out a hand. "No more questions. Everyone's here. Time to move this inside."

They dragged me toward the main entrance.

"Let him be," Lu called after them. "He won't run. There's nowhere to run to."

All they did was loosen their grip a little as we moved indoors through the entrance hall, which shuddered in the light of twenty or more candles strewn about its walls and alcoves. The wind whistled through the building, and the telegraph's familiar rattle drifted downstairs as the guards walked me up.

I guessed this was how a prisoner might feel on the way to the gallows, but I'd pay the price — any price — if they'd give Mum another chance.

The others followed us, Becky steering Mum up by her good arm, Sukie and Lu just behind. Mum looked as if she were in shock, unable to comprehend what she was seeing. Becky mouthed something to me, but I couldn't tell what she was trying to say.

I gave a start when I saw the hallway up ahead. The conference room door was open — it had never been open before. Another pair of guards stood outside, staring blankly at the opposite wall.

"That's where we're going?" I asked faintly.

"It's a serious matter," the guard on my left said.

After that, nobody spoke for a long time.

The conference room felt like a cave, a huge, cool space with hewn stone walls, a long oak table at its center with twelve chairs surrounding it, and above the table a giant crystal chandelier glittering with all the colors of light.

A black cast-iron fireplace stood against one wall, a log fire burning in its grate. At the far end of the room were three stained-glass arch windows, each depicting historic battle scenes — scenes from the eternal war.

There was more. The room's most remarkable features were the twelve portraits that hung on the walls, six on either side of the great table. The faces in the portraits were as old as time and white as death and constantly changing, dissolving from one set of features to another, as Mr. October's often did.

The twelve faces gave an impression of deep thought and disapproval, not a hint of a smile among them. They overlooked the room like jurors, twelve men good and true, anonymous as jurors because they were never the same when you looked at them again. They didn't keep still for a second.

"The paintings are alive," Becky whispered. "And I think I know who they are. . . ."

We stared in wonder at the faces of the nameless Overseers.

I was so absorbed that at first I didn't spot the movement higher up in the room. Just below the sculpted ceiling, which showed more scenes from the wars, a raven sailed from a darkened corner toward the chandelier. Spreading its wings, it glided gently down to perch on a chair at the head of the table. Its beady eyes surveyed the scene.

With a sudden flutter of feathers, the bird became Mr. October. He wavered a moment between two personalities, the elderly soul in white and the sharp-suited businessman, before settling into the one I knew best. Light from the chandelier crowned his shiny skull, and his face was as grave and rumpled as his worn-out suit.

He sat perfectly still, lost in thought. There were no jokes this time, I knew. No *gotchas*.

"Please be seated," he told the gathering. "This shouldn't take long, but it has to be dealt with. Will those of you with no business here please go out?"

All of the Vigilants but two left — the two who had brought me here. At last they let me go and moved to the door, closing it and standing before it to seal off the meeting.

We took seats near the head of the table. The living portraits stared down, cold and colorless. Seated beside me, Mum opened her mouth to speak, but then said nothing.

Mr. October rapped on the table.

"We're in a state of emergency tonight," he said. "This, as you know, is the night the enemy are at their strongest, and to make matters worse, a name was taken from here a short time ago. It couldn't have come at a worse time."

He glanced at me and I looked away, feeling his disapproval.

"It isn't the first time this has happened," he went on, "and we know from experience how damaging it can be. For one thing, we've had to divert valuable manpower to track what was taken. This at a time when we're already stretched to our limits. When things of this nature occur, it creates a chink in our system. Our defenses are broken. It lets the enemy in."

I didn't need to look up to know what the portraits thought. I could feel their frowns bearing down on me.

"So we have to shore ourselves up," Mr. October went on. "If they attack, we must be prepared. To this end we've called in all our part-time staff, and every Vigilant will remain on duty until further notice."

He paused, hoarse from speaking, and produced a glass of ice water from a pocket. He took a long sip before continuing.

"The other thing we must do," he said, "is balance the

books. As we sit here, the numbers are out of alignment. One has been called but not accounted for. The sooner we deliver that missing soul, the sooner we can clean up this mess."

I couldn't look at him. I couldn't look at Mum. I felt for her hand under the table and squeezed.

"Take me instead," I said weakly.

Mum tugged at my hand in alarm.

"What are you *talking* about?" she said.

"Beg pardon?" said Mr. October.

"It was my fault," I said. "We all know I'm the one who took it. I didn't think how it would change things and I didn't think how much damage it would cause. But I did it for a good reason, and I'd do the same again."

"But, Ben," he said, "that's hardly the point. There's no better reason for breaking the rules than to protect someone you love. But *your* name wasn't called."

"There has to be a way," Becky said. "A way to balance the books without taking this innocent woman."

Mr. October shrugged. "You should know by now, innocence has nothing to do with it. How many innocents have you shed a tear over since you started here? It isn't only the guilty who're called."

"All the same . . . ," she said.

He waved her to silence and pinched the bridge of his nose. Then his face cleared and he leaned toward me across the table.

"Before we proceed, Ben, I think I should have the item in question. The item you stole."

I hesitated. Across the room, the Vigilants stood to attention, hands on rifles. Mum looked at me as if she were beginning to make sense of what was happening.

"Go on," she said. "It's all right. I know what this man's saying and I'm proud — proud of what you did. But you should give it up now."

Her words tore a hole in me. I wanted to weep. "But you're going to get well, Mum. It's not . . . it's not your time."

Her hand held mine tightly.

If I didn't give it back, they would take it regardless. But I wouldn't let her go without a fight.

"Ben, please . . . ," Mr. October said. "The longer we delay, the better the opportunity the enemy will have."

Mum nodded, tears in her eyes. With a cry, I dragged the paper ball from my pocket and slammed it on the table in front of Mr. October.

"There! Are you happy now? Take it back! Just take it!"

A silence settled over the room. No one stirred or made a sound. The critical eyes of the living portraits softened. If they were content now, if they were relieved, I was anything but.

Mr. October took another sip of water and unfolded the crushed sheet, flattening it out on the table, then lifting it into focus nearer his face. Something flickered behind his eyes as he read.

"Hmm. Interesting."

It was the last word I would've chosen. "What's so interesting about it?"

"Sukie —" Mr. October began.

"Yes, he's still there," she answered before he could finish.

"Is the 4837 we brought in still in the waiting room? Then it's time he joined us so we can settle this matter once and for all."

Sukie was already on her feet. "On my way."

The Vigilants stood aside as she hurried out. The rest of us stared after her, bewildered.

"Would someone mind explaining what the heck's going on?" Becky said.

"Patience," Mr. October said. For the first time, the faces of the elders in their portraits were almost approving. Something had changed since he'd read the telegraph, and we were about to find out exactly what.

Everyone looked up at the sound of the door, the wind whispering outside as it opened and closed. And there was Sukie, coming inside with the one from the waiting room, the 4837.

Mum let out a startled cry. She might've screamed if she'd had more strength.

The burned man came forward to stand at Mr. October's side. His features were easier to distinguish now and seemed to be improving even as I watched, as if his appalling injuries were quickly healing.

"It happens all the time," Mr. October said. "The healing begins soon after the lost become found, and believe me, this man has been lost far too long. You were a difficult case right up to the end," he said to the man, "the way you bounced us across town all afternoon."

The man lowered his head in apology.

"I'm sorry." Even his voice sounded clearer now that the wounds to his throat were repairing. "I was afraid. I didn't know where to go."

And now the missing left side of his face was healing, and now the singed hair was growing back, and now I recognized him for who he was and cried out too, a cry from the deepest, darkest part of me.

"Ben Harvester," Mr. October said, leaning back in his seat. "Stand up and take this man's hand. Say hello to your father."

# 24

# THE BURNED MAN

The room held its breath. No one moved a muscle. Even the elders in the living portraits seemed stunned, their faces becoming ovals of billowing white clouds. I could have died of shock, like Andy Cale at Belsize Park. Standing up, I felt so far outside myself that I had to check my chair to be sure I wasn't still sitting there. Mum got to her feet too, even more unsteady than me, and I looped an arm around her before her legs could give way.

"I'm seeing things, Ben," she whispered. "Have I lost my mind, or is that really your father standing there?"

"You're not losing your mind, Mum."

"I'm so sorry, son," Dad said.

It was hard to think of this man as Dad, to imagine what he'd been through since I last saw him, walking away up the path with his suitcase, disappearing into the night.

But I knew him. I remembered him from the photo albums

we kept, from discs with his fingerprints all over them and books with his scribbled notes in the margins. Four years lost, but where had he been and where did he go from here?

"Donna," he said, and Mum stiffened against me. "I wish I could turn back time."

I looked at Mr. October, demanding an answer. I'd always had so many questions for him, but this was the only one that counted now.

Mr. October looked up at me, a sadness in his eyes. The empathizer.

"I know how hard this is," he said. "You always dreamed you'd find him again, alive and well and back on your doorstep. But it's better to know the worst than to live in the dark, none the wiser."

"But I thought . . . I thought we were here for Mum." I held her tightly against me. It would take every Vigilant in the house to tear her away from me.

"That's an intriguing point," Mr. October said, pushing the telegraph printout across the table. "Take a look, tell me what you think. It's quite enlightening."

As I turned the paper around, many-colored lights danced across it under the chandelier. I pulled the page into focus and prepared to read what I'd read before — but now the name, the only name on the list, was *Jim Harvester*.

Everything stopped. The only sound was muted wind in the hall outside the room and another, more distant howling sound I'd heard somewhere else but couldn't place. I was too overloaded.

"You should be in hot water for what you did," Mr. October said. "Not only did you take Ministry property, but you took the *wrong* name, a blunder if ever I saw one. If you'd filed this right away, we could've dealt with your father much sooner. We would've been spared this pantomime."

"That can't be right," I almost shouted. "That's not what it said. That's not the name I saw."

Was that a hint of a smile on his lips, a mischievous twinkle in his eye?

"See how easily mistakes can be made?" he said. "That's why we always stress careful reading and meticulous typing. Imagine the chaos if the wrong name were filed."

He leaned back, fingers drumming the table.

"Folks, the family needs private time," he said. "Time to share a few last words. I'll ask you to show respect and keep your voices low if you must speak at all. Sukie? There's something here for the files."

Sukie ran to collect the page from him, glanced at it quickly, then at me.

"Sorry for your loss, Ben, I really am. It's awful you had to find out like this. But the —"

"The telegraph never lies," I said.

She blinked, surprised, then started to the door.

So now the three of us stood at the far end of the room under the stained-glass triptych, forming a close circle, not quite touching. My gaze flitted between Mum, pale with shock, and Dad's still-healing face with its strong cheekbones and Roman nose.

Behind us, the great table and those seated around it looked miles distant and very faint, as if a veil had fallen between us.

"You've come a long way, son," Dad said, then looked dotingly at Mum. "We all have. And you have to learn to let go now. You've held on long enough."

She wiped her streaming nose. "This can't be happening. I don't even believe in ghosts."

"But you believe in me," he said.

"Yes, I do."

"Then that's all that matters. That's something to take with me when I go."

"We always hoped you'd come back, but not like this," Mum said. "I'd rather know you were living another life without us than see you this way."

"What happened, Dad?" I had to ask. It didn't feel so strange now, calling him that, but my chest felt as heavy as stone. "Why didn't you come back?"

"I tried to," he said. "The night I left, I knew that was all I wanted: to make things right, the way they used to be. But I also knew we needed time, your mum and I, so I made myself wait a month before calling to see if she was ready."

"But you never called," Mum said. "That was the hardest part. The not knowing."

He smiled a broken smile. "But I did call, you see. I called I don't know how many times. It must've been rotten timing, because you were always out or away when I rang. After leaving my friends in Newcastle, I moved to a B&B in Edinburgh. But the farther away I got, the bigger the pull I felt to come back. So I bought a ticket home. I thought if I could just see you up close, it would be easier.

"So I *was* coming back. I was on my way home when the accident happened, and everything I'd dreamt of went flying out the window."

"The train crash," I said, the heaviness increasing in my chest as I thought of Becky huddling down in the wreckage, playing hide-and-seek. *That* train crash.

Mum looked at me, aghast.

Dad nodded and lowered his gaze. "You may have heard of it, Donna — the crash on the East Coast line that killed so many passengers. But you wouldn't have known I was one of them."

"Oh God . . ." Mum's cry trailed off into space. I held on, keeping her upright.

The Overseers averted their eyes.

"It came without warning," Dad said. "One second I was watching the countryside go by, the next there was debris and glass everywhere, an inferno running through the carriage, panic and screaming. Then there was some kind of explosion. The impact threw me against the window headfirst, and I never left my seat after that. I was one of the few who never made it out in any kind of shape. No one could've identified us. I remember looking down through the furnace, seeing myself in the seat, everything turning black around me. I knew what the fire had done to me, but I didn't feel any pain, not physical pain. Only the pain of missing you and not being able to find a way back."

I looked at him, the burned man, the horror-film and comic-book fan. He looked as he used to, his features almost fully restored.

"We've missed you too, Dad. Missed you like crazy."

Mum nodded, speechless.

"I'm sorry for everything," he said. "For my stupid mistake, for leaving you without a clue. I tried to contact you so many times, I ranted and raved, but you never heard . . . not until that day in the classroom, Ben, when you saw me for the first time. I know I messed everything up, but you need to know I never loved anyone but you two. If I could take it all back, I would."

He paused, and I sensed an electricity in the air that told me our time was nearly over.

"I'm glad we had this chance," Dad finished. "I'm glad I could finally say what had to be said. But now we have to let go and move on. Can you do that, Donna?"

She shook her head in protest. "I don't want to."

"You'll learn how."

He touched her face, and a shudder ran through her as he wiped away her tears. He rested a hand on her bandaged arm a moment, looking into her eyes. Then he took my hand, and tiny sparks of lightning surrounded our fingers as we touched.

"Only thing is, I don't know what happens now," Dad said. "They didn't explain that. They said you'd know."

I looked at the conference table. No one reacted, least of all Mr. October, who sat with his head bowed and his back turned to us.

But suddenly I realized I didn't need his help for this. I knew, or thought I knew, without being told.

Inside the stained-glass windows, the warring figures seemed to be subtly moving, as if the aftershocks of their battles were still vibrating. But the pictures didn't show what I wanted. They gave no sign of a way out, a place where the departed were supposed to go.

"There," Dad said suddenly, looking past me. "Could that be the place?"

In the darkest corner of our side of the room, a fine-line crack of light had appeared, as fine as the crack between the walls in the alley. That had to be it. We looked at each other and knew. We started toward it.

Mum held herself back, as if she understood she couldn't play a part in this now. She could only look on as I walked Dad away, and as I did he half turned to look at her, and the look that passed between them seemed to speak volumes, saying everything they'd left unsaid.

We were nearly there. Even at close range the crack wasn't easy to see. But when I put out my hand, I felt something solid and cold, something very much like a doorknob. My fingers closed around it.

"Love you, Dad."

"I know," he said. The look in his eyes took me back years to the times when he sang me to sleep and read me bedtime stories. "Love you too, Ben. Wish I could say I'll be seeing ya, but you know this is where it ends. Take care of Mum."

"I will," I said, and then I opened the door.

The bright burning rectangle that loomed against the wall gave off a comforting warmth, so comforting I almost wanted to step inside it myself. But instead I moved aside, letting Dad pass. His last look seemed to say, *It's all right now. Everything's fine now.*

He didn't speak, though. He didn't hesitate. He walked into the golden-yellow beyond, just as Mitch and Molly had before him. The warmth engulfed him, and as he moved farther inside I began to lose sight of him. Then he was a part of the welcoming flames, and I closed the door and leaned against it, sobbing.

Slowly the room came back into focus. Mum watched me with tear-filled eyes, not knowing which question to ask first. I took her hand and the veil seemed to lift midway across the room as I steadied her back to the conference table.

Mr. October was already on his feet. The elders looked down on us, nodding their heads.

"Now do you believe me?" Mr. October asked the portraits. "A first-rate show, young man. Astonishing. If my superiors still had any doubts about you, you wiped them away with what you just did. So . . . how do you feel?"

"Dunno," I said. "Shaky. Empty."

"Understood. Still, it's good to have the chance to lay our own ghosts to rest. In time you'll be glad of your part in this."

Mum could only sniffle, still reeling with shock.

Mr. October turned to her now. "Our deepest sympathies, Mrs. Harvester. I know you're still recovering from one loss in the family and this must be hard to bear. These things have a way of coming all at once — it seems so cruel and unfair. But there's a new day waiting for you now, a very bright day."

Mum muttered something I couldn't quite hear. I gave her hand a squeeze.

"We should get you home," Mr. October said. "If you don't mind waiting while I speak with this young prodigy of ours, we'll have you on your way in no time. Lu? Becky?"

The girls snapped to attention.

I was reluctant to let Mum go, but I knew she'd be safe with them. The Vigilants stood aside until they'd passed, then followed them from the room. The wind sighed past the open door, and again I heard something else inside it: a mournful wailing.

Now that we were alone, Mr. October became serious and agitated, morphing back and forth between three different personas.

"There's something else you should know," he said. "I couldn't explain in front of your mother — she has too much on her plate already. But there's another task facing us now. Do you recognize that sound in the wind?"

It was louder now, a chilling howl from the depths.

"You heard it the night we saved the Willow children," he said. "It's the enemy mourning losses of their own. Your father may have slipped through their fingers, but they won't go away empty-handed. There's been an incursion. They're already inside the building."

Above us, the elders let out a collective groan. Something stirred in the pool of shade under the windows.

"What should we do?" I asked.

"Whatever we can." He reached out a hand, collecting his walking stick out of thin air.

A spider-shaped shadow crept out of the darkness across the room, shot up to the highest point of the wall, and spread itself out in a corner. The weave it threw across the ceiling seemed to suck light from the air.

As its web closed around the chandelier, the conference room fell into semidarkness. Other shadows appeared, stretching around corners, spilling out of the stone walls, sweeping across the living portraits to blot them out.

"Security!" Mr. October called.

The door was thrown open. Two Vigilants looked in, awaiting instructions.

"The enemy are here," Mr. October said.

And I was the one who'd let them in. I'd punched a hole in the Ministry's defenses when I'd taken that name. Somehow I had to make up for what I'd done, but for the moment all I could do was look on, helpless, as the demons tumbled out of their cover of darkness and into the room.

# 25

# THE INCURSION

They came in all shapes and sizes, from every unlit corner, spilling from the fireplace's gaping mouth, from cracks in the great stone walls. In the stained-glass windows the creatures portrayed in battle scenes came slowly alive, escaped their prison, and came flopping down to the floor.

Another door opened in another corner of the room. There was no welcoming light inside this one, though, only a pitch-black nothingness. A procession of Deathhead agents stormed out.

And worse: the Mawbreed, an entire nest of them, oozing through gashes in the stone floor and walls, sitting up out of the shadows. I hadn't forgotten how hideous they were. Their coiled, wormlike bodies were semitransparent, with pale fluids pulsing under the skin. Their limbs, with their bristling suckers, reached far and wide. The ravenous mouths they had for heads craned above them, tasting the air.

In no time the room was alive with them, demons of every description. I couldn't see the elders in the portraits anymore — they must've gone into hiding. If they had, I couldn't blame them.

A siren sounded, loud enough to shake the building's foundations. Clouds of plaster dust fell from the ceiling. Sounds of stampeding footsteps and discharging weapons echoed from the hallway.

I looked at Mr. October in distress. "This is on me, isn't it? I'm to blame for all this."

"What's done is done. Now that they're here, we'll have to deal with them the best way we can. Run me an errand, Ben — go and check the receipts room. This shouldn't be happening if Sukie has filed your father's card. The numbers may still be out of alignment."

I faltered, keeping an eye on a Mawbreed that had drawn too close for comfort.

"You're trying to protect me, aren't you? You're sending me out to keep me away from this."

"I *need* you to go. The name is high priority and must be filed by someone who knows what they're doing."

We retreated a few paces, keeping distance between us and the Mawbreed's suckered hands. Mr. October twitched his walking stick toward it, uttering something inaudible under his breath. The Mawbreed drew back.

"Go now," he said as a team of Vigilants crashed into the room from behind us. "Take care as you do, though. They may be everywhere. Remember what you've learned, Ben. Remember what you can do."

"Mum's still in the building. . . ." The full horror of that thought hadn't hit me until then. "If they're everywhere, what about her?"

"She's in the only safe place. You haven't been in the waiting room before, have you? The elevator music they play there is written in ancientspeak, with ancientspeak lyrics. They couldn't go in there even if they dared. Now will you please get along and do as I say?"

As I started away, a creature from one of the windows came scampering across the floor, silent and stealthy as a cat, with eyes and mouths surfacing all over its shiny black body. A half-dozen Vigilants closed around it, cutting it off from Mr. October.

At the same time, a sucker-covered arm flashed down from the darkness near the chandelier, looping around one guard's neck and hauling him screaming up to the ceiling.

His screams followed me from the room. The last thing I saw before stepping outside was Mr. October unleashing a fireball with a flick of his wrist. It detonated in front of the fireplace, trapping three invaders inside it, turning them into thrashing masses of flame.

The hostilities weren't confined to the conference room. Out in the hallway, a dozen Vigilants were caught in a free-for-all with twice as many Shifters. The plasma weapons seemed to have little or no effect on the intruders. One lizardlike demon took a hit to the neck that spun it around, dazing it only briefly before it came again, leaping through the air and changing in midflight to a jellyish form that fastened itself over the head and shoulders of the guard who'd fired.

Other guards and demons were locked in hand-to-hand combat — in some cases hand-to-claw or hand-to-tentacle combat. I threaded my way among them, past a Vigilant with an axe in his hands. He lifted it high above his head and brought it down on a Shifter, which turned itself into an eel the instant before the blade fell. Then there were two eels, sliding away in opposite directions, one growing a new tail, the other a new head. One snapped its jaws at my ankle as I darted past the dispatch room.

The receipts office door stood open just ahead. This far down the corridor was clear of fighting, but new shadows were shifting and crawling all through it. Whatever was inside them would soon come out. I had no time to lose.

The first thing I saw in receipts was Sukie, passed out in the chair, bent forward over the desk. Her head rested on the typewriter and she held a freshly typed card between her fingers. She was breathing but clearly out of commission. It only took me a second to work out why.

To the left, inside the door, a demon was standing over the telegraph — one of the Deathheads. It didn't see me at first but watched the machine as the latest list chugged out. They'd lost control of one soul tonight, and the demon was here to steal many more in return.

It seemed to sense me then and turned its head, narrowing its empty eye sockets into slits. The lipless mouth leered. I couldn't be sure if it was the one from the old Willow house or another just like it, but its decaying gray hands were fully formed and long-fingered.

"You," it said.

Without a thought I flung myself at it, hitting the creature full-on with my shoulder. It spun away and landed neatly on its feet, flashing out a hand that caught me squarely in the chest.

It was like being hit by a bus. The pain didn't even register until I'd flown back across the room, smashing into a bookshelf against the far wall. I slumped to the floor in a rain of books. A screaming pain drilled through my upper body. And now the Deathhead turned from the telegraph, crossing the room with a single leap to stand above me.

"We'll finish what we began," it said. "I'll be a cause of celebration in my domain when I take back your precious soul."

But only the Mawbreed could take living souls, I remembered. This one would have to kill me first.

I sucked in air, fighting an urge to close my eyes as the demon bowed over me. I mustn't look away. I had to think clearly.

*Use the gift,* I thought.

*Your God-given talent,* Mum's voice echoed through my head.

*Your developing skills,* echoed Mr. October. *Remember what you can do.*

The demon craned lower and nearer until I felt its foul grave-breath on my face. I'd remember this in my dreams, I thought, if I lived to dream again.

"Now then," it whispered, prodding my chest. A set of needling claws sprouted from its slimy fingertips. "One small incision here, another larger one there ... Your measly body's no use to us, but your life force is a topic of heated debate where I come from. You're leaving here with me."

It wasn't until then that I saw it, that I knew what to do. The gift wasn't something you thought about; in fact, the harder you thought about it, the harder it was to pull off.

*I wish I could do what you do.* Becky's words floated back to me from that first time, our first walk home from school. *Picture it in my head and put it down on the page as I see it. . . .*

That was the key. I'd always had it, one way or another. I'd had it, but I just hadn't known what to do with it till now.

All I really had to do was picture it. It was almost like drawing from memory.

The demon felt it. It seemed to sense what I had in mind. It lurched backward, opening its mouth wide and screeching as I got to my knees. Smoke rose gray and thick from the collar of its black suit. Its body began to quiver.

I pictured it now, seeing it clearly, holding it steady in my mind. Sometimes the sketches didn't work out as intended. Sometimes, as with the fire children, they were almost exact. What I was imagining now was happening right there in front of me. A rattle escaped the Deathhead's throat as its bony head began to melt.

Now I was on my feet again. The demon reeled away, thumping against a wall, both hands at its own throat. It stumbled past the telegraph machine, looking for an escape. But there was no escape for it now — only an exit.

What features the demon had ever had were now so blackened and warped out of shape that I didn't recognize it. I waited, but only a heartbeat, until it plodded another step farther into the corridor. It stood there, rocking on its feet, wailing from what was left of its throat.

"See you in the great beyond," it gargled.

"That's right. Take this back to your leader."

And with that, the sketch was complete.

The demon exploded in a great whoosh of dark red matter, a million tiny fragments of it blasting in every direction. A spray of heat and smoldering debris filled the space outside the door, then gradually dispersed until there was nothing left but red mist.

The siren was still screaming. I leaned across the desk.

"Sukie?" I said.

She looked lost in sleep, but managed a very slight nod.

"Nnn . . . be OK . . ." Her hand twitched the typed card toward me. "Take this. . . ."

I certainly hoped she'd be OK. The priority now, though, was the records office. The hostilities wouldn't begin to die down until I'd been there.

As I took the card from Sukie's hand, the telegraph stopped and settled, the new list protruding from its front. I couldn't leave the list out in the open. Others might come to steal it. It wouldn't be good to pocket it, either, in case anything happened to me.

I took it and hid it between two thick volumes on the shelf above the desk.

"Sukie," I said. "If you can hear me, the new list is between volumes one and two of the *Apocalypti Phrase Book, Unexpurgated Edition*, OK?"

"Nnn."

She nodded. She was coming around, but I couldn't stay. The fighting was still going on in the hallway and the Shifters seemed to have the upper hand. Two of them were arguing over a Vigilant's corpse as they both tried to extract its soul at once. Another guard was taking a beating from a creature that looked half man, half octopus. All eight of its hands were at his neck, and it threw him back so forcefully that his body left an imprint on the wall.

The records office was in turmoil too. The enemy had found a way in. Demons in shadow form soared about the airy white space, attacking drones on their rolling ladders, breaking open filing cabinets with pincer-shaped hands.

I saw a worker up in the heights seized and thrown aside like a rag doll before plunging fifteen floors, about two hundred feet, hitting the marble floor not far from me with a bang and a spray of red. Another was dead before he hit the ground, torn apart in midair by the intruders. His body came down in three separate pieces.

Meanwhile, the guardians of the records, the bats from the rafters, were defending their space. They dive-bombed the demons in packs of twenty or more, snapping and lashing with silver-needle teeth and claws. In every quarter of the vast room, airborne fights to the death were in full swing.

One misplaced name, one theft, had caused all this. I'd never be able to look anyone here in the eye again. And after what I'd done — I supposed everyone knew by now — the last person I needed to see was Miss Webster.

But that's who I was running to. Her little booth seemed impossibly distant, nothing but a soft smudge on the horizon. Crossing the floor toward it, I caught sight of a many-armed shape rushing down at me. The bats were on it in a split second, a small army of them tearing it to shreds. The shadow petered out like a snuffled flame and frittered away like dust.

"I hope you're very pleased with yourself," Miss Webster said sourly. There was so much spider activity about her head, her perm seemed to be moving by itself. "But there's nothing I can do, thanks to you. Can't you see all our staff are occupied? Your card will have to wait."

"It can't," I said. "The numbers — the numbers are out of alignment."

"Of course they are. I'm not a fool. And whose fault is that anyway?" She scowled across the room as another employee fell many floors screaming. Then she turned the scowl on me. "We can't process anything with all this disruption."

"I'm sorry, I didn't think —"

"That's correct, you didn't think. You'd better give me the card anyway. I'll hold on to it until someone is free."

"No," I said bluntly.

"What did you say? Give it here," Miss Webster said, brushing a cobweb from the tip of her nose.

"I'll file it myself. That's what I'll do."

"Don't be an imbecile. Look around you. This is unprecedented, unheard of. You're not even qualified."

But it was the only way. Balance the books and contain the incursion. I started from the booth, turning to ask one last question.

"Miss Webster, where are the *H*s? This has to be filed under *Harvester*."

She clucked her tongue and sighed dramatically. "If you had any sense, which you clearly haven't, you'd do well to wait. But if you must —" She broke off to check her ledger. "You'll find them on levels 53 and 54."

I hurried to the steps that spiraled up to level 1, daunted but knowing I had no other option. As I started up the staircase, a formation of bats clouded around me, circling my shoulders and head. At close range, their beady eyes and pink-fanged mouths were worrying, and at first I thought they'd come to attack — that they'd mistaken me for an intruder, or maybe they were demons in disguise.

But they had other ideas. They hovered there, waiting for my next move. They knew what I was carrying and what it meant. They'd come to escort me all the way.

As I climbed from level to level, the majority of the guardians stayed with me while one flew just ahead like a scout and another watched the rear. At each turn of the stairs, enemy agents swooped into range, looking for a way through, but the guardians were multiplying, sending wave after wave of reinforcements down on the shadow creatures, ripping and tearing the darkness apart.

The climb seemed to go on and on, but finally I dragged myself up the last few steps and stood on the platform below the first cabinets marked *HA* and looked out across the ever-growing space with the clouds just above me. I heard an explosion deep in the building — the beginning of the end, I hoped.

Then I rolled the stepladder into place, started up, and pulled out the fifth cabinet drawer from the top. There were more Harvesters here than I'd expected, each with its own folder and reference number. I found Dad's tucked away near the back.

As I opened the file, a second, more distant explosion rang out. Inside the folder was Dad's entire history, indexed and sorted all the way up to the fatal crash.

I couldn't read it now. I wouldn't be able to bear it. Someday, perhaps, I'd try. There was only one thing to do now, and my escort seemed to know. They parted and drifted away as I kissed Dad's card and slipped it inside a slot at the back of the folder, then closed the folder and filed it away.

The siren stopped immediately. The last intruders faded from view, their dark shapes shrinking into corners and melting away. The winged guardians swept up through the clouds toward the rafters miles above.

*It must be over,* I thought. The books were balanced, the numbers aligned. Shattered and close to tears — but I wouldn't cry yet, not yet — I began the long climb back down.

The waiting room was the first place I checked after the records office. Ancientspeak music wafted across the white-walled space, a weird kind of bossa nova with soft-spoken lyrics that made no sense to me.

Becky and Mum were together on a white two-seater sofa, watched over by a pair of armed, grim-faced Vigilants. Mum looked broken as she leaned against Becky, who was stroking her hair and whispering, "There, there."

"It's ending," I said.

Mum didn't hear me, but Becky looked up. "There's still some activity in the conference room. Lu just got called away."

"I'd better go."

"Don't," she said quickly. "It's under control. You did what you had to do."

"I'll be fine," I said. "I won't be long."

"Please, Ben . . . don't."

I couldn't begin to tell her what I'd seen in the last few minutes. Whatever she was worried about in the conference room couldn't be any worse than that.

"I'm responsible for all this," I said. "I mean *all* of it. I need to make amends if I still can."

Mum peered up at me then, just before I left the room. She didn't seem the least bit aware of her surroundings. Her eyes were glazed and far away.

"It's OK," I told her anyway. "Like Dad said, it's going to be fine."

Then I turned away, heading out along the hallway.

The fighting had stopped, but the aftermath was awful to see. Bodies littered the floor, Shifters and Vigilants alike. The walls were cracked and marked bloodily in several places. A scattering of gray-black ashes marked the spot where the Deathhead had fallen. A 11215 if ever I'd seen one.

The conference room was hazy with smoke. It rose from the floor, from burned-out defenders and demons. As I moved inside, it was hard to see much of anything at all. The few figures still standing were like ghosts in the fog. The place had been ripped apart, chairs scattered, the great long table split into two. It looked like the end, but now I heard movement in the smoke — a roar and a muffled scream, the sound of a Mawbreed ingesting a man's soul with one greedy gulp.

It wasn't over. The enemy were defeated, but they didn't know when to stop. I moved deeper into the smoke, half expecting them to lunge at me left and right. The first clear sight I had of anything was a Vigilant cowering on the floor, gazing up in terror at the Mawbreed looming over him.

I couldn't make it stop. I tried to picture something to save him, but it wouldn't come in time. The Mawbreed was fast, faster than a thing that size ought to be, and its drooling mouth covered the guard before I could blink.

Back along the hallway, the telegraph woke again with a sound like a backfiring car. Here came another list of names to add to the last, but there wouldn't be any record of the souls these demons were stealing.

*How many?* I wondered. *How many more?*

The smoke cleared just a little, forming a canopy under the ceiling, and I noticed another figure stretched out on the floor in front of me, dressed all in white, battered and burned. My heart slumped as I moved nearer and saw Lu kneeling over him. She was weeping and clutching his hand. She looked up as my shadow fell over him, then she looked back at Mr. October.

A fireball, or something like one, had torn straight through him. There were dark scattershot marks around his midriff and chest and a great deal of blood. For a minute — it could've been longer — my mind shut down. I couldn't think. Couldn't feel a thing. I prayed for a dark hole to open up so I could roll inside it and vanish.

"He's breathing," Lu said.

"No!" I knelt down, facing her. "Is he really?"

"I'm sure of it."

I let it sink in for a moment. Some relief. Still hope.

"What happened?" I asked.

She shook her head, uncertain. "He was like this when I got here. He rang, but too late."

Somewhere in the thick of the smoke, a Mawbreed growled. Another, finishing its meal, belched loudly.

"Too slow," Mr. October murmured. At the sound of his voice, Lu and I looked at each other, drawing the same short breath.

"You're alive," I said.

He tried to nod, but ended the movement wincing.

"Too slow," he repeated. "This body wasn't meant for combat. It hit me before I had time to change. There's a lesson in there somewhere, Ben. Never bring your mourning attire to a war zone."

His gray eyes held mine. His face muscles ticked as if he was trying to take on another appearance but hadn't the strength.

"Sometimes it's all too much," he said. It was the first thing I'd ever heard him say, a lifetime ago at Highgate Cemetery. Feeling through his pockets, I found a handkerchief and dabbed it around his damp face.

"You know what to do to finish this," Mr. October said. "And you know *how*. It's your time now, young man."

I knew very well what he meant. I had to visualize what I wanted so clearly that I could have sketched it.

His eyes fluttered shut. Perhaps he'd only blacked out. He still might survive. So I wouldn't mourn yet. I'd only feel what I needed to feel. All I needed now, as I got up to my feet and the seven remaining Mawbreed came into view, all I really needed was rage.

They dragged their great bulk toward us, leaving silvery snail trails across the stone floor. Seven red mouths gaped open, scenting us on the air. I took a step forward, bunching my fist around the handkerchief as the picture came fully together in my head.

It wasn't pretty, but it had to be done. It wasn't something I'd ever boast about, but I wanted it now more than anything.

"For my dad," I said, "and for Mr. October. For everything you've done here tonight. For everything you are."

Lu let out a gasp behind me as a tremor rolled through the room. Everything seemed to flicker and turn black for a second. *It's your time now,* Mr. October had said, and I wondered if I found the phrase book in my pocket and opened it the words might finally hold steady and be still.

It wasn't easy to watch when the Mawbreed began to eat one another. But I'd made this happen and I had to see it through.

It began when two of them ambushed another, turning on it from both sides, their ravenous mouths clamping down on it and devouring it in three, four swallows. At the same time, the other four went into a kind of standoff, facing one another for several moments before all flying in at once, chomping blindly, smothering one another with their suckered hands. Suddenly the whole nest of them were pulled into the same fight for survival. I'd imagined all this, I'd dreamt it up, but a part of me wished I hadn't.

Mawbreed fed upon Mawbreed until only one was left standing, and that one was so morbidly bloated that it couldn't move. It lumbered to and fro like a drunk, letting out a belch that would've drowned out the siren if it hadn't already been switched off. The creature gave me one last lingering look — if it could see anything at all, and I wasn't sure that it could — and opened its yawning, dribbling mouth as far as it could go.

Then it proceeded to eat itself.

I watched until there was nothing left to see. Wherever it went after that long last swallow, I'll never know. I felt drained as I came slowly back to myself and looked down on Mr. October.

"Will he make it?" I said to Lu. "Will he heal?"

She looked at me, stunned by what she'd just witnessed. It took her some time to find the words.

"What you just did . . . I never saw anything like it." Then she nodded, remembering the question. "There's a chance. His pulse is strong."

She glanced past me and across the room, eyes widening. I followed her look and saw what she saw: the last surviving enemy in the room.

Its shadow nimbled down the wall — the spider shape whose web had sucked out the light. When it reached the floor, resting in the shade below the windows, I almost lost sight of it. Then it spun itself a new form, a nearly but not quite human form with two arms and two legs that hovered above the ground in front of the stained-glass windows.

Its face wasn't clear to see, but I knew the general shape of it well enough, and I recognized the grating voice when it spoke.

"Next time," said Nathan Synsiter, the scarecrow, second in command to Randall Cadaverus. "Next time, Ben Harvester. We told you what would come upon you if you took sides in this struggle. Don't think it's over between us. Whatever else you do, don't fool yourself about that. We'll be back for full payment, with interest."

I was still trying to decide what to do with him — flip him inside out or make him explode — when he hurled himself at the glass, dissolving for an instant, then becoming just another frozen figure in an ancient battlefield scene.

This battle was over; the eternal war would go on. I'd taken only a small part, yet seen enough for a lifetime. As I turned from the windows, a medical team ran inside the room, followed by a crew of battered and bruised Vigilants. The medics ran to Mr. October while, behind them, Becky looked in from the door. My mother was with her. She looked OK, but I'd seen her look much, much better.

Becky slowly took in the scene, the carnage, the injuries to Mr. October, with mortified eyes.

"Oh my God, Ben, is he . . . ?"

"Not yet," I said. They were stretchering him away when I noticed Mr. October's fingers wiggle at his side. The movement reminded me of the first sweet apple he'd pulled from the air for me, and I thought, *You know, he may look fragile, but he's very resilient. Where there's life, there's hope.*

Lu scrambled to her feet and dusted herself off, then took my arm as we walked from the room.

"I'll take you home now," she said. "You did good, very good. But that's enough for one night."

"And what a night," Becky said. "What a Halloween."

We went out, leaving the empty conference room behind — empty except for the Overseers frowning down from their portraits at the carnage.

# 26

# A DISPATCH
# FROM THE MINISTRY

Well, that's what happened. It's everything I know, up to and including Halloween night at HQ.

So this is my dispatch from Pandemonium House, hidden away in a place no one will ever find it unless they know how to look. And you *do* have to look in just the right way, otherwise the walls on Camden Passage stay sealed and the alley beyond it stays hidden. It's a secret.

I'm recording this for myself, to try to make sense of it all. I'm typing it at the desk on the old Olivetti Lettera 22. Built in 1958, pistachio colored, it could've been anywhere in its life before it came here. It could've belonged to a famous author or to a war correspondent who carried it around the globe, or it could've been here all the time. Perhaps it's never left this place, and it's only ever been used to record the names of the soon-departed.

That's the part of the job I'm starting to like least. After what very nearly happened to Mum — and I still swear it was her name I saw that night, not Dad's — it hurts to type the cards. Whenever the telegraph spits out a new name, I know someone else somewhere else is hurting too, or soon will be.

You can't take these things for granted. You have to concentrate. I've learned my lesson and I know not to mistype the cards, not to misfile them, and never, ever to unbalance the books.

Two hours after we left the conference room, word reached us that Mr. October's condition had worsened. Ministry medics were holding a vigil while Sukie, who quickly recovered and returned to duty, kept a close eye on the telegraph, hoping and praying his number wouldn't come up.

I want badly to see him again, fully recovered. I want to see the twinkle in his eyes. Still, there are times when I think it would've been better if we'd never met at all. Life would've been simpler, at least. I'm part of the eternal war now. I've made a target of Mum as well as myself, and I have to be watchful every second. You never know what's waiting in the shadows.

"I'm not out of the woods yet," Mum said the last time we spoke, but she's slowly improving every day. Now that I think of it, she's seemed better ever since the moment Dad looked into her eyes and touched her arm. Maybe what she'd needed most of all was a chance to see him one more time. Closure, Mr. October had called it.

There's a postcard on the desk by the typewriter. Mum sent it over the weekend and it arrived in today's mail. It's from Lanzarote and pictures a rugged desert terrain, all gray and orange under a clear blue sky with palm trees and volcanic mountains in the distance.

Ellie's still waiting to hear about the condo, but they went anyway, and the long days of sunshine are working wonders, Mum's postcard says in very legible handwriting. She wishes I were there. She'd tried to persuade me to go, but my duties here will keep me busy until Mr. October returns. If he ever returns.

Mum isn't happy about my involvement. She probably never will be. After that night at HQ, I had to tell her everything, and she still hasn't come around to my way of seeing things. In time I hope she'll understand, that she'll support everything I have to do and be like Batman's butler, Alfred Pennyworth, or like Iron Man's confidante, Pepper Potts. But I don't see it happening any time soon.

Before she flew to the island, we used some of Aunt Carrie's money for Dad. It didn't feel right, Mum said, to buy a marker for a cemetery or churchyard in his hometown where we'd never see it. So instead we paid for a bench with a brass nameplate in London Fields. It sits to one side of a tree-lined path with a view of the Pub on the Park in one direction, and in the other direction a view of the house they're rebuilding on our street.

I sat on that bench on Sunday, a quiet morning, too cold for barbecues and sun lovers. I thought about Dad as I added him to my sketch pad, picturing him as I'd seen him for the last time, healed and at peace after four unspeakable years. I missed him and I knew I wouldn't see him again. He wouldn't squeeze my hand again or read me bedtime stories, and he wouldn't whisper to me on the wind with the dead, dry leaves blustering around me, because he wasn't there anymore. We're still recovering, Mum and me, we're still coming to terms. We know it will take quite a while too.

During Mr. October's absence, I've formed a close-knit team with Lu and Becky — one of the Ministry's best in the field. It's a punishing schedule, and now and again we see things we'd rather not see, such as the 63964 last night that none of us wanted to look at. But for the most part we keep good time and the work is rewarding.

At school it's been harder on Becky than me. Her gang is distant toward her now, she isn't part of the in-crowd, and they don't invite her to their houses so often. She's sad about that, but she knows that her true calling comes first. Most lunchtimes we go to the crypt and talk about things we've heard and seen on our shifts, but we never discuss Ministry business in school.

Raymond Blight gave Becky a push in the corridor the other day. I called him on it, but all I got in return was a look, that Raymond Blight look. And I thought, *If you had half an idea what I can do, Raymond . . . you wouldn't do that.*

"But that would be an abuse of power," Becky said when I brought it up. It sounded like something Mr. October might say. "People abuse the power they have every day, and it only gets the world into more of a tangle."

She was right, of course. Gifts aren't given out for no good reason. They're supposed to be used with care, not wasted away, and not abused, either. Besides, there are more important things to worry about than Raymond Blight.

Things like the work we do unseen every day. The war we're all caught up in. The threat Nathan Synsiter left me with before he jumped back inside the glass. It's a threat that stays with me all the time, because I know he means business and I know I'll see him again one day, and I know when I do we'll have to settle the argument.

But I have to stop now. The telegraph is working again. Another list is on its way and the machine rocks and puffs and shakes the room. I sit watching and waiting for it to stop, but it keeps on going. That's just the way it is sometimes. There's always more work, there are always more calls to make — and it looks like another long night ahead.

This list goes on and on and on.

# ACKNOWLEDGMENTS

Although I wrote every word myself, I couldn't have done it alone. I'm indebted to so many people for their support, encouragement, and patience while I worked on this book, and the chief suspects are:

Gill Wilkinson, who read it first and made many suggestions that helped so much with the final draft, and who introduced me to a London I hadn't known before — the canal walks, parks, and alleyways that play so large a part in the story.

David Gamble, for an inspiring Saturday morning mystery walk to Highgate Cemetery East, where the idea for this novel first took hold; and his lovely wife, Alex Mackie, for offering me use of the study in their home, where the early chapters were written.

Liz Webber, Pete Stone, Anne Wilkinson, Anuree DeSilva, Tina Hetherington, Helene Oosthuizen, Craig McCall, and all my friends in London, and Amy Garcia in Mateca, California — a terrific writer with a spectacular future. Thanks for everything, folks. I'm lucky to know you.

Thanks to my tireless UK agent, Mandy Little, at Watson, Little, to Maurice Lyon and the rest of the team at Frances Lincoln for their enthusiasm and great goodwill, and to Steven Chudney of the Chudney Agency and Nick Eliopulos at Scholastic for making this happen in the USA, too!

A special thank-you to Eileen Gunn and all at the Royal Literary Fund, whose kindness and generosity know no bounds.

I'm also grateful to whoever sold their unwanted Olivetti Lettera 22 to Islington antique shop Past Caring. It was love at first sight, £30 well spent, and the first draft of this book was typed on the same splendid machine used by Ben Harvester. *Ker-ching!*

Last but by no means least, the biggest thank-you of all to my parents, Betty and Stan, who never doubted my crazy notion of becoming a writer and supported me all the way. They're no longer with us and I miss them every day, but there's still a big part of them here between the lines on every page.